Rose, Rose, I Love You

MODERN LITERATURE FROM TAIWAN

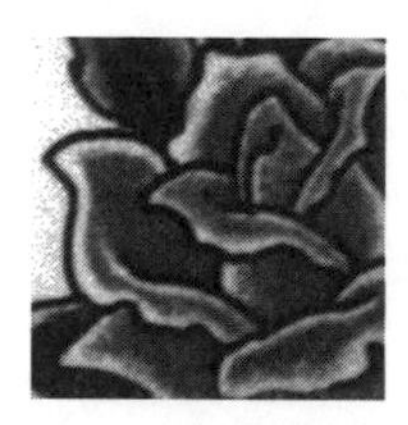

MODERN LITERATURE FROM TAIWAN

Rose, Rose, I Love You

WANG CHEN-HO

Translated by Howard Goldblatt

COLUMBIA UNIVERSITY PRESS

NEW YORK

Columbia University Press wishes to express its appreciation for assistance given by the Chiang Ching-Kuo Foundation for International Scholarly Exchange in the preparation of the translation and in the publication of this series.

The translator would also like to thank the Taiwan Council for Cultural Planning and Development for assistance in the translation and publication of this volume.

First published in Taipei by Yuan-ching ch'u-pan shih-yeh kung-szu, 1984
Republished by Hung-fan shu-tien, 1994

Columbia University Press
Publishers Since 1893
New York Chichester, West Sussex

Library of Congress Cataloging-in-Publication Data
Wang, Chen-ho, 1940–1990.
[Mei kuei mei kuei wo ai ni. English]
Rose, Rose, I love you / Wang Chen-ho ; translated by Howard Goldblatt.
p. cm. — (Modern literature from Taiwan)
ISBN 0–231–11202–5 (cloth) — ISBN 0–231–11203–3 (pbk.)
1. Wang, Chen-ho, 1940–1990—Translations into English. I. Goldblatt, Howard, 1939– . II. Title. III. Series.
PL2919.C426M4313 1998
895.1'352—dc21 97–33519

Casebound editions of Columbia University Press books are printed on permanent and durable acid-free paper.
Printed in the United States of America
Designed by Linda Secondari

c 10 9 8 7 6 5 4 3 2 1
p 10 9 8 7 6 5 4 3 2 1

Contents

Translator's Preface

Wang Chen-ho once revealed to an interviewer that his wife began but never could finish *Rose, Rose, I Love You*. "Why," she wanted to know, "do you have to write such trash?" Wang's daughter was even more direct: "It's so dirty!" she complained, looking over his shoulder as he wrote.

Well, so it is. But then what should we expect from a novel dealing with the training of local bar girls to service American GIs—who do not appear in the novel except in the fertile imaginations of the girls and their patrons—about to arrive on an R & R visit from Vietnam? Deftly combining farce and satire, plus a liberal amount of kitsch,[1] Wang Chen-ho has molded this "tawdry" material into the most raucous comic novel in modern Chinese literary history, a work reminiscent of John Kennedy Toole's *A Confederacy of Dunces*; here, however, Ignatius Reilly's noisy and intractable pyloric valve is replaced by the more common malady of flatulence in the novel's protagonist, Dong Siwen, a pompous high school teacher whose name means "one who understands refinement." As both the tar-

1. See Jeffrey C. Kinkley's "Mandarin Kitsch and Taiwanese Kitsch in the Fiction of Wang Chen-ho," *Modern Chinese Literature* 6 (1992): 85–113. This is the best and most comprehensive analysis of both "Chinese kitsch" and Wang's novel in print. Kinkley reminds us of Gilbert Highet's dictum on kitsch, that it "took a lot of trouble to make and is hideous." That, of course, is why it works so well as satire.

get and initiator of lethal satiric barbs, "Teacher Dong" takes his place alongside such comic tricksters as Joseph Heller's Milo Minderbinder, Hasek's "good soldier" Svejk, and, of course, Rabelais's Panurge.

First published in 1984, *Rose, Rose, I Love You* (the title of a popular song from the 1930s—see my note following the translation) offended and delighted contemporary readers in Taiwan at a time when the island-nation was coming to grips with the consequences of modernization, the heady beginnings of political liberalization after more than three decades of martial law and subjugation by Chiang Kai-shek and his heirs, and the breakdown of cultural traditions. Wang pokes delicious, and often scatological, fun at all of these, and more. In addition to a schoolteacher who trains whores, we are introduced to a doctor who cares more about fondling men and young boys than healing patients, a lawyer who turns the law into a weapon and a money tree, and a politician who strips naked at a campaign rally to show his constituents why they should vote for him.[2]

The setting of the novel is the coastal city of Hualien, a relative backwater in 1960s Taiwan. As in Joyce's *Ulysses*, the central action of *Rose, Rose, I Love You* takes place in a single day, and centers on the opening ceremony of a crash course for "bar girls to be" in a lovingly described Christian church that is then defiled by an assemblage of flesh-peddlers and the flesh they peddle, as "The Lord's Prayer" competes with visions of untold riches from a project with strong nationalistic overtones.

Yet with all the social misfits and buffoons who populate the novel, and the incongruous, madcap adventures in which they participate, it is Wang's ingenious use of language that sustains the comic exuberance of *Rose, Rose, I Love You* and "creates a cacophony of discourse, not only mocking Taiwan's multifarious culture, but also stressing the novel's rebellion against the monophonic system on which traditional orthodox novels depend."[3] A unique mixture of Taiwanese, Mandarin Chinese, Japanese (a consequence of fifty years of colonial occupation, 1895–1945), and English, and the even more interesting mix of people who use and frequently abuse one or more of those lan-

2. This and other revealing observations appear in an appendix to the 1994 Hongfan reprint of the novel by Hsiao Chin-mien, pp. 263–78.

3. David Wang, "Radical Laughter in Lao She and His Taiwan Successors," in Howard Goldblatt, ed., *Worlds Apart: Recent Chinese Writing and Its Audiences* (Armonk, NY: M. E. Sharpe, 1990), p. 53.

guages, afford Wang a wealth of comic possibilities, few of which he lets pass. Puns, spoonerisms (insofar as they are possible in Chinese), mangled foreignisms, malapropisms, and a host of other linguistic oddities pour from the mouths of Wang's characters, both the high and the low, to great satirical and farcical effect. For the translator, however, this feature presents a formidable challenge, which in turn requires a bit of explanation to readers.

Wang Chen-ho knew that few of his Chinese readers would be linguistically adroit enough to follow all the verbal twists and turns embedded in his novel, and found it necessary to help them along by including parenthetical definitions, clarifications, even foreshadowings of changes to come. For the foreign reader, the problems are compounded by both linguistic and cultural chasms far too vast for literal renderings. It has been my goal to replicate the tone where exact parallels between English and Chinese (or Taiwanese or Japanese or whatever) do not exist or where they miss the point altogether. Foreign words appearing in the Chinese text are italicized; mnemonic, and frequently outrageous, Taiwanese renderings of English and Mandarin words are given in comic re-creations in brackets; while other linguistic aberrations have simply been altered to produce an effect close to that of the original. I doubt that Wang Chen-ho ever expected his comic masterpiece to move beyond the linguistic realm—admittedly broad and amorphous to begin with—in which it was created; I hope that he would approve of this attempt nonetheless. Wang's premature death in 1990 (at the age of fifty) robbed not only Taiwanese readers but also a prospective readership throughout the world of a strong satiric voice, for while the locale and the incidents of the novel may be limited, human foibles all too easily transcend time and place.

I am grateful to Lin Pi-yen, Wang Chen-ho's widow (who surely has managed to read *Rose, Rose, I Love You* all the way through by now), and Yeh Pu-jong of Hong-fan Book Company for permission to translate. Thanks, too, to David Wang for choosing this novel to launch a series of Chinese fiction from Taiwan by Columbia University Press, whose Publisher for the Humanities, Jennifer Crewe, and editor, Leslie Kriesel, have been instrumental in seeing it into print. Taiwan's Council for Cultural Planning and Development and the Chiang Ching-kuo Foundation for International Scholarly Exchange generously supported the translation, for which I thank them. Finally, my heartfelt thanks to Sylvia Lin, who carefully checked the finished manuscript against the original and made numerous suggestions for improvement, and to whom I dedicate this translation.

Rose, Rose, I Love You

Chapter One

The Sino-American Theater was located on China Avenue in downtown Hualien, a scant few hundred yards down the street and around the corner from the city's red-light district. And that was where you would find Mercy Chapel, run by the aging mother of Dr. Yun. It was a neighborhood where good coexisted comfortably with evil. The chapel's door stood open all night long to give neighborhood sinners a shot at repentance. No wonder so many people visited the area time and again. You would, too, if you could taste the wicked delights of the flesh and the joy of salvation and rebirth in a single outing. But if you have the opportunity to come to Hualien these days—for pleasure, not business—don't waste your time looking for Mercy Chapel or for Dr. Yun's aging mother. You won't find them. Now, if you feel a need to seek repentance, I recommend walking a bit farther, say to a church on Sun Yat-sen Avenue or the one next to Taiwan Electric Company or that one at the foot of Huagang Mountain—houses that have been filled with the spirit of God for ages. They are all fine places to gain salvation and find Jesus.

Mercy Chapel occupied about 300 square feet of a single-story concrete building whose tile roof had begun to sprout clumps of green moss after a decade of weathering. Except for the rectory, where the pastor managed her affairs, the rooms were given over to fellowship, Bible study, prayer, and choir practice. When you passed beneath the words *Mercy Chapel* on the steel gate, you were confronted by a life-sized knotty-pine crucifix nailed to a limestone wall. Much of the red lacquer had peeled away to reveal the original wood color, transforming what remained into drops of blood that threatened to stain a four-by-seven-foot speaker's platform below. A brand-new pulpit, donated by Sister Li two weeks before the events recounted here—that is, three days before she was summoned by the Lord—stood in front of the platform, and an organ donated by yet another female parishioner occupied an entire corner. Rows of high-backed wooden pews, so old and beat-up they seemed ready for the grave, fanned out all the way to the rear. The offering box by the door, on the other hand, was strong and dauntless as it dispensed powerful whiffs of guilt to all who passed by without stopping. But while the offering box was old yet sturdy, the bookcase behind it looked like a sickly old man about to topple over. The gilded Bibles, the hymnals, and the psalm books were brand new, all having been recently received through the mail from an overseas religious order. Alongside the rickety bookcase stood a small wooden door. Open it and walk ten feet or so, and you would reach an outhouse, one of those old-fashioned hole-in-the-ground types where, when you squatted down, the smell just about bowled you over; then you looked down and had a bird's-eye view of piled-up shit and swarms of wriggling maggots.

It would be another four or five years before the Hualien Municipal Office would discover, to its astonishment, the advantages of cesspools and would urge the city's residents to fill in their latrines and install flush toilets, even offering a 5,000 New Taiwan dollar subsidy. But by then Dong Siwen was already up north working for a TV station in Taipei, having given up his job as English teacher at the Hualien high school. In Taipei, he happily busied himself with newspaper and magazine articles, writing stuff like: "Ah ah! How I miss Hualien's old-fashioned privies! Especially the clang of an iron scoop when it strikes the sides of a cement latrine late on a quiet night! Such a lovely, memorable sound. Ah! Ah! When I recall the clang clang of an iron scoop on a cement latrine, I succumb to homesickness! (A lie. He was not from Hualien originally. Rather, he grew up in Restoration Township, near Hualien.) I am overcome by melancholy!" (Another lie, for he was never one of those mawkish, sentimental types.) This particular essay was filled with "Ah! Ah! Ah!" from start to finish, but, ah, it still won a literary award. Ah!
The courtyard fronting Mercy Chapel was quite spacious, a good 200 square

feet or so. A pair of breadfruit trees, unique to Hualien, stood in the courtyard, one in front, one in the rear. Both were a rich, clean green—dense lotus-sized leaves that spread out in tiers, one on top of the other, to form a thick emerald cloud that all but blocked out the sky. Wonderfully inviting in the summer, the trees had evolved into favorite cooling-off spots for local residents. Clusters of golden yellow decorated the overhead sunshades—from a distance they looked like grapefruits—which the Hualien residents called *bochiloo* (probably an aboriginal word for breadfruit). When the fruit was at its ripest, gusts of wind sent it thudding to the ground, where the scaly golden rinds would split to reveal white fleshy fruit, like manna sent to Moses by God. The fruit was fair game for anyone sitting in the shade below, who would take it home to peel and boil it in fresh water with some dried minnows, which gave it a flavor like it says in the Bible: biscuits dipped in honey.

Beyond the breadfruit trees stood a whitewashed wall roughly five feet high. On one side of the gate, the words *God Loves All His Children* were painted in black, each word a commanding presence that yielded before no one, as if it were impossible for anyone *not* to be loved by Him. A bulletin board on the opposite side of the gate displayed announcements for "Fellowship," "Bible Study," "Prayers For The Sick and Disabled," "Seek, seek, seek, seek the Holy Spirit," and so on.

I have taken pains to describe Mercy Chapel in some detail because it is an important setting in the novel. But please don't assume that this tale is in any way tied up with Christianity, for in fact it is unrelated to any and all religions. It does, however, have more than a passing relationship to off-color rituals, so put your mind at ease and read on!

It was nearly nine o'clock in the morning when a large contingent of people filed into Mercy Chapel. None was a believer, and none qualified as a friend of the church; most were here for their first walk with God. They were the people who ran neighborhood brothels. Besides the whoremasters and madams from such second-class establishments as Lovely Ladies, Tender Town, Peony Pavilion, and Happy Hamlet, the managers of the elite bordellos, the so-called Big 4—Garden of Spring's Black-Face Li (male), Stumpy Courtesan of Night Fragrances (female), Big-Nose Lion from Rouge Tower (male), and Valley of Joy's Sister Red Hair (female, of course)—all showed up. And they were just the ones who came in person. Also arrayed around the pulpit were baskets of fresh flowers; squeezed into all available space, they had been sent not only by these first-time parishioners, but also by an assortment of legislators and bureaucrats who were too busy to make an appearance. Truly, they comprised a garland of exquisite color! Most of the red cards on the flower baskets conveyed one of two sentiments: "Congratulations on the Grand Opening, May Riches Flow Your Way" or "Spring Breezes Bring Rain, Education Without Discrimination."

But this contingent of visitors to the church had not come for morning prayers or to seek the Holy Spirit or even to listen to a sermon. They had been invited to attend a 9:30 indoctrination—not Bible study, but a "Crash Course for Bar Girls."

I'll bet that took you by surprise!

The teacher for this "Crash Course for Bar Girls" was none other than the local high school English teacher, Dong Siwen. Surprised? Teacher Dong's name, Siwen, means "refinement," but it belied his outward appearance. Standing not quite five and a half feet tall, he weighed as much as a super heavyweight, except that the pounds were distributed less equitably, owing to his aversion to exercise; his ample hindquarters and enormous belly made him look like anything *but* an English teacher, in fact were better suited to a general affairs department head who was on the take. Surprised? Well, I have an even bigger surprise for you: Teacher Dong was the spitting image of Shi Song, you know, the fellow who always played the TV clown; that combined with the similarity of physique—the word *blubbery* leaps to mind—well, if you didn't look closely, you might indeed mistake him for Shi Song himself.

Not only that:

1. Owing, perhaps, to his industry in studying a foreign language, even Siwen's Mandarin had a decided Western twang. And the greater the intellect or educational background of the person to whom he spoke, the more inclined he was to pepper his speech with words from translated novels: *What rot—I'm delighted you share my view—This is my considered opinion—He simply doesn't know what he's saying—I am so very proud of you—I was pleasantly surprised* . . . and the like poured from his mouth, making it difficult to listen to him and awkward to have to. Sometimes, like ducks listening to thunderclaps, no one could understand a word he said!
2. No matter how busy or tired he might be, and whatever the weather or the day of the month, he never forgot to take 3,000 milligrams

of vitamin C (he'd read a medical report somewhere that heavy daily doses of vitamin C were invigorating, but could not be sure if that included enhancing his virility); he never ate food that had been in his refrigerator more than a week, for fear that it had become carcinogenic; sorry, but he never used plastic eating utensils, having heard that plastic releases carcinogens when exposed to high temperatures; and he refused to eat meat barbecued on metal grills—cancer again. He would not use laundry detergents until absolutely necessary (ordinary folk like us didn't know until the end of 1981 that there were coarse and fine detergents, and that the coarse ones were far more dangerous)! Each night at bedtime, without fail, he cleaned the spaces between his teeth with twelve inches of dental floss, sawing it back and forth to ward off periodontitis. With such meticulous attention to personal hygiene, no wonder his body weight was going the opposite direction of TV program quality: in his case, up.

3. Teacher Dong was slightly over thirty, yet still a bachelor; so to meet his biological needs without getting into any sort of trouble (by this I mean contracting syphilis or some other venereal disease, herpes not included. Back then, like the rest of us, herpes didn't mean a thing to him; he'd never even heard of it), on the first and fifteenth of each month, as if it were a sacred rite, he locked himself in the school's bachelor dormitory and prudently pleasured himself, as conscientiously as someone taking a prescribed medication: on time, precise dosage.
4. Hard to say if something was wrong with his digestive tract, or if it was a genetic condition, but he was almost ceremoniously flatulent, day and night. Sometimes stentorian, sometimes silent.

Surprised?

Wearing a dark blue suit and a Christian Dior silver-gray silk tie—a gift from Councilman Qian—on this day, Dong Siwen actually did look sort of refined. He was leaning against the offering box, which stood about desk high, gazing fixedly out the door. The fruit on the breadfruit trees is coming awfully early this year! Who'd have thought that my "bar girl class" would actually get underway today, the fruit of my efforts? He was as nervous and excited as an actor mounting the stage for his debut performance. Summer had just arrived in Hualien, with light breezes morning, noon, and night, and low humidity—the best time of the year. But Teacher Dong felt hot all over, as if these were the sweltering dog days of summer; sweat filled his armpits and soaked his forehead. He took out a handkerchief and mopped his brow. God, how I could use a cigarette! Stuffing the handkerchief back into his pocket, he reached into his right suit coat pocket and felt around.

Cigarettes? No such luck!

Reluctantly he recalled that he'd quit smoking. Three weeks earlier, the health department had come to his school with a documentary on smoking and lung cancer. Given his deep-seated fear of cancer, before the film was half over he was in such a state of terror—you'll pardon me for using crude yet appropriate language here—that he nearly released a thunderclap of wind and a torrent of piss. As soon as the film ended, he announced with heroic determination that as of that day he was ending his love affair with tobacco.

Boy, could I use a cigarette now!

He turned to size up today's guests, trying to guess who among them might be a smoker. Most looked exactly like people in the flesh trade ought to look; they were bunched in twos and threes in back pews, sitting up straight and not moving a muscle, like folks in the presence of God ought to sit. A few stood under the arched windows, glancing out cravenly, as if Satan awaited them on the other side. The fiftyish Big-Nose Lion, who managed Rouge Tower, was dressed like a cabaret performer: bright red sport coat, flashy green bell-bottoms, slicked-down, dyed black hair combed straight back to expose every inch of a still-narrow forehead; his nose, worthy of the nickname, was so big that at first glance his face seemed occupied by little else. He and the managers of a couple of second-class brothels were standing five or six feet from Teacher Dong, studying epigrams tacked to the wall next to them: "Don't put off till tomorrow what you can do today," "What ye sow, so shall ye reap," "Stride forward, head high and chest out," "Be open in how you act, and fair in all matters." Big-Nose Lion turned and whispered to the other two:

"Brilliant! That calligraphy is a work of art! And the messages, well, what can you say! The place really does look like a classroom with those up there."

The compliment caused Teacher Dong some unease, for the epigrams had been tacked up in the dead of night by his four assistants. If only they hadn't been so rushed, he wouldn't have had to settle for a harum-scarum job. In addition to the epigrams along the sides of the room, the front was decorated with four large words cut out of red cardboard: Propriety, Justice, Honor, Shame. A piece of floor-length scarlet flannel dangled in front of the pulpit, and a three-by-four-foot blackboard (back then Magic Marker boards hadn't yet made an appearance) stood beside it. . . . Mercy Chapel did indeed look like a classroom.

Teacher Dong had known Big-Nose Lion only a few days, and each time he saw him, the man was puffing away like a train engine. Now this fellow's got to have cigarettes on him.

"Aniki." (He used the Japanese word for older brother, since that's what everyone else called him; why not follow the crowd?) Waiting until he saw Big-Nose Lion look his way, he asked loudly, "Got a smoke?"

"Smoke?" The befuddled look caused Big-Nose Lion's face to shrink, and seemed to enlarge his already prominent nose.

Teacher Dong scissored two fingers and raised them to his lips. "Got any smokes?"

"Yeah—sure." A bit of hesitation there.

"Can I have one?"

"Huh?" That really stumped Big-Nose Lion, whose face continued to shrink, making his nose grow even larger. "Teacher, are you asking—is it OK to smoke in church?"

"Who says we can't?"

"Hey! Hear that?" Big-Nose Lion blurted out gleefully, like the class dunce who has accidentally solved a tough math problem. "You heard him. We can smoke in church!"

Like a magic incantation, this outburst breathed life into the crowd. Those with cigarettes whipped out their packs and lit up; those without smoked O.P.s. Big-Nose Lion preferred his gold-plated pipe. In a flash, out came pent-up chatter and laughter, as if these neophyte churchgoers had come not to pray, but to party.

The man called Ah-cai, a second-class whoremaster, handed Teacher Dong a second-class American cigarette—a Camel. But as Dong put it up to his lips, he stopped and handed it back ruefully.

"I quit."

"Smoke it, what's the difference?"

Siwen steadfastly shook his head, which was revisited by scenes from the documentary shown at school. From that day forward he would keep his vow to treat his body like fine jade and never rekindle his love affair with tobacco, not even a minor flirtation. When he later went to work at the TV station, he submitted one of those "ten-thousander" reports (in this case it was well over ten thousand words, including, of course, plenty of "Ah!"s and "Ah ah!"s) to the station manager, asking him to forbid employees from smoking on the job and fouling the air (he actually used the word "fouling," which was standard at the time, although in March or April 1983, magazines and newspapers abruptly began using the word "polluting," for reasons that escape me) for nonsmokers. With unassailable logic, he declared: Nonsmokers have an inalienable right to be smoke-abhorrent. Ah ah! This right must be respected, ah! He was the first person in that crowd to use the term "smoke-abhorrent," and where he got it is a mystery. The station manager had sure never heard it, and even now, as late as 1984, you can scarcely find a soul who has. Which is why the station manager can be forgiven for laughingly tossing the "ten-thousander" into the wastebasket. (Dong was actually lucky the man "laughingly" threw it away, and not "angrily." Don't you think so?)

Refusing the cigarette, it seems, was no insignificant event, and it had a soothing effect on Siwen; sweaty armpits and a damp forehead ceased to be much of a problem. A couple of the chattier guests crowded up to tell him that if he hadn't spoken, they might have thought that Shi Song himself had come to Hualien.

"Teacher— "

"Hm?"

"Will they really come?"

"You mean Councilman Qian and that bunch?"

"No!" Stumpy Courtesan, the motherly manager of Night Fragrances, shook her head vigorously, propelling the dangling gold earrings back and forth beneath her tiny ears. She had a tiny body so light that when she stepped on the mat of an automatic door, nothing happened. However, though only forty-four years old, she possessed alarmingly oversized breasts (I'll let you in on a secret: she'd had implant surgery in Taipei, but three years and eight months later her Marilyn Monroe tits suddenly started migrating, and even after a prolonged hospitalization, they stubbornly refused repatriation). She wore a bright yellow maxi-skirt, and her glistening hair was combed straight back into a bun at the back of her head, covered by a black hairnet, and adorned with a red velvet flower; her face, all rouged and powdered, beamed as if she were in church to get married. "I'm not worried about Councilman Qian, I know he'll come. I'm talking about—" She reached back to touch the artificial flower and smiled through pinched lips, introducing crow's feet at the corners of her mouth. "I'm just afraid that the GIs might not come to Hualien for their R & R!"

"Yeah, what if they don't come—" That from Black-Face Li, manager of the first-class Garden of Spring, a man who looked like a stick of charcoal, with a face as dark as the bottom of an old wok, a rail-thin body (excessive masturbation, perhaps?), and his customary black martial-arts outfit. In the days to come, whenever an American GI on R & R ran into him in the Hualien bar, the startled comment would inevitably be, "Aha! So there are Chinese negroes, too!" Well, our Chinese negro was standing beside Stumpy Courtesan, chewing incessantly on betel nuts, his mouth stained with the red drool as if he'd vomited a bowlful of blood.

"If they don't, won't we do what the Hakka call 'shoe fur'—you know, suffer?"

"What the hell are you worried about?" Big-Nose Lion blew a mouthful of smoke in his face. "It's been in all the papers, right there in black and white. The American GIs have already left Vietnam by ship. So what's the problem?"

"I know that's what the papers say—"

"Hold on, Teacher!" Stumpy Courtesan interrupted. "Hold on. What I'm saying is, there's a war in Vietnam, right? Well, what I'm saying is, what if the Americans get their butts kicked—"

"On the contrary," Dong Siwen cut in, switching to Mandarin, a smug look on his face.

"Huh?" Stumpy Courtesan shook her head uncomprehendingly, setting her dangling gold earrings in motion once more and initiating a series of round-trip expeditions by her Marilyn Monroe tits.

The other guests shared her bewilderment: "What are you saying, Teacher?"

"What I'm saying—" With a smug grin, Dong Siwen switched to Taiwanese for their benefit: "It's the opposite of Americans losing the war! The opposite of losing the war, of course, is *not* losing the war! Heh, heh, heh, how could a superpower like America lose a war?"

"Oh!" They nodded their heads. "So that's it!"

"Teacher is a learned man! He doesn't talk like us," Ah-cai volunteered in Mandarin with a thick Hakka accent.

"On the contrary. Ha!" A thunderclap of laughter from Big-Nose Lion. Now you know where the "lion" in his name comes from. "A very interesting way to put it."

"Well, if that's the case—" Before Black-Face Li could finish, he flew to the doorway and propelled a mouthful of bloody betel-nut juice onto the carpet of green grass, then flew right back. "So the American GIs in Vietnam are definitely coming for R & R?"

"On the contrary of the contrary," Siwen said with a laugh.

"Hold on! What did you just say, Teacher?" Stumpy Courtesan cozied up and punched him lightly on his meaty shoulder. Her heavy bracelet glinted. "I don't get it!"

"You're joking, right? How could you not get something so simple?" Another thunderclap of laughter from Big-Nose Lion. The pipe clasped between his teeth quaked like a child in a thunderstorm. "On the contrary of the contrary means the opposite of the opposite of what you said, which takes you right back to where you started. Isn't that right, Teacher?"

Without waiting for Dong Siwen's answer, Stumpy Courtesan snuggled up like a schoolgirl and aimed another playful punch at his shoulder, her gold bracelet glinting again. "Teacher, don't talk—don't talk with such refinement, all right? When you turn things upside down like that, you make a dumb old broad like me feel like she's got a swollen head!"

Feeling very pleased with himself, Dong Siwen stroked his jowls, up one side and down the other, like massage therapy.

"The warship bringing the GIs is scheduled to reach port Saturday afternoon at two. Everyone, from the mayor and the county boss to the municipal representatives and county councilmen, plus a contingent of students and another of local citizens, will be there to greet them. Do you folks realize how much work all those people, from the mayor to the county chief, and from the municipal representatives to the county councilmen, have put into getting things ready for these GIs—"

"How many are coming?" Black-Face Li blurted out. "One day the papers say a hundred, the next day it's two hundred."

"Yeah! How many? If it's only a hundred, it's hardly worth the effort."

"How many, Teacher, do you know?"

Eyes staring in anticipation, they awaited Dong Siwen's answer. But he was in no hurry. He fished out his handkerchief to mop his sweaty face before stating with calm assuredness:

"Three hundred."

"So many?" Stumpy Courtesan and a few of the second-class whoremasters and madams nearly shrieked their astonishment. "Three hundred? Really?"

"Are you sure about that?" His question asked, Black-Face Li ran out to deposit another mouthful of bloody betel-nut juice on the carpet of green grass.

"That's what the telegram said. Three hundred American officers and men stationed in Vietnam are coming to Hualien for some R & R. If the telegram said three hundred, then three hundred will be here, no more, no less. That's how Americans do things—one means one, two means two, unlike the peddlers in our marketplace, who are always giving short weights."

Siwen spoke with enthusiasm, drawing out the last comment with studied slowness, as if to allow his listeners a chance to hear the humor in it; then he paused to give them time to react. But damned if not a single one of them laughed, or even smiled, at his little joke. Was he disappointed? To be sure. But like a dedicated scientist, he refused to abandon his experiment.

"Um—believe it or not," he continued with unabated enthusiasm, "in order to give our GIs the royal treatment, everyone—from the mayor to the county boss and so on—is so busy they don't even have time to sweat!" He clamped his lips shut and surveyed his audience, a tiny smile on his fat face, eyes closed to a squint. Still no one laughed. *Damn!* he cursed inwardly. A bunch of stones. Undaunted, he tried again, this time enunciating each word carefully: "Believe it or not, in order to give our GIs the royal treatment, everyone—from the mayor to the county boss and so on—is so busy they don't even have time to sweat!"

My God! None of them laughed. Another inward curse: *Damn.* What a bunch of stones! Undeterred, he made an impromptu correction: "They're so busy they don't even have time to shit!" That was more like it. Those obstinate stones should get a kick out of *that.* With hope swelling his breast, his eyes swept the faces of the flesh peddlers. Not a snicker. *Damn,* nothing but stones. He licked his lips and decided to abandon gentility: "County boss mayor councilmen so busy they don't even have time to get laid!" That ought to do it. Or will it?

But he'd barely opened his mouth when Big-Nose Lion broke the silence. "Three hundred is a hundred more than the two hundred we were expecting, do you realize that?"

Damn! Dong Siwen's eyelids slid downward. He couldn't bear to look at those blockheads, those stones, any longer.

"Wow! A hundred more!" some of the second-class whoremasters and madams said admiringly.

"Not ten, not twenty, but a hundred more!"

"Ai—wow—wee—a hundred more, can you believe it? What great news!" Was that the manager of Valley of Joy, the one everybody called Sister Red Hair? Siwen looked up. It was her, all right. Somewhere along the line she had left the other guests and was standing behind Black-Face Li like a towering tree. As she blurted out "What great news!" she shoved the charcoal stick, Black-Face Li, aside and stepped up next to Big-Nose Lion.

God, is she big! Monstrous hips, no waist, a mop of fiery red hair held down by a cluster of gold hairpins, and a bright red rose stuck behind one ear; rippling biceps emerging from an imported vest she'd bought at a consignment shop in Taipei made her look like a lady wrestler, and no man who laid eyes on her could escape with his masculine dignity intact. Anyone who hooked up with her slinked away before a month was out, worn to a frazzle. By 1981, her business had spread all the way to Taipei, so twice a month she went north to check things out, traveling on the newly expanded Northern Rail Line. With inexhaustible energy, she showed up in restaurants and clubs on Linsen North Road on the arms of strapping young midnight cowboys; sooner or later, every one of those gigolos screamed bloody murder, and if they saw her they took cover, as if she were an avenging angel.

"Great news! We're getting more than we expected! You know, don't you, that all that olive green spells folding green for us!"

Everyone laughed, happy at last. Big-Nose Lion roared like the king of beasts after a kill.

By then everyone was talking at once, pulsating with excitement.

"That's the truth, for crying out loud. Olive green spells folding green!"

"Olive green spells folding green, that's the ticket!"

"Anybody know the conversion rate for U.S. dollars?"

"Forty!"

"Forty? Don't give me a heart attack! Are you saying that one U.S. dollar equals forty NT?"

"More than that on the black market!"

"How much more?"

"At least forty-five."

"No!"

"I'll drop dead if I'm lying."

"Hey, try this out. One GI fuck means one U.S. buck."

"That little? Says who?" This time Ah-cai spoke in Mandarin, albeit with a thick Hakka accent.

"How much are you going to charge them for a night with your girls?"

"U.S. dollars or local currency?"

"American GIs, U.S. dollars. What else?"

"I'd say—"

"We shouldn't be carrying on like this in church!"

"What's the difference? They have weddings in church."

"Drop dead! What the hell is that supposed to mean?"

Ha ha ha. They couldn't have been happier.

Damn! Blockheads, every one of them. Dong Siwen turned to look outside. All they know is money and a piece of ass. No *sense of humor* at all. *Damn!* A bunch of stones, blockheads every one.

"You Big 4 are really on top of things!" Ah-cai looked admiringly at Big-Nose Lion, Sister Red Hair, Black-Face Li, and Stumpy Courtesan. "You've got it made. Your brains work faster than ours. First you open a bar to rake in the foreigners' dollars, then you set up a training session for bar girls! Well, you've got my respect. I'll bet that by joining forces, you Big 4 will make a killing. I take my hat off to you. Aniki—" He gazed into the face (at the nose is more like it) of Big-Nose Lion. "If you have any more good deals in the future, how about letting us second-class folk taste a bit of that honey?" He switched to Taiwanese for this last sentence, lowering and softening his voice in the process, almost flirtatiously, very uncharacteristic for a flesh peddler.

The other second-class whoremasters and madams jumped in with their opinions:

"Right! Aniki, we're all in this together."

"Together, through thick or thin."

"When the Big 4 team up, us little guys, like Black-Face Li says, are left with 'shoe fur,' as the Hakka say, to suffer!"

"No way!" A pout appeared on Sister Red Hair's blood-red lips.

"Aniki!" Ah-cai gave Big-Nose Lion the thumbs-up. "No wonder you're the big honcho. I hear that opening the bar and training bar girls was all your idea. You're amazing, Aniki!"

All his idea, my ass! On the contrary! Dong Siwen shot a contemptuous look at Ah-cai. *Damn!* No wonder he's a second-class whoremaster. He sure talks like one.

With the hint of a smile on his gold-pipe-enhanced lips, Big-Nose Lion was about to reply modestly when Ah-cai continued: "Aniki, you Big 4 are really going to make a killing this time! Wow! And in U.S. dollars, no less! Like you'd died and gone to Heaven!"

"Ai—wow—wee, Hualien's never had a real bar before, this is the first time. We're a bunch of amateurs at this. And talk about problems! Ai—wow—wee, so much trouble, you'd never guess. And all the money we've sunk into this! Make a profit? We'll thank Buddha if we don't lose our shirts." To help make her point, Sister Red Hair threw out her hands, palms up.

"No false modesty now, Big Sister."

"I'm just telling it like it is."

"Hold on." Stumpy Courtesan switched to Mandarin to sound a little more refined, her one chance to show that she'd read a book or two. "I really don't care if we turn a profit. I'm just worried that the GIs won't come. If they don't, then all our work will have gone for naught!" In order to impress her listeners, she repeated herself: "All our work will have gone for naught!" After patting Dong Siwen on his meaty shoulder, she switched back to Taiwanese. "But we have this great news. Teacher says they're coming for sure. We won't have to worry ourselves sick over spending all that money!"

Damn. Go ahead and worry yourself sick, I don't care!

"Teacher, you said you got a telegram, right? What I'm saying what I'm saying is say it again say it—"

With a loud harrumph, Big-Nose Lion said, "You said I said he said, what the hell's wrong with you?"

"No, what I'm saying is the teacher saw a telegram from Vietnam, isn't that right?"

The now-deflated Dong Siwen merely grunted "Um, um."

"Ai—wow—wee, a telegram from Vietnam! Ai—wow—wee." Sister Red Hair reacted like a worshipper who has just seen a vision of Christ. Joyfully she shook her head, as if not daring to believe the good news; the artificial rose behind her ear leaped and bounced excitedly.

"Who got the telegram, Teacher?"

"That's right, who got it?" A clump of ashes—hard to say whose—landed on the shoulder of Big-Nose Lion's red sport coat. Sister Red Hair reached out to brush it off; as she did, the muscles in her arm popped and rippled as if a mouse were loose under the skin.

"Oh." Seeing himself once again the focus of attention, Dong Siwen felt his pulse quicken; his face reddened and the strong willowy scent of his Yaminagaya hair tonic seemed to saturate the air around him. "It was sent to the county boss."

"The county boss? Not to you?" The questioner, a second-class madam, flicked the ashes of her cigarette onto the newly swept and mopped hardwood floor.

"The county boss the county boss, of course the county boss, why would they send it to me? Just so you'll know, it was written in bean-sprout squiggles [English], but our county boss can't even say A-B-C, Dog bite pig-gy—" Finally someone laughed. In line with his award-winning diction, Siwen should have said: Ah! Ah! That's nothing to sneeze at, ah! A couple of the second-class madams laughed like sows in heat—oink-oink-oink, oink-oink-oink. "Now tell me, how could a county boss like that understand a telegram? Tell me, am I right? How could he possibly understand it?"

The next opinion was not long in coming. "How about his staff, you know, his secretary, or his assistant secretary, his department heads, people like that? At least one of them should know dog bite pig-gy!"

Even more laughter this time, with the volume turned up on the oink-oink-oink, oink-oink-oink mating calls.

"On the contrary. They're just like the county boss. They may know a lot about our master Confucius, but nothing about those red-haired barbarians!"

Sister Red Hair didn't lose a beat: "Ai—wow—wee, are you talking about me? Teacher, me and the county boss go way back!" She pointed to her own nose.

"Idiot! Are you even listening?" Big-Nose Lion gave her a steely look.

Sister Red Hair returned the look, but turned coquettish: "I was just joking with the teacher, you know." This woman, who looked like the bandit innkeeper in *Men of the Marshes*, had a soft touch when she needed it. Surprised?

The "you know" still hung on her lips when Teacher Dong Siwen recaptured the initiative. "All they know is bean-curd writing [Chinese], not a thing about bean-sprout squiggles. The county boss had to go looking for Councilman Qian—"

Another interruption: "That makes sense. Councilman Qian's been to college."

"He should know dog bite pig-gy, if anyone does."

More laughter. This time some of them even slapped their thighs.

"Aniki, aren't the county boss and Councilman Qian sworn brothers or something?"

"I hear they drank chicken blood together."

"So they *are* sworn brothers."

"Sure, that's why I went to Councilman Qian to get a license, because he and the county boss are sworn brothers."

"Really?"

"Ai—wow—wee, if not for Councilman Qian, God knows if we'd even have a bar."

"Really?"

"Aniki here wore himself out getting the green light on this. Mother-humper! When bureaucrats say they won't give a license, they won't give one. Mother-humper! All those Keelung and Kaohsiung women, they're mother-humpers too! Money's all they care about. They don't give a mother-humping shit about doing something for the country!"

"This is a church, Black-Face Li, so stop with that mother-humping nonsense!"

They all laughed, everyone but Siwen. The second-class madams really oink-oink-oinked up a storm, as a few late-arriving second-class whoremasters and madams walked in the door. Spotting all the hilarity, the latecomers gathered round to see what was going on. "What's so funny?" they asked. "What are you talking about?"

Teacher Dong took advantage of the first little pause to have his say.

"Councilman Qian didn't study English in college, he studied animal husbandry—animal husbandry, you know, raising cows and pigs. His specialty was breeding swine—" Fearful that someone else might be waiting to jump in, like a bolt of lightning that strikes before you can plug your ears, he forged ahead: "Breeding swine! A whaddayoucallit, a porker poker!" That sparked a number of shocked "Ha ha ha"s and a "Really?" or two. Even some sighs. "Ah! So Councilman Qian studied porker poking! Strange, I never thought you had to go to college to do that." Siwen ignored these comments and went on, speaking faster and faster. "So he couldn't figure out couldn't understand what sort of hormonal crap the telegram was talking about. That's why he came looking for me why they came looking for me, to help the county boss read the telegram help the county boss read the telegram and translate the bean sprouts into bean curd so the county boss will know the county boss will know what's what. I remember clearly that the telegram said clearly that three hundred GIs are on their way—"

"Aniki!" Ah-cai's voice rang out so loud he might as well have been a first-classer, but that was the only way he could bring an end to Teacher Dong's frenetic rambling. "How much are you going to charge the GIs?"

That question really got the crowd talking.

"Right! Do we make them pay U.S. or NT?"

"Ai—wow—wee, you already asked that."

"U.S., of course." Another staccato comment by Black-Face Li, and another dash out the door to deposit his betel-nut juice on the grass.

"What do you think? You're doing business with Americans, and they spend U.S. dollars."

"Will you tell us what you people are talking about?" the late-comers—all second-class flesh peddlers—asked in unison.

No one paid them any attention.

"Wow!" Ah-cai blurted out, beaming with admiration. "U.S. dollars!"

"How much?"

"What?" Big-Nose Lion stared at the inquiring guest.

"What I mean is, how much do they pay each time?"

"Each time?"

"What I mean is, how much will you charge the Americans to get laid?"

"The going rate?" Ah-cai asked with mounting enthusiasm.

"First-class rates?"

"Um." Big-Nose Lion gave Siwen an imploring look, hoping Mr. Refinement would come to his rescue.

But before Siwen could answer, another whoremaster spoke up.

"I say three hundred apiece!"

"U.S.?" one of his cohorts asked.

"No, stupid, local currency!"

"That's not even eight U.S. dollars. Why should they get such a bargain? Those big-nosed GIs are coming here for one reason: *s—e—x*."

"That's right, he's right! With their big tools, they ought to pay extra, just to be fair. Am I right? Besides, if we're not careful, they might sneak a Vietnamese rose past us. We'd be crazy not to charge extra!"

"What the hell is a Vietnamese rose?"

"You don't know? Where the hell have you been? Vietnamese rose is a super v.d."

"Ai—wow—wee, you bunch of pot-bellied idiots, keep talking like that in church, and you'll go straight to hell."

This caused an uproar of hilarity, with Big-Nose Lion leading the pack, as always.

Damn!

Dong Siwen staightened up and aimed his enormous belly outside without even taking pains to give the clamoring guests a parting glance. Black-Face Li fell in behind him to noisily deposit yet another mouthful of blood-red betel-nut juice in the lush green Korean grass. The cuffs of Teacher Dong's suit pants came just that close to being an unintended target.

Damn!

"Where are you going, Teacher? The girls—oh, I mean the trainees—will be here any minute." Black-Face Li was standing in the doorway, wiping drops of betel-nut juice from his mouth with the back of his hand.

"I'm going to see if Councilman Qian and the pastor have arrived."

"The pastor? She's coming too?"

"Yes." Siwen headed for the breadfruit tree.

The spacious courtyard of Mercy Chapel was generously planted with Korean grass, tender and green as a rice paddy. Clusters of rich azalea blooms, some red, some purple, lined the base of the wall. Only here, only in this courtyard, had Teacher Dong not disturbed a single blade or moved a single twig.

As he sat on a bench under the breadfruit tree, he heaved a sigh and bit down on one of his fingers. *Damn!* All your idea, Aniki? Heh heh heh. Could you have managed that bar without me? Could you expect to get a single U.S. dollar out of those GIs without me? *Damn!* At that moment, a fart escaped, a loud one, as if in protest against the inequity of it all.

He looked up into the tree, where new leaves flourished like ears of maize, soft green with specks of yellow peeking through, fresh and clean as if washed by a gentle rain. The leaves shuddered as a breezy gust of wind swept through, rustling softly. This reminded him of the one tenacious problem he had not been able to resolve over the past couple of days: When the *bar girls* greet the GIs at the pier, what should they sing? It ought to be something lively. "Mountain Green"? Not bad, not bad at all, but somehow not quite right. "The Blue Streetlight"? Too sappy, probably not to the foreigners' liking. What, then? They can't sing "Bitter Wine Fills My Cup" or "The Past Lives Only in Our Memory." How about "Wonderful Taiwan"? That's it, they can sing "Wonderful Taiwan"—another gusty breeze set the leaves of the two breadfruit trees rustling—but it might require a bit too much artistry from this bunch of girls. Could they handle it? Besides, it could be too somber. Yes, a little too somber for GIs on R & R. (What a pity that "Children of the Dragon," "Plum Blossoms," and "Hymn to the Republic of China" weren't written at the time. Otherwise, Dong Siwen would certainly have thrown them into the pot of his cogitations. You can bet on it.)

Chapter Two

As Big-Nose Lion, Black-Face Li, Stumpy Courtesan, and the brawny Sister Red Hair were getting ready to leave, Big-Nose Lion took his gold pipe out of his mouth and smiled at Dong Siwen. "Teacher, everything is in your hands. Do what you have to, and spend as much as you need, no problem."

Stumpy Courtesan patted Siwen lovingly on his meaty shoulder. "It's all up to you now. We've already shaved half the head. The bar's ready for business on the corner of Nanking Road and Avenue of Universal Love. It's all made of speckled bamboo. Come take a look when you have a minute. I mean it, half the head has been shaved."

"That's right, half the head. That includes the tables and chairs, which have already arrived from Taipei. And now we find out that—"

Sister Red Hair burst in: "Ai—wow—wee, Aniki, enough about that! After all—" She spun around and smiled fawningly at Siwen. "It's all up to you, Teacher." She reached out to pinch and tickle Dong Siwen's flabby chest. My God! Even Amazons like that know how to flirt! Poor Dong Siwen's face flushed hot, and he couldn't utter a word. All he wanted to do was pass wind.

"No problem," Councilman Qian said over and over as he saw them off—no problem. "No problem!"

After the Big 4 brotheliers were gone, the spacious sitting room was left exclusively to Dong Siwen and

Councilman Qian (the councilman's wife had flown to Taipei that morning for some shopping, and wouldn't be back for a week or so). The two men sat on English blue velvet armchairs, facing each other across a large black-and-green marble coffee table, the current home of one of Mrs. Qian's flower arrangements, several teacups whose contents had been reduced to dregs, and a marble ashtray overflowing with cigarette butts. The councilman summoned his *obasan* [maid], who emptied the ashtray, wiped the table, and took away the used teacups, quickly returning with two cups of freshly brewed tea. After she left, Councilman Qian took off his sport coat and tossed it onto the sofa, then loosened his tie and undid the top buttons of his shirt to reveal a clump of black chest hair and release the imprisoned sour smell of underarm sweat. Dong Siwen's brows twitched. The obasan had slid a silver canister up next to Dong Siwen's teacup, just beyond the reach of Councilman Qian, who gave Siwen a sign with his eyes and motioned to the dish, eliciting an Oh! from Siwen; he scurried to push the dish to the other side of the table. Councilman Qian took out a *Kent*, lit it, inhaled, and pulled a long face.

"What sort of mosquito tactics are you up to?" he said in Taiwanese slang. Then he switched to Mandarin: "Did you take the wrong medicine today, or what?"

"Me? What did I do?" Dong Siwen gnawed his fingernail, a puzzled look on his face.

"Act your age. Who ever heard of a grown man, and a teacher, at that, biting his nails? Don't you care if people laugh at you?"

"What did I do, Chief?" Embarrassed, Teacher Dong drew his hand back and rested it on his knee. "Why should people laugh at me? I didn't take off my pants, or anything."

Councilman Qian let a laugh escape, but quickly regained his stern demeanor. "Did you or did you not agree this morning over the phone to spare no effort on this? Then tonight, in front of everybody, you go and—"

The telephone behind the pinewood screen interrupted him—ring-ring, ring-ring. Chief Qian didn't budge.

"In front of everybody," he continued, "you started hedging big time, coming out with all those maybe this and maybe thats. How come?"

Ring-ring, ring-ring, insistently the telephone rang on, in accordance with the three precepts of Mr. Ye Gongchao: Hold your temper, maintain your dignity, and achieve your goal, no matter what—ring-ring. The goal must be achieved. Ring-ring. Councilman Qian got to his feet. "Stay right there!" he said sternly before disappearing behind the screen.

"Hello! Hello—um—" The telephone had achieved its goal of eliciting a response from Councilman Qian without losing its temper or compromising its dignity. "The police have dropped the charges? Good, good. Why thank me? Oh, by the way, I've been meaning to tell you I've already worked things out. Starting from the fifteenth of next month, the highway buses will discontinue service to Beipu Airport. Seastar Trucking will have the route all to itself—they still want to pass a budget, don't they? They wouldn't dare say no now—right! Tell Ah-zhu and that bunch to get everything ready. The fifteenth of next month will be here before you know it, not many days left—as for the right to operate on the Huadong Highway, the county head and I—" From here on, Councilman Qian, who ran his own trucking company and was honorary chairman of the board of Seastar Trucking, dropped his voice so low it sounded like pillow talk, words not meant for others' ears.

Dong Siwen was feeling a bit more at ease, experiencing one of those rare quiet moments. Chief Qian had come down on him so hard all day that he couldn't even recall how many meals he'd eaten. Or if. Which is why the moment was so satisfying. Not only was he spared the sound of the man's voice, but his nostrils were given respite from his b.o. Siwen raised up ever so slightly and released a fart—an audible one.

He picked up his tea and sipped it slowly. My, what delicious tea! He took a big gulp, put down the cup, and sat back, arms folded across his chest, to leisurely survey his surroundings. He noticed that Chief Qian's second-story sitting room had recently been enhanced by the addition of a sandalwood bar, loaded with a dizzying array of foreign liquor, row upon row of exotic, eye-catching bottles.

Councilman Qian's residence was a fairly new three-story building at the foot of Restoration Avenue, away from traffic. Each floor occupied about 1500 square feet of space, and each could brag a sitting room. The second and third floors were the family quarters for him and his bride of less than six months. His parents lived on China Street, where they ran a fabric shop. Servants occupied the ground floor. When he had visitors, such as merchants with whom he had business dealings or those who wanted his help, he entertained them here on the second floor, where they could talk freely. Guests for a game of mahjong went straight to the top floor, where awaiting them were a mahjong table, mahjong lamps, a mahjong set . . . everything a player could ask for, nothing was missing—nothing, that is, but a place for books, since the word for books sounds like the word for "lose." Common citizens were greeted on the ground floor, in the service area, so as not to force the voting public to negotiate the stairs. In Siwen-ese it would be, Ah! Ah! A man deeply rooted in the ways of popular mores, ah!

The ground-floor furnishings were considerably more austere than those upstairs: Naugahyde sofas, squat tables made of inferior lumber, rattan chairs so old they were rubbed shiny (these you could not buy anywhere, and had been supplied by Mrs. Qian, who had her servants claim them from the garbage dump near the Mingli public school, and even then it took some doing). Downstairs visitors were treated to black tea that cost a mere fifty New Taiwan dollars a catty! For this brilliant suggestion, they had Teacher Dong to thank. At first, Chief Qian opposed the idea: "Why should we act like paupers? We can afford better." Then, with a couple of loud snorts, he switched to Taiwanese: "People will die laughing at our phony act."

This outburst had sent Dong Siwen into a fit of fingernail chewing; his cheeks puffed out as if he had stuffed apples into his mouth. He always did that before saying something momentous, words that must be articulated in perfect dot-the-i's-and-cross-the-t's Mandarin.

"Chief, you're a damned candle, that's what you are! If you're not lit you don't shine. There are *at least* two *advantages* in doing it my way. First, you'll be seen by the people as an 'honest and upright civil servant.' Second, you will create the illusion in the eyes of most people that even though you're a councilman, you're no better off than they are. They'll be able to identify with you that way. Chief, please don't forget one important thing, that allowing the people to identify with you will consolidate your grassroots support for the future. Unless you're not interested in getting reelected, it is to your distinct advantage to take my advice to heart."

No one could accuse Chief Qian of not wanting to get reelected, so he did indeed take Siwen's advice to heart; in fact, he went even further by dressing more appropriately than before. In the winter, when he met with his constituents, he normally wore a dark blue pullover unless it was particularly cold, in which case he added a twill jacket in the color of a military uniform. In the summer he wore only a T-shirt, the collar and underarms of which were invariably soaked through; if his perspiration output fell off a bit, he ran into the bathroom to add a little tap water to the mix (he alone could take credit for this particular strategy), giving the impression that he was serving his constituents every minute of the day. If he was prevented from adding his "sagely" water, he merely took off his shirt and went downstairs to meet his constituents stripped to the waist. For this remarkable ploy he could not claim credit, however. No, it had sprung from the fertile imagination of his schoolmate—from middle school all the way through college—Dong Siwen. In fact, during the campaign for councilman, Siwen even advised him to walk down the street soliciting votes stripped to the waist. At the time, needless to say, Qian opposed the idea.

"Are you nuts? You want me to walk around half naked?"

"Why not? Afraid to show off your tits, little girl?"

"You must be out of your mind! Who'd vote for me if I did that? Take it from me, I won't get a single vote that way."

"On the contrary."

"They'll vote for me?"

"Sure they will."

"I don't see why."

"If you're willing to walk around shirtless, and the other candidates aren't, what does that say to people? Can you figure that out? Chief, you're dumber than I thought if you can't even figure that out. It says, 'I'm a man of action. But the other candidates aren't.' From that point on, you'll be saying things the other candidates don't dare to say, and you'll be broaching topics they won't touch. Whoever has the courage to say things, do things, and broach topics is the one the voters will cast their sacred ballots for. And you can't even figure out something as simple as that. You really are dumb!"

"But doesn't going around half naked look bad? (Back then the word *image* had not gained popularity. Otherwise he would have said, "But wouldn't that tarnish my image?")

After a quick "Aiya!" Dong Siwen explained himself again with a "You'll do what the others won't," and "They don't have the guts, you do," until at long last Chief Qian uttered a reluctant "I'll give it a try." Seeing the chief give his consent, Dong Siwen breathed a sigh of relief. "Talking to you wears me out." Lifting himself ever so slightly off his seat, he sealed his happiness with a fart, another audible one.

"Hmph," Chief Qian grumbled. "Talking to you wears *me* out! After listening to your sermons, I have to endure a gas attack." He shrugged his shoulders and glanced up at the ceiling, with its painted flowers and birds, then lowered his eyes until they were resting on Dong Siwen's ample belly. He blinked, patted the sofa he was sitting on, and started laughing. "It looks like Qian Mingxiong will have to fucking sacrifice his good name just for an extra vote or two."

The campaign posters underwent a change, turning a suit-clad candidate into one who was naked from the waist up. Chief Qian had a taut, muscular body—the back of a tiger and the waist of a bear, and the hairy chest of a European. When the revealing posters first went up, people thought they were advertisements for a virility tonic. Except for the obligatory lines, "I respectfully ask for your vote" and "Candidate number seven, Qian Mingxiong, bows in gratitude," which were left untouched, the remainder of the text was changed to "I am Agent 007, daring to do what others will not. Up to the stars and down to the seas, I am fearless. Vote for me, you won't be sorry." The printing was crude and black, the words a series of clubs. At each political rally, Qian stood up and roared, "I am Agent 007, straight out of the movies. I take on everything my opponents shy away from" and "What others won't do, I will." A loud and intimidating roar.

At his final political rally, he shouted over and over, "What others won't do, I will—what others won't do, I will—"

But his political mantra was cut short by voters at the foot of the stage.

"What will you dare to do? Tell us that!"

"Just what is it you dare to do? What will the others shy away from? What will you do, tell us that."

"Right! What the hell will you dare to do?"

Bursting with excitement, he shouted, "What others fear to say, I'll say. What others fear to do, I'll do. Where others fear to tread, I'll—"

"All talk!"

"What is it you'll dare to do? Show us!"

"Right, right, right, show us!"

"All we hear is 'dare dare dare.' Big deal!"

"Show us what you're made of!"

"Show us!"

This unanticipated development stopped Qian Mingxiong in his tracks.

"Um—um—um—" was the best he could manage, while his face turned red as a ripe persimmon and his underarms flooded with perspiration. At the foot of the stage, his campaign manager squeezed his eyes shut, not wanting to be an eyewitness to the collapse of the sky. But leave it to Dong Siwen to keep his wits about him. His eyelids fluttered for an instant, then he muttered, "I've got it!" Without a word to the campaign manager, he rushed up onto the stage and whispered something to the dumbfounded Qian Mingxiong, who reacted like a penitent who had just heard a horrible blasphemy. Staring bug-eyed at Dong Siwen, he found himself incapable even of "Um um um um." Without another word, Siwen simply patted him on the shoulder and started down off the stage, to a clamorous outburst all around.

"Hey, Shi Song's here!"

"He's come to boost the campaign!"

"Hey! Fat man Shi Song! Fat man Shi Song!"

"Shi Song the clown!"

"Shi Song, Shi Song! Give us a leap! Let's see one!"

"Give us a leap!"

"Give us a leap! And a twist!"

Before Siwen had time to clear up the confusion, someone near the stage stood up and shouted, "You're all wrong!" The crowd quieted down. "That's not Shi Song, that guy's an English teacher right here in Hualien."

The "rectifier" sat down.

"He's right," someone agreed disappointingly. "He's absolutely right. Shi Song wears glasses when he isn't onstage. That guy isn't wearing any."

"Good observation," Dong Siwen remarked in Mandarin. "You get an A-plus."

The crowd laughed.

"But he sure looks like Shi Song," someone else commented. "They're both fat."

"Of course we look alike," Siwen said as he alit from the stage. "We're twins, didn't you know that?"

"Really? Is that true?" more than one curious person asked.

"On the contrary."

"Huh? What did you say?"

Dong Siwen just shrugged his shoulders and smiled craftily. "Sorry, I don't repeat myself."

More laughter.

When he was back in his seat, Siwen looked up at Chief Qian, who was watching him closely, fixedly, the shocked look in his eyes gone. That was a relief to Siwen, who finally felt good enough to permit the sweat to ooze out of the pores on his forehead. Eventually, the campaign manager, who was sitting next to him, opened his eyes; he leaned over and asked, "What did you say to him?" Before Siwen could reply, Qian Mingxiong had begun to speak.

"Ladies and gentlemen, young and old!" He paused to let his eyes slowly roam the faces of the audience. Dong Siwen, having taken a college course in public speaking, knew how important it was to *pause* before a *climax* or before delivering the central *message*, in order to gain your audience's undivided attention. Qian Mingxiong had learned his lesson well. A hush fell over the people who had come to hear the campaign speech, and their eyes widened as they gave him their attention.

It appeared to Siwen that Chief Qian was about to do exactly as he had suggested. Happy again, he was dying to pass wind. So he shifted his hindquarters just enough to let the fart escape silently into the air.

Sensing that he had paused long enough, Qian Mingxiong cleared his throat.

"Fine!" he bellowed. "Since you've got yourselves all worked up, I, Agent 007, Qian Mingxiong, candidate number seven, will give you what you want. That way you'll know that candidate number seven is a man of his word." Another pause to gaze bright-eyed at all those voters craning their necks in eager anticipation. This pause was briefer than the first one. "Take a good look!" he thundered as he tore at his shirt and undershirt with both hands until—presto, there he stood, naked to the waist, his shirts draped over the speaker's platform.

A shocked little girl standing near the stage screeched: "Daddy, look, he's naked! Aiyo, shame on you, shame shame on you!"

Some of the onlookers nearly fell over laughing.

Dong Siwen's Chief Qian thrust out his hairy chest, raised his chin defiantly, looked down his nose at the people below, and stood there with his hands on his hips like one of those itinerant boxers who peddle tonics in Taipei's Wanhua District.

"Well? Do you still think I'm all talk?" A broad smile showed how pleased he was. "Qian Mingxiong, candidate number seven, has shown you what he's made of, proving he's the man for the job, the one you should vote for. Now you know that Qian Mingxiong says what others dare not say and does what others dare not do."

"Says who?" someone shouted from below. "It's just a shirt. Big deal!"

"Right! Right! Anyone can take off his shirt."

A young man in his twenties in the back row stood up, to everyone's surprise, and shouted: "If you can do it, so can I!"

Even before most people had time to turn around in their seats, the young man was naked from the waist up—he only had on a sport shirt, with nothing underneath, making it easy to show up Qian Mingxiong, his speed proving he was even "bolder and more daring." There was scattered applause as the audience urged the young man to go up onstage with Agent 007, Qian Mingxiong, and see whose chest was bigger. Qian, not shaken in the least, waited patiently for the clamor to die down.

As for the excitable, half-naked youngster, he was all ready to run up onto the stage, and would have if one of the candidate's aides hadn't shoved him back into his seat and held him there.

Deprived of a good show, the voting public grew restive again.

"What's so daring about taking off your shirt in public?"

"Right, who couldn't do that? Big deal!"

"I don't know about that! Ask one of the women."

"Why not? Strippers even whip off their underpants, one-two-three!"

Female members of the voting public shrieked their displeasure: "Drop dead, you!"

"Big belly, short life! How can you say things like that?"

"Anybody who talks like that should have a son without an asshole!"

At that moment, candidate number seven Qian spoke up calmly. "Ladies and gentlemen . . ." Private conversations at the foot of the stage continued unabated, so he turned the volume up. "Ladies and gentlemen—ladies and gentlemen—"

Little by little the conversations died out, as people turned to hear what he had to say now. Under his breath Dong Siwen muttered, *Good!* Chief Qian was improving, much better than at the beginning of the campaign, when he'd freeze the minute he got up onstage. Even a simple statement like "I am Qian Mingxiong, candidate 7" came out "I, Qian Mingxiong, can do it 7 . . ." which was met with roars of laughter. And that happened more than once. Now he was in control of the situation, and it had taken him less than two weeks! A quick study, that's for sure. No more panic attacks by Chief Qian; now *he*, Dong Siwen, was the rattled one, as he chewed his fingernails nervously, and his legs, each the size of a small child, shook mightily. The campaign manager's eyes darted back and forth between him and Chief Qian as he muttered to himself: a prayer? a sutra? Could have been either.

"Stripping to the waist is no big deal, you got that right. Now if . . ." Qian Mingxiong lowered his voice and rubbed his belly. Everyone held their breath as their eyes snapped open wide. "Now if . . ." he repeated in a low voice as he pointed to his waistline. "Now if I took off my pants, would *that* be a big deal? Is that something anyone might do?" An "Ahhh" of wonder arose from the first row, while from the back came the shout, "Speak up, we can't hear you!" Qian Mingxiong responded by raising his voice: "What I said was, if—if—I took off my pants, would *that* be a big deal? Is that something anyone might do?" Even the sound of breathing was stilled in the crowd below. "Of course your answer is, stripping to the waist is no big deal, but taking off my pants, now *that* would be a big deal! Anyone can strip to the waist, but no one would dare take off his pants in public. No one, that is, except the fearless Agent 007, Qian Mingxiong. Only me!" He paused again, and the stillness below the stage intensified. Now he had the audience in the palm of his hand. "Watch me!" he said as he stepped out from behind the podium and, without a wasted motion, carefully removed his shoes and socks, neither too quickly nor too slowly, as if stripping to music. The voting public stared wide-eyed, not daring to blink for fear of missing a second of the show. The lips of the campaign manager, who was sitting near Dong Siwen with his eyes squeezed shut, never stopped moving in whatever prayer he was intoning. Maybe the Rosary, or maybe the Great Mercy Sutra, or maybe—. By the time the election monitor sitting in the front row was on his feet waving his arms frantically in warning, Agent 007, Qian Mingxiong, had tossed his pants to the side and was tugging at the last stitch of clothing between him and nakedness—his underpants. Everyone in the audience craned their necks, waiting breathlessly; that included women whose eyes were shut, as if they dared not look, and those who held their hands over their eyes and peeked out through the cracks. The smile on Dong Siwen's face was of a satisfied man who had turned raw genius into a work of art!

"You can't take those off, don't do it!" The election monitor had moved to the foot of the stage, where he thrust his arms heavenward and waved frantically. "You can't take those off!" Terrified that Chief Qian might not heed his warning, he nearly flew to the steps to the left and rushed up onto the stage like a cop chasing down a thief. He was headed straight for candidate number seven Qian to stop him. Dong Siwen made a new assault on his fingernails. Take them off, Chief, take them off! he pleaded silently. Hurry up, take them off! Hurry, hurry! Shit, why won't you hurry!

In the split second before the election monitor reached his objective, candidate number seven Qian turned his backside to his voting public and, in less time than it takes to tell, stepped out of his underpants and stood there in his birthday suit. He took them off! He's naked as a jaybird! He hasn't got a stitch on! The crowd roared—Waaa—and some of the women could be heard to blurt out "Drop dead, you!" or other such exclamations. Flash cameras came alive, blazing in the hands of reporters; the poor election monitor, his hands spread out in front of him, was dumbstruck for a moment before gathering his wits about him and rushing over to where the discarded trousers lay, scooping them up off the ground, and wrapping them around candidate Qian's naked ass so tightly that his prey couldn't get free. Forgetting that he should be shutting his eyes, Qian's campaign manager sat there with his mouth hanging slack, his prayers and sutras also forgotten! Dong Siwen could barely keep from running up onstage to plant a big kiss on Chief Qian and tell him jubilantly, *I am proud of you!* Oh, so proud! Grinning from ear to ear, he shifted in his seat and released a proud, sonorous fart. Unfortunately, the people around him were too caught up in the sight of the bare-assed Chief Qian to savor the spreading odor.

The election monitor had but one thing in mind: dragging candidate Qian down off the stage. But his determined prey shoved him away and turned back to display his nakedness to the crowd below. The election monitor, dutiful to the end, came charging back and once again wrapped the trousers around the candidate's exposed member. As Chief Qian fought the man off, he bellowed to the voting public who had gathered to hear his political views:

"You saw that, didn't you? I, Qian Mingxiong, candidate number seven, am not all talk, am I? I did what I said I'd do. candidate number seven has the guts to do what no one else will do and say what others are afraid to say! I, Qian Mingxiong, candidate number seven, am Agent 007, the man in the movies, who walks where others fear to tread! And that is who folks like you need, the man you should vote for—"

The panicky election monitor could not drag candidate Qian down off the stage, no matter how hard he tried. Back and forth the two men vied, this way and that, until the struggle finally wore the election monitor out and his arms hung limp at his sides, allowing the trousers wrapped around candidate number seven's midsection to slip down. They were back on the floor!

Waa waa waa! Waa waa waa! There was candidate Qian's black pubic hair! Right there in plain view! The people were dumbstruck. Distaff members of the voting public, pale faces showing their shock, screeched as if they'd seen a ghost in the dark of night. Their male counterparts, on the other hand, lapped it up, quick to editorialize:

"You can't call *that* small!"

"Ho, I'd say it was a size large!"

"That's one even a Yankee could be proud of!"

Chief Qian was like one of those actresses who, years later, acted in so-called social-realist (soft porn) movies and turned nudity into stardom. Not only did he trounce his opponents, but in the process he earned a nickname of which he could be proud: Pantless Qian.

After his election, Qian began doing what others dared not do, as promised. At the first hint of an energy crisis, he made a direct appeal to all married compatriots as part of an innovative plan to conserve energy: since married couples sleep together, it made perfect sense for them to bathe together (the idea came from Dong Siwen, who had stumbled upon it in a British newspaper). At a council meeting, he held forth on the benefits of married couples sharing a bath: it saves water and electricity, one person can wash the other's back, it's very romantic. . . . The next day, newspapers big and small devoted an entire page to this breaking story, even ran his photo. Who'd have guessed that one bold utterance would propel him to the status of the most celebrated city councilman in the country?

For decades, a host of people had wrung their brains dry in an attempt to land prized bus routes, and every one of them had failed. But our Pantless Qian was no ordinary man; he had been daring to do what others dared not even try on the city council for less than a year when every prized bus route was handed over to the Seastar Trucking Company (needless to say, Seastar made it worth his while, with stock options and the like). The nature of his daring? "If you don't give me the bus routes, I, Qian Mingxiong, won't let you pass your budget!" (This clever move did not originate with Dong Siwen.) Many such bold moves sprang from the mind of Pantless Qian—as numerous as the hairs on a cat's back—but this isn't the place to troop them out for your acclaim.

Dong Siwen sipped his Dragon Well tea as he gazed admiringly at the handsome sandalwood bar, then took another sip, marveling over how delicious it was. Just delicious! He knew Chief Qian would be grumbling at him pretty soon. Who'd have guessed that the chief would take a casual, meaningless comment so seriously, and actually invite the Big 4 to his home to put their scheming heads together? What a surprise that had been!

"Siwen, I need a favor." Chief Qian had phoned him at school shortly after nine that morning. "You're the only person in the world who can help me on something."

"What is it, Chief?" He was so flattered there was laughter in his voice. "What is it? Tell me, what could possibly be so urgent?"

"It's a long story, a very long story."

"Then give me the short version. You're going to have to tell me what's up sooner or later!"

"Here's the deal—you're not too busy to talk, are you—oh, no classes, that's good—so here's the deal—" Like an official at a briefing, Pantless Qian laid out the particulars, briefly and to the point. As soon as the heads of the Big 4 heard that American GIs in Vietnam were coming to Hualien for some R & R, they devised a plan to open a bar to entertain the Yanks. One of them sent to Taipei for bar girls while another one applied to the county government for a permit. They assumed that getting a permit would be a snap, and were surprised when the county government buried their request; apparently no one in all the centuries since the legendary Pangu separated heaven and earth had ever requested a permit to open a bar in Hualien. Lacking a precedent, they simply postponed any decision. The news perplexed Dong Siwen, who "ah-ah"ed and "oh-ah"ed over the phone. That bunch of tawdry panderers sure know how to use their heads, Dong Siwen was thinking. Nothing tawdry about their imaginations!

"So they came looking for me. They were a big help in my campaign, so of course I felt obliged to intercede on their behalf. And of course, I got them their permit."

"And of course they found a way to show their gratitude."

"It wasn't much."

"How much? I'd be interested in hearing."

"Only twenty percent of their stock. That's all, twenty percent. But you know, in order to keep me from worrying about this whole business, they've given me a blank check. You may think they're in a tawdry business, but they know the meaning of the word *honor*!"

Dong Siwen clicked his tongue a few times before exclaiming, "*Wonderful! Wonderful!*"

"But you know, now there's been a snag."

"Like what? Second thoughts? Holding back on the money?"

"No, that's not it. The money's no problem. The problem is, the Taipei bar girls don't want to come, they won't—" Councilman Qian paused while he searched for just the right words. "They don't want to come here to perform their services."

"They don't want to take their cups to another table!"

"They don't want to come here to perform their services."

"Afraid there won't be enough money?"

"No, it's not the money. It's the distance and the short term of service—only a week. Besides, the bar girl business is booming in Taipei these days, so they're not willing to leave. All their emissary has to show for his time in Taipei are a couple of scuzzy whores who can tend bar. What good is that? Oh, and that's not all. What do you think those scuzzy goddamned Taipei whores said? You'll blow your stack at this. They said their biggest worry about coming to Hualien was earthquakes!"

"What did you say?" Dong Siwen blurted out, blowing his cool, not his stack. Some teachers grading papers in the office stopped writing and looked up.

"They're afraid of goddamned earthquakes. Whores who've been laid a thousand times think their asses are worth their weight in gold! That bunch of know-it-alls said that all Hualien's got are earthquakes and typhoons, and that performing their services could get them killed."

"Damn!" Switching to Mandarin, Dong "the refined" was anything but. The other teachers in the office were looking at him again, and a couple of the women wrinkled their noses as if a foul odor had hit the air.

"Construction on the bar is nearly finished, you know, right there on Nanking Road, in that vacant lot across the street and down a ways from the

Heaven's Omens Theater. And you know, don't you, that the custom-made bar and the tables and chairs have already been delivered. Not to mention all that imported booze! Then some scuzzy whores tell us they're not coming! Lousy cunts!"

Realizing that his fellow teachers were eavesdropping, Dong Siwen lowered his voice. "Sounds like you'd better cut your losses and get out!"

"Get out? This is no time for jokes! They've poured a lot of money into this!" By this time, Councilman Qian was mixing his Mandarin and Taiwanese indiscriminately.

"It's their money, what the hell does that have to do with you? Oh, right, I forgot. You're worried about your twenty percent, aren't you?" (Using 1981 street talk, he could have said, "You're worried about your oh-point-two cut, right?) Dong Siwen was a teacher, after all, and it was important for him to dot his i's and cross his t's in proper Mandarin.

"That's not what worries me."

"On the contrary!"

"Enough already! I'm about to shit my pants, and you're joking around! That's you in a nutshell. All we've got is a week, you know. The GIs will be here in one week. Now do you see the urgency?"

"Taipei's got its tea-tasting establishments, so why not open a wine-tasting establishment here?" Pleased with this suggestion, Dong Siwen chewed on his fingernails as his eyes swept the office to see if the other teachers were still listening. They were busy correcting student papers—too bad. Apparently they had lost interest.

"You can operate other businesses without women, but not this one. For this business, it's long live women!"

"You've got a point. I guess that means the bar won't open."

"Oh, it'll open, all right. I told them we don't need those Taipei girls, so not to worry. There's no shortage of girls right here in Hualien!"

"That's right, Chief. You tell them there's nothing wrong with the local products."

"My thoughts exactly. I'll have the Big 4 pick some of their best-looking girls to service the Yanks!"

"Chief, I'm not just flattering you when I say that's one hell of an *idea* you've got there. That's it, use girls from the Big 4. Girls from the Big 4, that's the ticket. They're all battle-tested, aren't they? They won't have any trouble servicing those fighting GIs from Vietnam. And that puts them on a par with the best of Taipei. Who needs them? You can't tell me they've—" He lowered his voice and looked around again to see if the other teachers were eavesdropping. "They don't have two you-know-whats, do they?"

"Mother of all ancestors! I thought you were a teacher. How can you say something like that? Selling her you-know-what isn't all it takes to be a bar girl, don't you know that?"

"Well, sure, they have to know how to drink."

"Drink? That's no problem. Anyone can drink."

"What else is there?"

"They have to know some English. The girls at the Big 4 flesh mills—" Dong Siwen laughed so hard at that—momentarily forgetting where he was—that all the other teachers stared daggers at him. "—don't have any trouble selling their wares. And they know to drink. But they don't know a word of English, and that's the rub."

"Oh!" A lightbulb went on in Dong Siwen's head. Then, regaining his refined, scholarly demeanor and not forgetting to lower his voice, he said, "I thought you meant writing poetry and novels."

"Poetry and novels? Shit! I'm talking about English conversation."

"English conversation, that's easy. A snap. All you need is a little training."

"A little training. That's it?"

"I wouldn't lie to you, Chief. A little training, that's all you need. Let me explain. The issue here is that the girls want to sell you-know-what, and the Yanks want to buy some you-know-what. A business transaction, that's all it is—" On the other end, Councilman Qian muttered, "Shit, what's with all this you-know-what stuff? Aren't you taking this 'refined' business a little too far?"

"How about holding off with your brilliant opinions until I finish? What I'm trying to say is, everything revolves around the buying and selling of you-know-what. Don't tell me you can't understand that. Give me a break, what do you say? I'm in the school office, Chief, so I have to watch my language! All right? Whether you get the picture or not, the buying and selling of you-know-what is what this little play is all about. Which means that if the girls learn how to say three things in English—"Hello," "How are you?" and "Want to do you-know-what?"—everything is A-OK! You're not sending them to Vietnam to negotiate with the Viet Cong or attend a meeting of the UN

Security Council, so who needs to be fluent? Three phrases—"Hello," "How are you?" and "Want to do you-know-what?"—is plenty. Beyond that, it's what they do, not what they say. Actions speak louder than words. Am I right, Chief?" All this he said in a tiny voice, of course, but his face glowed with pride.

"All I know is, you're the only person I can count on for something this important."

Without getting the drift of the Chief's comment, Siwen plowed ahead with his lecture: "Chief, just teach them those three phrases, and everything will be *OK*! Three little phrases will guarantee you a thriving business. The dollar bills will come rolling in!"

"Siwen." Councilman Qian's tone of voice was a clear sign that he had made up his mind after careful consideration. "I really need your help on this."

"How's that?" Dong Siwen cranked up the volume without meaning to. Some of the teachers put down their pens and stopped working so they could get an earful.

"*You* can train the girls from the Big 4 to speak English. I'd like you to teach them as much as possible, and not just three phrases."

"Me? How can I do something like that?"

"If my pork-belly drill instructor can't do it, who can? Have you forgotten that you're an English teacher? A full-fledged graduate of Taiwan University's Department of Foreign Languages!"

"Where am I supposed to find the time, Chief?"

"That's no problem. I'll request leave for you. Come over to my place tonight, and we'll talk things out with the people from the Big 4."

"Chief, I—"

"You don't want to help me, is that it? Have you forgotten that you're a consultant for my company?"

"Don't get me wrong, Chief—"

"Then it's settled. Eight o'clock tonight at my house. Oh, and I'll have Huang, my bookkeeper, bring over an advance on this month's consulting fee—Hm? OK, fine, I'll send money to your father in Guangfu. Who'd have guessed that a meaty fellow like you could be such a filial son! Oh, right, it's time our meaty Siwen got a raise. Shit, this is no time to be polite. What's wrong with showing my gratitude with a little extra cash? Why thank me? I should be thanking you for helping me get elected! Shit, a little extra cash isn't going to kill you!—My meaty Siwen. Tonight, eight o'clock sharp, got that? And have dinner before you come, got that?"

"Aiya, you don't even want to feed me, is that it?"

"I'll make it up to you after my old lady comes back. Have you got it? Be on time, you hear me?"

"All right."

"You said you'd do it." After wrapping up his secretive phone conversation, Councilman Qian came out from behind the Japanese-style pinewood screen and sat down next to Siwen. "So what's with the cloak-and-dagger stuff as soon as the heads of the Big 4 are around? 'This won't do, that's no good,' like you won't agree to anything! What's the matter with you?" He took a cigarette out of his silver humidor and lit it. "They said they'd cover all your expenses. You won't be out a penny. Not to mention the thirty thousand yuan for your troubles. Thirty thousand! Not enough for you? Thirty thousand for less than a week's work. That's six or seven months' teaching salary, do you realize that? A great job like this, and you want to think it over! Have you taken the wrong medicine today, or what?"

Shrugging his shoulders in reply, Siwen looked happily into Chief Qian's angry face and raised a finger to his lips, but quickly lowered it for fear that Chief Qian would give him hell for chewing his fingernails at his age.

"Say something, will you?"

But Siwen, laughter tucked into the folds of his fat face, kept his mouth shut, and merely turned his blubbery head to one side to move his nose out of the way of the strong vinegary smell rising from Chief Qian's armpits.

"Oh, I know!" Councilman Qian said as he pounded his fist into the sofa. "It's because they're lowly prostitutes, isn't it? Not good enough to be your students!"

"Oh, please!" Siwen replied in defense of himself. "Teachers aren't the snobs you think we are. Anyone who wants to learn can be our students. Didn't Confucius himself say we should provide education without discrimination? Education without discrimination!"

"Then how come you made things so difficult for them a while ago, hemming and hawing like that?"

"There's something you don't know, Chief." Now if this had been one of those popular musicals, Dong Siwen would have struck a pose and broken into song about now. But instead of singing, he just giggled. "Why make it sound like my patriotic duty? This isn't about going out to kill off commie bandits, after all. Besides, with people like that, you have to make them think you're stooping to their level because you have to, not because you want to. Not only that—not only that, it's important to let that bunch of whoremasters and madams know they can't get intellectuals to do their bidding just by throwing a little money around!"

With his cigarette hand, Councilman Qian pointed and said with admiration written all over his face, "Who'd have thought that a numbskull like you, with that pig brain of yours, could be so clever and calculating?"

Delighted by the comment, Dong Siwen felt the need to pass some celebratory gas; leaning ever so slightly, until his right cheek was off the sofa, he let one fly. Oh, a loud one!

Embarrassment forced him to turn away from Chief Qian's gaze and stare at the brand-new, handsome bar. Graciously pretending he hadn't heard, Chief Qian kept on smoking and kept on talking. "Siwen, time's a-wasting. How much is it going to cost? How many people do we need? Where do we start? It's time to work out the details." He picked up his tea, took a big gulp, and carried it over to the head of the stairs, where he shouted down to the obasan for a refill.

They talked for a long, long time. And the more Siwen talked, the faster the inspirations came, and the more his confidence grew; he kept writing and drawing things in a little notebook. As for Councilman Qian, the more he talked, the closer he felt to that oh-point-two cut, which kept his spirits high.

At a little before two in the morning, Dong Siwen abruptly smacked himself in the head.

"Of course! Chief, we've got a problem."

"What's that?"

"Where am I supposed to stay?" At that moment, he looked like a man discussing matters of grave national concern.

Councilman Qian put down his teacup and stared at Siwen. "Don't you have a nice place in the school dormitory?"

"And there's the problem."

"Are your hormones acting up again? What are you talking about?"

"Boy, are you dumb, Chief! How do you expect me to use my school dormitory to engage in this kind—this kind—" He was too embarrassed to say it.

"This—what?"

"How can you expect me to use my school dormitory room to engage in this sex business?" He spat out the words, as if he had only to get them out quickly for them not to belong to him.

It took Chief Qian a while to absorb this.

"Shit!" He pounded the table admiringly. "I'm no match for you. You may be big and dumb, but you're one sly fox—" He took a sip of tea and cast a sidelong glance at Siwen. "You could stay here at my place—" No, that didn't feel right. He sighed a time or two, then turned very businesslike and said, "I'll arrange for you to stay at that newly opened hotel, and it won't cost you a thing. It's on the Big 4, every penny of it." His face softened into a smile. "That ought to clear up that problem. Sex in a hotel is how it's supposed to be, right? Am I right?"

Chapter Three

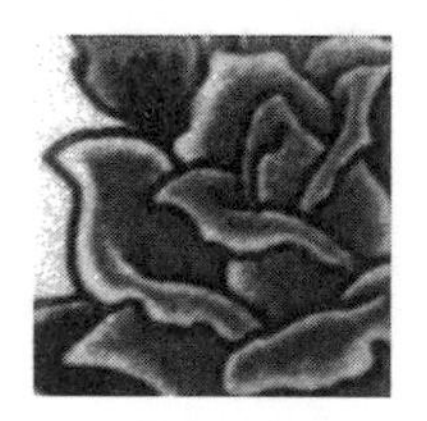

It was a third-floor hotel suite whose sixty or so square feet were covered by a dark red carpet. Curtains in front of the French windows had fist-sized red roses on an apricot yellow background. With the curtains open, wind swept in to make dancing bouquets of the roses. By looking out the French windows you could see all the way to the breakwater past the far edge of the city. It was a beautiful day, with sunlight glinting off the blue ocean. Just off to the right, rows of lush green eucalyptus trees on Huagang Mountain seemed so close you could reach out and touch them. But in a scant few years, the skyline would be broken up by buildings four stories high and higher from one end of Hualien city to the other, and if you felt like looking out the hotel window at the breakwater or at the eucalyptus trees on Huagang Mountain, then, Ah ah! Impossible, ah! (I wrote that in award-winning Siwen-ese.)

Now while the hotel had only three floors, it was the first one in Hualien to actually use the word *hotel*, and the first lodging house equipped with modern facilities (high-class places like the Astor, the Generalissimo, and the Universe had not yet appeared on the scene): every room was air-conditioned and came equipped with a coil-spring mattress, a functional headboard, a bedside lamp, a telephone, a TV (color, of course; Hualien's relay stations were up and running by then, and programming from all three Taipei stations was available), a sofa, and a tea table. And a desk stocked with stationery printed with the hotel's logo, address, and phone number, all for the writing and reading needs of the guests. Siwen was thinking that all the place needed was a copy of the King James Bible to be perfect—world class! There was, of course, a sit-down flush toilet, a full-sized bathtub with hot water at the turn of a tap, and toilet paper on dispenser rolls. Why, the bathroom even had porcelain tile walls! Admittedly, not everything was the best that money could buy, but for Hualien at that time, the array was a real eye-opener. During the first two weeks after the grand opening, swarms of local residents had come to gawk at the new hotel, some actually spending four or five hours on a train from the countryside just for the privilege of having new vistas opened to them. Thanks to Councilman Qian, this was where Siwen would live *and* work. The choice of a top-floor room was Siwen's. He was taken by the pink walls, his preference for which drew sarcastic comments from Chief Qian about how he never thought a big, dumb porker like him could be a romantic at heart!

But romance had nothing to do with it! Siwen had once come across a newspaper item about a woman in America who had discovered the benefits of pink: how its properties could revitalize the fatigued and weary, mellow the irritable and irascible, and inspire and stimulate the downtrodden; it was even effective in getting bad people to put down their knives and take the path of goodness and mercy. . . . Naturally, the item was accompanied by refutations from several hardboiled scholars. After reading this story, Siwen not only saw pink in a new light, he developed an infatuation with the color. Years later, he got married and covered the walls of his house, from the living room to the bedrooms, with pink wallpaper. Even the ceramic tile in the bathroom was pink—exactly why is hard to say. To lessen the strain on his body, and his mind, through improved bowel movements, maybe? After going to work at the Taipei TV station, he even wrote a soap opera revolving around the color pink and all its benefits: if you wanted a baby boy, you had a baby boy; if you wanted a baby girl, that's what you got; kids who grew up in pink houses never learned bad habits, and lazy kids enrolled in pink schoolhouses were eager to learn. . . . It was called "Ah ah! Pink, ah!" Before the daytime drama had run its course, many businesses had already painted their offices pink. Naturally, some local schools painted the walls of their slow-learner classes bright pink. And just as naturally, a considerable number of families jumped on the bandwagon and painted their houses pink, inside and out. A journalist wrote in one of the newspapers: "It's a pink cyclone!" And Siwen was the creator of that cyclone! Absolutely unimaginable!

Absolutely unimaginable! That he would move into a third-floor suite in Hualien's first hotel—the first to offer sit-down flush toilets—chosen by Councilman Qian as the place to train his bar girls! And that was just the beginning. Councilman Qian rented a room on the second floor as an office and sent four of his clerks to serve as Siwen's assistants. Within hours of moving into the hotel, Siwen was suddenly, and rather astonishingly, reminded of the biblical story of how Jesus miraculously cured the lepers, one that his professor had introduced in a Survey of Western Literature course: "And it came to pass, as he went to Jerusalem, that he passed through the midst of Samaria and Galilee. And as he entered into a certain village, there met him ten men who were lepers, which stood far off. And they lifted their voices, and said, Jesus, Master, have mercy on us. And when he saw them, he said unto them, Go show yourselves unto the priests. And it came to pass that, as they went, they were cleansed." He recalled it as if he had seen it with his own eyes and heard every word. And that's not all that astonished him: immediately after recalling this story, he was treated to the incredible sight of forty or fifty girls from the Big 4 coming to meet him. They stood far off, lifted their voices, and said, "Teacher, have mercy on us!" He opened his mouth, he really did, and said: "Ah ah! I really truly have mercy on you all! Which is why I'm going to do everything possible to save you, ah! Cleanse you. Do everything within my power to train you to be the best bar girls you can be, ah! You must work hard and study hard to reap the greatest rewards from your training. That is your goal! Ah ah! Your standing in society will soar! Your lives will soon improve!" (Back then no one used the term "quality of life." If they had, Dong Siwen would certainly have added a sentence: "Ah ah! Before long, your quality of life will definitely improve, ah!") Ah ah! Incredible that a response of that caliber could flow from his mouth, ah!

It is quite possible that the pink walls had worked their magic to stir up his sense of compassion, to give birth to thoughts of good deeds, and to instill in him the determination to elevate this training course to a state of perfection, as if to say, "If I don't enter hell, then who will?"

A state of perfection!

Now that the goal was in sight, clearly in sight, he roared like a lion in his pink room: fear no hardships, stride boldly forward, reach your goal, never stop (four phrases, no more, no less, a la the MGM lion, which always roars four times).

Without wasting a minute, he summoned his four assistants and spent the next two days and nights studying problems with unrelenting diligence, part of the time in his pink suite and part in the second-floor office, eventually hammering out a detailed plan of action. In Siwen-ese it would come out like this:

"Ah ah! This great endeavor, unprecedented in the history of Hualien, will be undertaken by Siwen, who will oversee its development from cradle to full growth and vigor, ah!"

Chapter Four

"—Teacher, what's that you're saying? Huh? How come I can't understand a word? Ya—wn—" Big-Nose Lion yawned grandly as he spoke into the telephone receiver, his eyes tearing up in the process. His wife-in-waiting, A-hen, perched beside him on the red satin sofa, also yawned while filling his pipe with some American Mixture 79 tobacco.

"Ya—wn." Big-Nose Lion tried again. "Oh, you're speaking American! Well, that's why I can't understand it. Teacher, you talk American like a native! And I'm not the only one who says so. Even Chief Qian says your American is world class! I'm not just saying that to make you feel good. I'm telling the truth. I want you to know how grateful I am, Teacher, that you are helping us out like this. I was telling Black-Face Li and the others that we couldn't have made a better choice. No need to be so polite, Teacher, we four really owe you this time. Now don't talk like that, please don't—that's right, Teacher! If there's anything we can do, just give the word. And don't be so polite, we'll cooperate any way we can. Um, all right, I'll choose the fifty girls you asked for right away, all eighteen-year-olds, just as you want. Eighteen-year-old girls, the flower of youth, good, that's a nice way to put it. All right, all right, no one over twenty—don't you worry, Teacher, I'll remember every word—good, that's the way to do it, all right, I'll get on it right away, right away—"

Big-Nose Lion hung up the phone and yawned again, so grandly that his nostrils seemed to stretch all the way to his earlobes. A-hen pointed at him with the now-full pipe, which glinted in the light.

"The sun's about to rise in the west! Aniki sure knows how to talk, so refined and polite, so respectful to the teacher—" Flashing her long almond-shaped eyes, she mimicked the way he had been talking on the phone, humbly and respectfully: " 'Don't you worry, Teacher, I'll remember every word, I'll remember every word, I'll remember every word.' "

"That's enough. Since when did I repeat myself three times? You'll never catch me talking like that!"

He snatched the pipe away from A-hen, who picked a French cigarette lighter up off the table and lit it for him. A couple of good puffs brought his face to life, and the sleepy, half-drugged look disappeared. He sagged into the sofa beside her like a collapsed pagoda. "Whoever heard of such a mother-humping chatterbox! And a teacher, no less! First thing in the morning, before the sun's even up, he reaches for the telephone and screws up our day. Doesn't he know that people in our business are night owls, that we never go to sleep before dawn? I barely close my eyes and he's on the mother-humping phone. Woke you up, too, didn't he? One mother-humping phone call is all it takes. He says whatever pops into his head, and now he's called three times in half an hour. Who can sleep with all that racket? First he asks for twenty girls, then thirty, now it's fifty, and this many or that many are supposed to be mother-humping aborigines. How come? That's how you get a fair representation of Hualien's unique ethnic makeup, he says. Shit, whoever heard of a teacher being so damned *kadan ja nai* [fickle]. He changes his mind so often he can't stick to a single idea. Handing this business over to him—" Another mighty yawn, with his nostrils making a new assault on his ears, then: "—I tell you, I'm worried."

"So get someone else," A-hen said through her fingers, which were stifling a yawn of her own, as she scooted up next to him and touched his bare chest—not yet slackened by advancing age—with a hand on which the nails were painted bright red. "All it takes is money."

Her fingers slipped upward and began twisting the hair under his arm. Ticklish as always, he squirmed away. "There's no time. And how do we find someone who can speak American like him? Besides, he's Chief Qian's boy, and I'm not about to offend *him*." Her hand was busy again, this time with his nipple. "Shit, he's bringing all those U.S. dollars our way, so we'll just have to go along with him!" He pushed her hand away and stood up, naked as the day he was born, with the exception of a baggy pair of linen boxer shorts. Cupping the bowl of his gold-filled pipe, he said, "Go make me some ginseng tea while I get dressed. You know, tomorrow—that's right, tomorrow—our dear teacher wants to start the training, which means I've got to get moving if I'm going to choose the girls in time."

Big-Nose Lion wasn't wearing a Western suit, so he threw a bright red vest over a lavender shirt—the buttons were made of pale green Taiwan jade—slipped on a pair of bright yellow bell-bottoms with blue stripes and a pair of silvery white shoes, then slicked his hair, dyed jet black with a high sheen, from front to back. He topped off the ensemble with his gold-filled pipe and shades that covered the top half of his face: a fashion statement that made him look like a character right out of a movie, not someone meant to be out in the sunlight.

After drinking down the ginseng tea, he picked up his 007 briefcase and walked to the door, but didn't quite make it before the telephone called him back—ring-ring ring-ring. He tossed his briefcase down on the sofa and reached out for the phone but was stopped by A-hen, whose grumbles accentuated the insistent ringing.

"That has to be your dear teacher calling again! Tell him you're on your way to work, and if he wants to talk, he can call you at the Rouge Tower. And tell him not to call here again. We can't take much more of this! After going at it all night, how am I supposed to get any sleep if this damned teacher keeps calling! I need sleep to recharge my batteries, you know." She yawned until you could see the gold cap on one of her molars.

Sure enough, it was Dong Siwen. This time, instead of coming up with a new figure for trainees, he called to inform Big-Nose Lion that after discussions with Chief Qian, they had decided that the best place to hold the training sessions was Mercy Chapel, run by the aging mother of Dr. Yun, his old classmate. It was spacious enough, quiet, and a lot more convenient, since it was close to the Big 4. They had decided to turn the main hall of the church into their classroom, and had already made the arrangements. (Big-Nose Lion wanted to object, but what could he say at this point?) The rent was settled at five hundred yuan a day (at the time, a three-bedroom apartment with living room and dining room went for something in the neighborhood of seven or eight hundred a month). Siwen asked Big-Nose Lion to be sure to stuff five hundred into the offering box every day, without fail. Finally he said:

"Make sure every girl is at least five-foot-one. Absolutely no one under five-one. If they're too short, their customers might mistake them for teenagers! And who has the guts to do you-know-what with a teenager?"

"You-know-what? Just what is you-know-what?" As soon as he said it, Big-Nose Lion got the picture, and burst out laughing. "Oh, *that's* what you're talking about! When you speak in Mandarin, teacher, I don't always get every word, like a duck hearing a clap of thunder!"

"This is important, Aniki, absolutely no one under five-one—" Dong Siwen continued to make his point in Mandarin, as if that were the only way he could keep the conversation on the proper level. "You know, don't you, Aniki, that if a girl's too small, then her you-know-what will also be too small. I've got that right, haven't I? And if her you-know-what is too small, how's she going to *match* up with an American? The *size* will be all wrong, am I right or aren't I?"

Big-Nose Lion was indeed a duck hearing a clap of thunder—for he didn't understand a word the man said. "What's that you're saying, Teacher? I can't understand a word of it. Are you talking American again? You're not? Oh—oh—oh—ah—" By now he was laughing so hard that his nostrils seemed about to fly up into his ears, and his pipe nearly bounced out of his mouth. "Ha ha, I guess it takes a teacher to work out all the details, after all—Teacher, I'm not just being kind when I say that with you in charge, we can't lose, simply can't lose—no politeness, now. I'm just telling the truth—Teacher, don't you worry, I'll do everything you want, just the way you want it. I'm on my way out the door right now to take care of everything, take care of everything—that's right, if you need to talk to me, call me at work."

As soon as he hung up the phone, A-hen asked him what was so funny, but by then he was laughing so hard his face scrunched up into a mass of wrinkles that looked like one of those weather maps that would one day become so popular on TV weather broadcasts. Finally he finished telling her all about you-know-what, laughing the whole time, then shook his head in exasperation. "I can't believe I actually heard a teacher talk about such unrefined things. Weird, really weird!" (This final comment *he* uttered in Mandarin!)

Big-Nose Lion picked up his 007 briefcase and started out the door. A-hen grabbed his arm. "I'll fry you some eggs. You should eat something before you leave."

"Forget it."

"It's still early, not even seven-thirty."

"I said, forget it!"

She looked up at him with anticipation in her almond-shaped eyes. "Will you be back tonight?"

Cupping his pipe in one hand, he blinked hard a time or two, as if trying to clear his slitty eyes. "I guess so." He blinked a couple times more. "Tell you what. I'll spend the week here at your place. The teacher plans to use that lady pastor's church for the training sessions, you know. It's only a few steps from here to the church, which will make everything easier."

Chapter Five

A-hen didn't get out of bed until the obasan came to do the laundry and make lunch, sometime around eleven o'clock. After brushing her teeth and using the toilet, A-hen began putting on her face—some red here, a little white there, then some eyebrow pencil, nice and long, and eyeliner beneath her long, almond-shaped eyes, and finally bright red lipstick—until you would have thought she was making herself up for a part in a Peking opera. That done, she told the obasan to brew a cup of coffee—no cream or sugar. That was her usual breakfast—a cup of black coffee. For some strange reason, over the last year or so she had been putting on weight, certainly not what she had in mind. In recent days, Big-Nose Lion had begun teasing her about how well-fed she looked, and wondering how a woman not yet thirty, with no children, could have a waist as broad as her hips. As part of a reducing plan, she went to the courts at Huagang Mountain twice a week to play tennis. At three hundred fifty NT an hour (by 1982 that had shot all the way up to eight hundred!), most people considered it pricey, but not her. Just think, when she was one of the hottest items around, a half-hour session cost her john four hundred or more! And that for lying down and taking it easy! Now, several years later, aerobic dancing had made its way into Taipei, and as soon as she heard it was a sure-fire way to slim down, she took off for Taipei—hang the expense—to enroll in a class. No one could have been a more conscientious aerobic dancer, and still her body weight acted like a sovereign nation, taking orders from no one.

She finished her coffee and made some phone calls to arrange that afternoon's mahjong game—at the home of Mrs. Zhu, whose husband was a bank manager—then gave the obasan money to buy pig's knuckles to braise for Big-Nose Lion's dinner. Finally, she placed a long-distance call to Star Beauty Shoppe in Taipei (the word *star* here was not the name of the beauty shop, but came from "star high school," and is what most people called the place); at the time you couldn't direct-dial long-distance, so she had to wait until the call went through. She told Manager Cai she'd be in Taipei on Monday and would stop by the beauty parlor the next day; she asked for an appointment with the overseas Chinese beautician, Franco, insisting that he make time to do her hair. Hualien beauty operators were much too rustic for her tastes, so she was forced to travel to Taipei once a month to get her hair done. If Franco was unavailable, she asked for Stephen Kano, the Filipino. Those two stylists always got a thumbs-up from well-to-do Taipei women with names like *Stella* [si-diao-le—dead as a doornail], *Anne* [ai-ni—love ya], *Ruth* [le-si—driven to death], or *Helen* [hai-ren—assault and battery]. If they thought the two men were *ichiban* [tops], then so did she. Their fees, of course, were also ichiban, but that didn't matter to her. Money? She had plenty. Just look at Big-Nose Lion and his pot of gold, the Rouge Tower! As long as there were men on this planet, he didn't have to worry about an income. All this business about skyrocketing oil prices, downslides, economic slumps—none of it had the slightest impact on him.

Several years later, two years or so after the fall of Vietnam, Big-Nose Lion's sex appeal would vanish and a hard object would wilt, giving the lie to the theory of so many experts: "Live long, use it hard." And that was when A-hen would begin making regular trips between Hualien and Taipei. By then the Star would no longer be called a beauty shoppe; all such establishments would be referred to as hair salons. A-hen would regularly make appointments at several of the salons—new wave, avant-garde, ahead of their time—where not only would ichiban stylists like Franco style her hair, but where young—and very muscular—hunks would give her a shampoo and a massage, plus the latest gossip. If she liked her shampoo "boy," she would follow the lead of the well-to-do Taipei ladies—Anne, Stella, Ruth, and Helen—and take him out on a date, a romp with an ichiban hustler worthy of the name.

It wouldn't be long before one of those ichiban hustlers presented her with a dose of v.d. (no, not herpes). Soon afterward, she would wholeheartedly make a gift of it to another ichiban hustler, who would pass it on—sub rosa, of course—to one of Taipei's well-to-do housewives, who even had a Filipina servant. This housewife, not daring to attain the distinction alone, would share the gift with her beloved husband, who in turn would bestow it upon one of his favorite co-workers (a man). . . . The multiplication process would not stop at this point, no, it would even make its way to Los Angeles (the city to which that well-to-do housewife would emigrate). But Big-Nose Lion would be completely shut out of the gift-giving. Apparently, there is an upside to male droop after all, wouldn't you say?

A-hen sat slouched on the sofa, her feet up on the coffee table, with the hem of her yellowish-green sleeveless Western dress hitched up all the way to her thigh. She was smoking an American menthol cigarette, feeling very laid back, now and again blowing smoke rings, one, then a second, and a third . . . she watched their progress, one after another, getting bigger and flimsier, fading away, then gone. . . . After a while, she flipped the butt toward the wastebasket next to the wall; it missed and fell to the floor, but instead of going over to pick it up, she made a phone call.

"Hello—hello—is Ebony Chicken in? Who's this? A-su? You don't know who Ebony Chicken is? All right, I'll tell you. Ebony Chicken is the woman you work for—now do you know? All right, MAY I ASK YOU PUH-LEEZ, is she in? She is? All right, PUH-LEEZ ASK her to come to the phone—" She took her feet off the table and, still holding the receiver in one hand, sat up straight, hugging her knees with her free arm. Her dress was still hitched up around her thighs, and anyone sitting across from her could have seen her pretty red panties, in fact, couldn't have avoided seeing them.

"What do you mean, who's this who's this? You've forgotten who A-hen is? You don't recognize my voice? Is there something you can do for me? Aiyo! Please, enough of that phony courtesy! My dear boss lady, there's nothing you can do for me, but there is a LIT-TLE matter I'd like to discuss with you. What did you do with those two blouses you were making for me? They turned out, like they say in Mandarin, a damned mess! You followed the pattern you showed me? Well, if you followed the pattern, the sun has finally risen in the west! They're a damned mess, I can't figure out what they are. You followed the pattern? Hah! Lucky I dropped by yesterday to check them out, or I don't know what you'd have turned them into—yesterday afternoon, around three or four o'clock! You weren't even there! A-su was alone in the shop. The problem? *Ah-so desu!* That's a good question. Let me tell you, boss lady, there are many many problems. Go get the blouses, then we'll talk about them in detail, O-KAAY?" She lowered her head, causing several locks of shiny black hair to cascade down over her penciled eyebrows. She brushed them back with her free hand, then began picking the skin between her toes, whose nails were the same bright red as her fingernails. She kept at it for a while, then shifted her attention to her armpit, which she scratched and rubbed, before looking up and holding the receiver right next to her glossy red lips.

"Ready? Now, boss lady, see that yellow one? I didn't say I wanted buttonholes, so why'd you put them in? Are there buttonholes on the pattern? Well, are there? Then there's the collar. What's that supposed to be? Is there an inside seam? You were supposed to put one in. The whole thing's wrong, you know that, don't you? Now let me ask you this. You know how a collar has a hem? How come you can't do that? Like that white one you made for me last time. Add a flap, put it on the inside! If that isn't bad enough, the collar's too small and the bustline's too tight. Small collars are out of fashion, you know that, don't you? And blouses without hems are ugly! What kind of collar lies flat on the shoulders? It should stand up. You know what you are? An ebony *ghost*! Drop dead, I mean it! You know perfectly well I said I wanted it to stand up, but the way you did it, it's a drop-dead kindergartener's muffler. I tried calling you last night, over and over, but couldn't get through—I'd like to know who you were having such a nice romantic chat with! Drop dead! All night I tried, but I couldn't get through. I'll drop dead if I'm lying. Ebony Chicken, I made it clear that I wanted only master tailor Yali to work on my clothes. Those girls of yours weren't to touch them—Yali did the work? You GA-AVE THEM to him?" She raised her fist, just aching to use it. "That's strange! What? Why you, that mouth of yours. . . . Quit changing the subject. What I want to say is, no visible buttonholes, please. Why do you insist on putting buttonholes in it? That's crazy! I want you to change it—you can't? Why? Tell me—then put the buttonholes on the inside! You know, hidden buttons. You can't? I find that hard to believe. If you put the buttons on the inside, they'd be hidden by the flap. Impossible? What do you mean, impossible? Then use snaps. Don't give me that nonsense! Then there's the collar with black flowers on a white background. It's all wrong. How come it's so short? How am I supposed to wear a skirt with something that short? Ebony Chicken, you listen to me. The sleeves are too narrow, I want them looser. And the shoulder pads, I want the collar to stand up above them. Don't do anything yet, wait till I come over. I said don't do anything, I'll be right there. I told you what I wanted. The pattern was perfect, then you go and mess things up—every one's the same, every one of them's messed up—well, you can just drop dead, you ebony ghost!"

She slammed down the receiver, displaying the "hate" that made up her name, A-hen.

Chapter Six

"You're going out? You're going out to have more clothes made? Only last week you—all right, fine, it's up to you, I don't care. I don't dare tell you what to do, A-hen. I'm Big-Nose Lion, and I don't even get a little time to show my affection for you. But take my advice and get clothes that are a little roomier, so you won't grow out of them after you wear them a time or two. You won't? Oh, no? You'll see when it happens. Have you eaten already? You haven't? A cup of coffee, that's all? That's not such a good idea. Don't be so concerned about your weight. You'll ruin your health if you don't eat.

"Have I eaten? Have *I* eaten? Just saying it pisses me off. I haven't had so much as a drop of water since I left your place. Lucky for me I drank that ginseng tea. Otherwise, that teacher would have me in my grave by now. You know, he's run my ass off nonstop till this minute. That's a fact, that is a fact! —You're not busy, are you? No *tennis* today? Oh, it's tomorrow, that's good. We can talk, then. While I'm at it—eat? How could I eat anything now? While I'm at it, there's something I want to discuss with you. What? I'll tell you. Our Mr. Dong is a real pain in the ass, for crying out loud! I've never seen anyone more pig-headed, never in my life! And him a teacher, no less! Some English teacher! He says whatever pops into his head. I don't know what kind of mosquito he's turning into."

(Years later, in 1982, the man's opinion of Dong Siwen

would not have changed a bit. The Ministry of the Interior would be making a big push to ban video games, and as someone interested in making a pile of money in any shady business, naturally he would be seriously impacted by this situation. A-hen would often overhear him grumbling against the Ministry of the Interior: "What kind of mosquitos are they turning into? First they say they're banning video games altogether, then they change their mind where unlicensed ones are concerned. They say they're going to revoke licenses in May, then make an announcement that they won't start till July. So July rolls around, and they say it won't go into effect until the first of the year. They tell us they're going to buy the machines from the licensed owners for thirteen thousand, then when the time comes, they decide not to buy them after all. What kind of mosquitos are they turning into? They're just like Mr. Dong, the English teacher, saying whatever pops into their heads.")

"But it's kind of funny when you think about it. Just listen! I'll start from the beginning. As soon as I left your place, I hailed a pedicab, you know. The minute I arrived at work (he was modest enough to avoid saying "The minute I arrived at the office"), I got on the phone to Black-Face Li, Stumpy Courtesan, and Sister Red Hair, and told them to come over right away. Hell, they were still in bed when I called. Talk about living right! I said they had five minutes to get out of bed and get over here. Would you believe it, they showed up five minutes later! Faster than soldiers scampering for morning muster! You should have seen it! They didn't even have time to wash their faces or brush their teeth. Their hair was a mess, their faces were grubby—they were like refugees on the run. You've never seen the likes of it. Stumpy Courtesan and Sister Red Hair usually look halfway decent, but today, without washing up or brushing their hair and no makeup at all, well, shit, they looked like a couple of ebony ghosts! That's the truth, I'm not making it up. That face on Stumpy Courtesan, boy, too bad you missed it—black and green and yellow all mixed together, a dead ringer for an unpeeled mango. But, but maybe I shouldn't be talking about this to a jealous old vinegar vat like you. Now, don't get in an uproar, don't do that! All right, I'll tell you the rest. Stumpy Courtesan was in such a hurry to come over that she forgot to put on anything under her blouse, know what I mean? Well, without one of those, you know, a bra, well, you could see everything. I tell you, those tits of hers are big enough to choke a horse! Who'd have thought that someone no bigger than a little girl could have tits the size of an American housewife's? And so smooth and soft! Touch them? Are you out of your mind? I don't do stuff like that! Smooth and soft was just an impression, just some crazy thought. Oh? How come you're so quiet all of a sudden? You're not saying anything. Oh! You're jealous! Ha ha ha, so you're actually jealous. And crazy. How could I find *her* attractive? An ebony chicken like that, how could I fall for her? Not to mention her age. Fall for her? You're out of your mind! Cross my heart, I never said her tits were nicer than yours. All I said was they looked like drop-dead balloons, so big they scared the hell out of me, like an American housewife. How could tits like that be nicer than yours? Truth is, nobody has nicer tits than you, not too big, not too small, like a couple of pomelos. OK OK, that's it, I won't say any more!

"Yes yes, Black-Face Li came too. As soon as he walked in the door, know what he wanted? Betel nuts. I don't chew the things, so how could I have any around the place? Without his precious betel nuts, he sat there fidgeting the whole time, like a dope fiend. He didn't speak more than a sentence or two before his eyes started watering, and before long he put his head down on the table and fell asleep. No talking to him. So I sent someone out to buy some. Now where are you going to find betel nuts at seven or eight in the morning? They ran up and down every street in the neighborhood, but no one was open for business. Finally they got some. Guess where? At the train station! So after I went to all that trouble to buy his precious betel nuts, guess what he said when I handed them to him. I tell you, there's no pleasing Black-Face Li. He said we bought the wrong kind. Bought the wrong kind! Hualien's betel nuts are small, grainy, and tasteless. He won't chew them. Only big, tender nuts from Shuangdong. Shit! That's Black-Face Li for you! That's right, that's it exactly, a chicken with a crooked beak trying to eat rice. Yeah, sure we bought some for him. We swapped the little ones for big, tender nuts from Shuangdong. The extra cost didn't bother me, but do you know how much time we wasted on this little farce? A whole half hour. With people like that, nothing ever gets done.

"Once Black-Face Li popped a couple of those Shuangdong betel nuts into his mouth he was ready to go, laughing and talking throughout our meeting like a new man. Shit, we wasted a whole half hour over him and his precious betel nuts. And you know, it took me all of ten minutes to solve our problems. How many girls each company is supposed to send for training, the conditions and qualifications for each girl, things like that, I took care of it all.

Not like our pig-headed Mr. Dong. I'm a go-getter, ten minutes, that's all it took. If I'd let it go on a little longer, I hate to think what condition my bathroom would have been in, thanks to Sister Red Hair. She headed straight for the toilet as soon as she walked in the door, and then kept going back every few minutes. I don't know if she had diarrhea or if the Red General had paid a visit—what are you laughing at? Did you just call me a dirty old man? Ha ha ha! OK OK, stop that, stop saying that. It's OK, I'm calling from a secret room. Even the ghosts don't know this place. No one can hear me.

"When the meeting was over it was time for me to go pick out my girls, so I told them they had to leave. I wasn't about to let them stay another minute, or else my bathroom—OK OK, filthy, filthy, I won't say anything more about that, I promise. At the meeting I told the three of them they had exactly one hour to choose their girls and send them here in a group, you know what I mean? Then I'd take them all over to Dr. Yun's place. For what? For a checkup. To see if they're clean or not. Our Mr. Dong made it clear over the phone that the girls who were chosen not only had to be in the flower of their youth, but each had to have the face of a flower, and had to be as clean as a flower, as clean as a magnolia blossom—not a hint of anything unclean. He reminded me that we'd be servicing American GIs this time, soldiers fighting in Vietnam, not a bunch of horny locals. What would we say if one of them carried back some of our filth with him? He insisted that I take all the girls over to Dr. Yun to be examined. No dirty ones. Dirty ones are out. That's right, you're right. That's what I said, exactly what I told him. And what do you think his answer was? 'What makes you think the regular exams at the health clinic are reliable? How can we believe anything those people say? You have to take them to be examined by Dr. Yun.' He said Dr. Yun's medical skills are top of the line. Dr. Yun was Councilman Qian's classmate, his too. So of course he'd say that. But on the other hand, he made sense. We're servicing American GIs this time, after all! Nothing but the best and the safest for them.

"Ha ha, just the thought of it makes me laugh. Really laugh. The girls were still in bed, so I had Mengxie [wet dream] roll them out of bed and send them into the lobby, where I could line them up and choose the ones I wanted. Boy, you should have seen them scurry around the place. They were shouting, 'Surprise police inspection! Surprise police inspection!' The johns who were still in bed with them scooped up their clothes and ran bare-assed into the back. I didn't want things to get out of hand, so I yelled, 'There's no police, take it easy!' It took a few shouts to calm everyone down and bring the bare-assed johns out of the back, clothes in hand, their weapons hanging between their legs. Shit, they're not afraid to get a little on the side, but they split at the first sign of cops. Sure, that's what I told them: 'This is no hotel or unlicensed whorehouse, it's a class-A brothel, licensed by the government. An authorized enterprise that pays its taxes every year. We're completely legal, so there's nothing to worry about.' After hearing me out, the girls started yawning, you know what I mean, and headed back for some more sleep. The ones whose johns were still hanging around were eager to head back to their nuptial chambers—what do you mean, they're not nuptial chambers? The girls had their bridegrooms beside them, so why aren't they nuptial chambers? OK OK, no more of that, I'll change the subject. When I saw them all leaving, I told Mengxie to drag them back so I could tell them I was going to select some to undergo training to service the American GIs. They couldn't believe their ears. That's right! I thought they'd be jumping for joy. Not a peep. When it finally sank in, a bunch of them started jabbering away. What were they saying? Listen to this! They said things like, 'I'm not going to sleep with no American! We don't speak the same language, they've got yellow hair and blue eyes, and their noses are like beaks. You expect me to sleep with freaks like that? Aiyo! Don't make me puke.' That's what they fucking said.

"So I turned real mean-like and shouted: 'What are you bitching about? If I hear any more trash talk about the American GIs, I'll stop being Mr. Nice Guy.' As soon as that gorilla Mengxie heard me bellow like that, he whipped off his belt and snapped it in the air, scaring the hell out of the new girls. I tell you, it was a riot. The old pros didn't bat an eye, and I saw sneers on some of their faces. Little Yuanyuan actually burst out laughing. Who's Little Yuanyuan? You don't know? Don't tell me you don't know her, the girl who took first prize in last year's competition. She took on a hundred johns in one day, shattered the old record. Oh, now you remember. Right right, when it was over, she couldn't drag herself out of bed for a day and a night. Finally she had to get up to pee. But it was worth it. She won a gold medal that weighed three ounces. She's the one who laughed out loud. She even tried to calm the new girls down: 'Don't be scared, if they're going to punish someone, this isn't how they do it.' She knows her business, that's why she won the gold medal. Mengxie was just doing that for show, trying to assert his authority. But I had to laugh at the way the new girls were shaking in their boots. Who in his right mind would punish someone like that? A leather belt leaves marks. Do you think I'd do something like that? Hell, those stupid girls don't realize that their bodies are worth their weight in gold. What kind of idiot would sacrifice those fair, white bodies of theirs? Stop worrying. I told you I'm in my secret room, there's nobody else around. Hell, turn those bodies into a mass of scars? What a bunch of dumb girls I've got! If I wanted to punish them, I wouldn't use a fucking leather belt. Never have and never will!

"Hold on a moment, I need a sip of coffee. My throat's dry as a bone from all this talking.

"Hell, we've got better ways than that to punish someone. Probably more than any criminal division, and that's the truth. I don't have time to go into detail now, but our punishment is swift, it fits the crime, and it's plenty severe. Give me one minute, and I'll have them writhing on the floor screaming for mercy. Hell, not only that, what makes it perfect is that I don't leave a single mark, no evidence.

"Hold on again, I need some more coffee. This Brazilian stuff is terrific!"

(Here Big-Nose Lion went on to describe the way he punished the girls, and believe me, it's as shocking as you might imagine. I'm not going to repeat it here—I don't want to scare you off, and I sure don't want to give you any ideas. Painful as it is, I'm going to delete this "stirring" passage completely. I hope you understand.)

"—That doesn't interest you? No interest at all? OK OK! I'll shut up if you're not interested. How's that? Hell, that sneer was frozen on Little Yuanyuan's face. And she kept looking at me out of the fucking corner of her eye. That really set me off, so I walked up with this mean look on my face and all, and I said, 'You think you're hot shit, don't you? You say they're a bunch of freaks, is that it? Well, what makes you think those freaks will give you a second look? You're an old hag, you know that? Nobody wants the likes of you. Those American GIs are in the market for eighteen-year-olds in the flower of their youth, you know that? And how old are you? Well into your twenties. Hell, you're the last thing those freaks will want. You think you're hot shit, well, you're wrong!' And that wasn't all I said. 'You want to join this beauty contest? Wait till the next time you come around in life!' Boy, you should have seen her. Her veins were popping, she was so mad. She didn't say another word, just turned on her heel and went back to her room. Maybe I should have gone a little easier on her. I sure didn't mean to set her off like that. I guess I went too far. You ask why? I'll tell you in a minute.

"I tell you, it wasn't easy, but Mengxie and I finally managed to choose fourteen girls between the ages of eighteen and twenty. That's right, fourteen. Since we're bigger than the other companies, I chose a couple extra. The other three companies each chose twelve. Altogether that makes exactly fifty. Every one of those fourteen prostitutes knows how to 'boar pour more,' I'm not kidding you. You know, that alphabet they learn in grammar school—right, that's it, the phonetic spelling—oh, it's 'bo po mo'! Shit, to me it always sounded like 'boar pour more'! Every girl we chose knows how to—oh, hell, it's easier for me just to say 'boar pour more'! They know how to boar pour more, and they can write a little. Two of them went to middle school, so they even know a little A-B-C, Dog bite pig-gy! And that's not all! They're like flowers, every one of them, just like flowers. Now why do you say that? That's ridiculous! How could I? How could I fall for any of them? They can't hold a candle to you! Those little girls? As soon as I say anything about some other girl, you jump up and down. What am I supposed to do? A big vat of vinegar is what you are. You should know by now that you're the girl for Big-Nose Lion. You, A-hen! You know that, don't you? Lie to you? I should drop dead if I'm lying to you! OK OK, no more of that kind of talk. I'll tell you something funny, all right? What's that? You have to pee? OK, go on, hurry up—What? You changed your mind? Aren't you afraid you'll pee your pants?

"Listen to me. After we chose the girls, I told them to go wash up and get dressed, that as soon as Stumpy Courtesan and the others' girls came over, we were all going over to see Dr. Yun. I told them they could put on their make-up, but not to take too long. So one of the girls says to me—just listen. She says she's got a john in her room who's waiting to take care of business, so what's she supposed to do? She was the only one of the fourteen who had an all-nighter. The only one. So I said to her, 'Shit, the sun's up already. You want to take care of business now? Forget it. Go tell the john to put his pants on and go home.' She says he's already paid, and she can't just tell him to hit the road, she'd be embarrassed to. So I said, 'That's weird, the guy's been in your room all night, one whole night, and he hasn't done a thing?' She just shook her head. 'Can't he get it up?' That's what I asked her. 'Can't he get that thing of his up?' And she said, 'That's not it. It's the way he wants it. He likes to wait till morning to take care of business. The guy said he can get a good look when it's light out, and that way when he takes care of business he won't make any mistakes.' That's right! That's what she said. Ha ha, I damn near fell over I laughed so hard. In this business, even if you don't have eyes you can feel your way around to keep from entering the wrong door, right? You don't know? You say you don't know? Wise ass! Now listen up. I told her to tell the john to go take lessons from a blind man. Besides, ours is a nighttime operation. 'We don't do business in the daytime, we'd offend the gods if we did. And if you offend the gods, they send lightning down on your heads. You tell him to put his pants on and go home, understand?' What did she say? She said he'd already paid for a whole night, and if he didn't take care of business and just put on his pants and went home, she'd be mortified. 'What do you mean, mortified?' I said. 'He spent the night with you, so he got his money's worth.' But she said, 'It'll only take a minute. I can finish him off without holding up the rest of you.' I really blew my stack when she said that. I screamed, 'The devil's really knocked you down this time. Use your head! From now on you're going to be servicing American GIs, a different class of clientele altogether! Different, you understand? You can't be coddling some john off the street, you know?' She saw I was really pissed, so she backed off, muttering to herself like one of those opera singers.

"Well, she hadn't been gone a minute before I started worrying that that john of hers might pressure her into getting what he came for, which would waste everybody's time. So I told Mengxie to come along with me to her room and check things out. Mengxie led the way, swaggering along. You know how he is. Give him something to do, and he puffs himself up and struts that big ass of his, just like the police during the Japanese occupation. While he was swaggering along, like Generals Fan and Xie, the two warrior gods, he kept snapping his belt in the air. Like any underling with a swelled head. It didn't take us more than a minute until we were standing outside the girl's door, just in time to catch her coming out of the room carrying a basin of water, still warm. She was shocked to see us standing there, but that passed quickly, and she smiled to me and whispered, 'Aniki, I took care of things. He's getting dressed now, he'll be out in a minute.' Then she walked out back with the basin of water. I tell you, I was one surprised man. That fast? They took care of business in less than three minutes! And during that time she had to get undressed and get dressed again, then make sure that thing of his was all cleaned off. A space rocket isn't any faster than that! Don't you agree? You don't know? You really don't know, or are you just saying that? Heh heh heh! Well, I didn't believe her, so I walked up and sneaked a look inside. Hell, the john was putting on his pants. He was still naked from the waist up, and his face was all lit up, happy as a clam. He was even whistling some fucking tune. That made a believer out of me. They did it, and that's a fact. Hard to believe anyone could be *that* good. So I followed her into the bathroom, where she was squatting on the floor using the same warm water she'd cleaned that thing of his with to wash her . . . OK OK, I'll skip the details.

"I need some more coffee, hold on a minute.

"Know what she said? 'Aniki, I told you it would only take a minute to finish him off.' So I patted her on the shoulder. 'You're a real pro!' I said. Hell, if all the girls had her skills, we'd do a land-office business! Figure it out for yourself, go ahead. I told her she was a cinch to take first prize in this year's competition. She could easily break Little Yuanyuan's record. A-hen, it never occurred to me that this new girl would be one of Rouge Tower's treasures. Find out when she's got some free time? Why should I do that? What? Ah-ah-ah! What the fuck are you thinking? I can't do that! Those skills of hers are reserved for johns, not for the teacher! You know that, don't you? OK OK! No more nonsense!

"—Yes, yes they did. Within the hour, Stumpy Courtesan and the other two—talk about efficiency, they treated my orders like military commands—within the hour they sent the troops they'd chosen over to my place. And every one of them knew their boar pour mores, they could write a little, and they were flowers, every one of them, noses and mouths just the way you like them, especially the aboriginal girls, all up to par. I couldn't find fault with any of them. This lineup of beauties, hell—Hualien's never seen the likes of it. Aiyo! Are you crazy? Why the hell would I want to take one of those aboriginal girls home with me? After we counted heads, I told A-yong and Mengxie to escort the girls over to Dr. Yun's. I figured I was home free and could send out for something to eat. So wouldn't you know it, Teacher Dong picks that moment to call me on the phone. What did he want this time? You'll get plenty thin from laughing when I tell you, no need to knock yourself out playing *tennis* anymore. First he asked if we'd chosen the girls. When he heard that everything was taken care of, and that they were already on their way to Dr. Yun's, he told me to run out and call them back, all of them.

I turned and told Black-Face Li to run after Mengxie and the others. What was the matter? Listen, I'll tell you. Mr. Dong asked if we'd checked bust sizes when we chose the girls. I asked why we had to do that, and he said the Americans like big-busted girls, the bigger the better. So we had to make sure all the girls had tits, and big ones at that. Hold on, just listen. He even said that *both* tits had to be big, not one big and one small. Heh heh heh, pretty funny, don't you think? He's one teacher who hasn't been around much. Have you ever heard of a girl with one big tit and one small one? What did I say? I told him, 'You didn't say anything about that this morning.' But I gave him my word that every girl we chose had tits, and he said, 'Just having tits isn't enough, Aniki, they've got to be big, I want big ones. Please, Aniki, please replace all the ones with small tits.' So that I could do a good job for him, I asked how big the tits should be, what was I to use as a standard. He said if they were the size of pomelos, that was big, and if they were the size of Grass Mountain tangerines, that was small. Ha ha, this time he answered me like a pro, no rank amateur, a real tit man. He said to choose girls using pomelos as the standard—of course! Yes, that was the first thing that crossed my mind. So I said, 'What if there aren't enough to fill the quota? There aren't that many girls between eighteen and twenty to begin with.' Without even taking time to think, he said, 'Aniki, if you're afraid there won't be enough, then make up the shortage with girls from the previous generation. As long as they've got pomelos, you can send them for training.' That knocked me for a loop, I tell you. So I said, 'You mean you'll even take forty- and fifty-year-old *mama-sans*?' 'That's not what I meant,' he said, 'that's not it at all.' So I said, 'The next generation after twenty-year-olds will be forty- or fifty-year-old mama-sans, won't they?' Hold on, just listen. He said no. Then I heard him laugh over the phone. 'Aniki,' he said, 'I thought women were your rice bowl.' Those were his exact fucking words. If he hadn't been a teacher, I'd have hung up on him.

"He said, 'Women,' then he laughed some more. 'With women, a generation is five years, you follow? So with twenty-year-olds, the previous generation will be twenty-five. The previous generation for them will be thirty, understand?' Shit! Have you ever heard anything like that? What a joke! According to him, A-hen, since you're thirty, that makes you this group's grandmother. Ha ha ha, Grannie A-hen! What a joke! Don't you think so, Grannie? How should I know if he was making it up as he went along, or if he was telling the truth? That's not all, Grannie. Before he hung up, he told me again that if there weren't enough twenty-year-olds with big tits, I should choose some from the previous generation, some of the older girls. Then he said, 'But, Aniki, absolutely none from the generation before that. Keep that in mind, Aniki.' So Grannie, the way things stand, you're out of the picture. The Yanks will just have to do without you. No big deal? Well, you'll still get your chance. Right! I'll get to that in a minute, don't worry. I've got plenty of good news for you, my dear Grannie, just listen.

"This Mr. Dong of ours is a real pain in the ass. He says whatever pops into his head, and he's driving me nuts. Sister Red Hair, Stumpy Courtesan, Black-Face Li, and me, Aniki, the four of us, we ran our fucking asses off (hell, that Stumpy Courtesan never stopped grumbling, drop-dead this and drop-dead that), we ran our asses off trying to find enough qualified girls. Of course we did it Mr. Dong's way. Every girl was at least five-feet-one-inch tall—we eyeballed it! Who's got the Yankee leisure time to run down a tape measure? If they looked tall enough, they were in. Every girl had a set of pomelos—hell, some were the size of grapefruits! Of course we replaced all the ones with tangerine tits, all of them, every one. The youngest among them is eighteen, the oldest twenty-six. In Mr. Dong's terms, that's two generations under one roof! I said, two generations under one roof! One generation every five years for grown-up girls, that kills me! Oh, right, I forgot to tell you. That Little Yuanyuan is a real dumb-ass! Remember how all those pomelo grannies were bitching about freaks at first, how they refused to service the Americans? Well, they were still saying they wanted no part of it, but I gave them hell until they shut up and went to their rooms to doll themselves up. All except that drop-dead, dumb-ass Little Yuanyuan. At first she absolutely refused, then she sneered at me and said, 'Aniki, didn't you tell me I'd be in the beauty contest in my next life? Well, then, come see me in my next life.' Now that was just a bunch of talk, but she threw it right back at me. Give her hell? Not me! She's the Rouge Tower champ, our money tree! She's like one of those canaries on TV. Give her hell? What if she turned on me and moved to some other house? That way I'd win the battle but lose the war! Besides, those tits of hers are like a pair of button-tipped pomelos, not too big and not too little, a perfect match to her name, Little Yuanyuan—little round ones. Ha ha ha, little round ones. Nothing like those *round* things of Stumpy Courtesan—big round ones, like basketballs. They scare the hell out of a guy!

But, hell, those tits of Little Yuanyuan's—there you go again, the minute I start talking about some other woman you turn into a vat of vinegar, I don't know what I'm going to do with you. And then? Then I sweet-talked her till I turned blue in the face, and finally agreed to her conditions. What? You're a raving lunatic! Agree to marry her? That's ridiculous! You're the one I love, don't you know that? For crying out loud, you! Of course she agreed. Even the heart is just a bodily organ. As Aniki, by being honest and open with her, and keeping my voice down, I gave her plenty of face. How could she make a scene after that? How could she not agree? I'm telling you, A-hen, even the heart is just a bodily organ.

"—Ten o'clock, at ten o'clock sharp, Mengxie and Black-Face Li took the fifty lucky girls over to see Dr. Yun, and I thought my biggest headaches were behind me. So I opened a bottle of Napoleon brandy—people say it's the best you can buy, but who the hell knows? I poured everyone a full glass, and was raising my glass to Stumpy Courtesan and Sister Red Hair, now that we could relax a little, and I'll be fucked! All morning long we ran our asses off, didn't even have time to take a leak—just listen, OK? We were just about to drink, when, I'll be fucked! We haven't seen the first U.S. dollar, and we're ready to drop! What happened? Just listen. We were about to take our first sip, our very first sip, when Black-Face Li comes running in gasping for breath, and the minute he sees me, he says, 'We've got problems, Aniki, big problems.' We put down our glasses and asked him what was wrong. I figured our Mr. Dong had dreamed up some new idiotic plan. Just listen. Black-Face Li heaved another sigh. He was still chewing those Shuangdong betel nuts that I, Aniki, bought for him. He says, 'The doctor has an emergency at the provincial hospital, and can't make time for us. No way to examine the girls.'

"Stumpy Courtesan and Sister Red Hair started in with their 'What'll we do? Oh, what'll we do?' but I grabbed the phone and called Mr. Dong, who was just about to call me. He said, 'Aniki, I know everything. Dr. Yun doesn't normally go to the hospital on Mondays. But there was an emergency, so he had to. But that's all right, Aniki. Hurry up and take the girls over to see Dr. Wang at the harbor. Chief Qian already cleared it with him. He's waiting for them now.' Wait, there's more. He told me to hire a bus to take the girls over to Gangkou. Now who the fuck needed him to tell me that? Did he think we were going to walk all the way over there, like some parade to celebrate Taiwan's restoration? Am I right? Then he told me that Dr. Wang is Hualien's v.d. specialist. What the fuck do you use for friggin' brains? He's a specialist treating v.d., not a specialist *with* v.d. The girls are in good hands with him. So he said—just listen. 'This Venereal Wang is one of Chief Qian's bosom buddies.' Did you hear me? Bosom buddy means close friend. Ha ha, dragons and phoenixes seek out their own kind. A perfect match: a man known for taking off his pants and a doctor called Venereal. How do you like that?

"Of course I did, I sent Black-Face Li right out to hire a bus, which he managed to do just in time for Mr. Dong's next phone call. What did he want? Listen, and you'll see why I nearly blew my stack. I ran my ass off all morning long, just so he could call up to say excitedly—in Mandarin, no less—'Aniki, I wonder if you've thought of something, something very important.' What was it? Listen up. He asked me if we'd checked to see when the girls had their periods. Why'd he want to know that? Just listen. I told him that's something we hadn't considered. 'Oh, no! Big trouble! Lucky for us it occurred to me, or we'd be in ichiban big trouble, ah-so desu!' He then proceeded to tell me to quickly check each anointed girl—anointed, that's what he said. It's the same thing as chosen. He wanted me to hurry up and ask the anointed girls when they had their periods, then replace the ones who were expecting theirs next week, including this Friday and Saturday, replace every one of them with girls who already had their periods or who didn't expect a visit from the Red General for at least two weeks.

"Our Mr. Dong sure has an eye for the finer points; no wonder he's an English teacher! Of course they're finer points. If the Red General throws up a blockade, how are the Yanks supposed to enter town? Well? Our Mr. Dong wasn't finished. 'Those guys are coming all the way from Vietnam for a little R & R,' he said, 'how can we supply them with unclean girls?' Well, that made sense to me, but it meant that the four of us still had our fucking work cut out for us. Huh? Oh, no, no, I didn't see Sister Red Hair use my toilet again. Who's got that Yankee leisure time! I just watched her run back and forth until sweat was dripping from her face. It took time, but eventually we kept the girls who deserved to be kept and replaced all the others. Then what? Then we found out we came up short, that's what, at least ten short. Who had time to find replacements? So we had to go to Lovely Ladies next door and the Fairy Flower and Magnolia Mansion across the street to borrow some girls. We had to promise them all sorts of things before they finally said *OK*.

The Big 4 actually borrowing girls from fucking second-class whorehouses. If the word ever gets out, people will die laughing!

"Well, we barely got the girls on the bus when that granny-humping Dong called up to speed us along. I tell you, he'll be the death of me yet! He says whatever pops into his head. If not for all those U.S. dollars out there, I'd have hung up on him. He said he'd had a brainstorm, something that was incredibly important. Just listen. He said that some of the GIs coming on R & R will probably be looking for girls who are a little older, ones with motherly ways. After spending all that time making war, they'll be missing home and their mothers. 'So, Aniki, you might as well go easy on the age limit, expand it by a generation or so.' He's the one who set the fucking age limit, and now he tells me to go easy on it. This English teacher of ours sure knows how to give orders. How old? Just listen. He told us to choose seven or eight girls around the age of thirty, but no older, and no more than seven or eight, about one out of every eight. Pretty ones, he reminded me, and not with their periods. He said the GIs will be pleased to see a lineup of three generations under one roof, thrilled even. Leave it to him to think that up. (Now if this had been 1983, Dong Siwen would have referred to the lineup as a three-in-one combination of old, middle-aged, and young.) So now, A-hen, my little granny, you're qualified, aren't you? I'm not kidding. Just listen. Hell, we were off and running again (it was no picnic, I tell you), until we rounded up seven or eight decent-looking grannies who weren't having their periods. Right, we returned those girls intact to their owners, every one of them. And you know Li Damu from the Magnolia Mansion? Well he was so unhappy about the return his face scrunched up like a fucking crab!

"By the time we got the girls on the bus it was almost eleven-thirty. Something that could have been done in two fucking hours wound up taking us four or five, one whole morning, for crying out loud.

"Oh, right! There's something I need to discuss with you. You know we don't have more than a couple of thirty-year-old grannies working for us here. How many men are willing to spend their hard-earned money on grannies unless, of course, they're as pretty as you? A-hen, you are one beautiful woman, and that's no lie! OK OK, I'll shut up. So as I was saying, what worried me was that some of the girls might not pass inspection. Young ones, no problem. If we can't replace them, we can always borrow from the other whorehouses, and anything's possible as long as we make it worth their while.

It's those thirty-year-old grannies who worry me. If one or two of them don't pass, where am I going to find replacements, you tell me that. Not to mention our teacher Dong's requirements that they be like flowers or like jade, not having their period, that they have tits like button-tipped pomelos, and that they know their boar pour mores. Like looking for a needle in a haystack. Am I right or aren't I? But, but we have to find some reserves, no matter what. That way, anybody who doesn't pass inspection can be replaced by one of the reserves.

"Sister Red Hair and Stumpy Courtesan thought that sounded pretty reasonable. Sister Red Hair said she's got an adopted daughter who's not bad looking. Her husband died recently, so if we need somebody to help out, she's available. And Stumpy Courtesan said she has a good-looking twenty-nine-year-old niece. She's married, but we can call her over. I feel pretty good with those two in reserve, but I'd feel even better if I had one more—three all together. And that's what I want to talk to you about. A-hen, who else can we find to put in reserve? Think about it. Think real hard. You can't think of anyone? You really can't? So now what? What am I going to do now?

"Who? Tell me who. You can't think of anyone? Listen to me, A-hen. I've thought of someone, someone perfectly qualified to be a reserve. Who? You want to know who? Are you sure? If I tell you, you'll give me hell. You won't? Promise me you won't? You won't? Then I'll tell you. Now listen. The person I'm talking about is, it's, it's you! I said it's you! You see, you see, you said you wouldn't give me hell. It's no big deal—now listen to me. Just treat it as a form of entertainment, like playing *tennis*. You can learn some English from Teacher Dong, increase your knowledge, and what's wrong with that? Hang out with some Americans, drink a little, dance with them, you know, the good life. Good, clean fun. Am I right or aren't I? And it's only for two weeks. One week of training, actually five days, and a week with the GIs. Just treat it like a two-week vacation. Besides, you'll only be a reserve, and they may not send you, after all. Think it over. I'm not going to force you into anything. Only do it if you want to. What I'm talking about is a great opportunity. You can learn some English, you can service the Americans, and you can have a great time doing it.

"You're passing it up? Too bad. But there's something else I need to talk to you about. To open this bar, I had to put up all my capital, which means I'm going for broke on this one. You know what that means. For starters, you can quit *tennis* for a while. You already paid the instructor? So you paid him. That little bit of money doesn't matter. Give it some thought, OK? Some careful thought, OK? I'll come stay with you tonight. Oh, I already told you that this morning? I said I'd stay with you all week? See what being around that pain in the ass has done? My memory's shot. Oh! Good, I like the sound of that! Braised pig's feet. That's great, just great! A-hen, I want you to think about what I just said. I won't force you. Do it only if you want to. That's right, you said you had to pee real bad. Go on, go do it. Huh? You don't have to now? You peed your pants? Really? Heh heh heh. You're quite the kidder."

Chapter Seven

At a meeting held in Dong Siwen's pink suite, the four assistants reported on the progress of their work:

1. Student questionnaires, attendance cards, and daily journals that Siwen had told them to design (the girls would be asked to write down what they learned each day and how they felt about it. All fifty girls would fill in their names, and that's about it) had been printed and would be bound and sent over that afternoon.
2. A dance teacher had been hired to teach the girls a variety of steps. Negotiations were underway with a makeup specialist and a hair stylist; no problems were anticipated.
3. Everything necessary to turn Mercy Chapel into a classroom was in readiness; work would begin that night.
4. Student notebooks, ballpoint pens, pencils, erasers, and clipboards had all been purchased.

After complimenting them on their efficiency, Siwen gave them their new assignments. First and foremost, he told them to split up and visit shops, jewelry stores, markets, and the like to check the prices of all sorts of ordinary goods, jewelry, food. . . . They were also to check the going rates for pedicabs and *taxis*, and were to be as precise as possible.

"Oh, right, don't forget the local marble handicraft shops. And don't write down the prices marked, those are for the tourists and include thirty percent commissions for the tour guides. Even at half price, their stuff is still too expensive." Dong Siwen impressed upon the four assistants how crucial it was not to give up until they had extracted from the marble handicraft shops a reasonable price for their products. "Once the information is in hand"—here Teacher Dong was especially emphatic—"once the information is in hand, you must scientifically compare, analyze, and sum up your findings, then prepare a Chinese-English price list, which we'll print up and distribute free of charge to every *GI* who comes to Hualien as a welcoming gift. With this 'Hualien Goods and Services Price List' in hand, a '*Huh? No way!*' reaction from our visitors will greet anyone who tries to fleece them." And that was only the beginning. Teacher Dong planned to list telephone numbers for the Hualien Police Department and district station houses on the inside back cover of the handbook, right above a reminder in English, in red, that if a *GI* thought he was being cheated, he could call any of the above numbers to have the dispute settled quickly and with a minimum of inconvenience. The back cover would be a full-page advertisement for the new bar for which Siwen was the sole midwife. In addition to the address, the telephone number, and a glowing description of the place, the ad would include photos of some of the prettiest girls dressed in cheongsams; he insisted that the dresses have high collars and thigh-high slits up the sides, just like the ones worn by stewardesses on *CAT* Jade Express flights. He told his assistants, all junior college graduates, to get to work right away, making sure the handbook was absolutely perfect, and to see that it would be ready before the first GIs arrived. He stressed repeatedly the point that money was no object, that quality was the only consideration. "*Understand? Just think of it*, we're performing a diplomatic function for the nation! We are obliged to treat our guests with the very best, ensuring them a pleasurable holiday. We must do everything in our power to ensure that our guests take home with them an unblemished impression. *OK?*"

Chapter Eight

As soon as the four assistants left on their assignments, Siwen made a phone call to Councilman Qian.

"I'm glad I finally got hold of you, Chief. I tell you, finding you is harder than getting an audience with the emperor. I've been calling this hotline of yours all morning. Oh, so you've been at the station house interfering with police work, have you? Who for this time? Some hooligan who was running a gambling operation? Crap. You're really something! (Except for the popular 'Crap' in Taiwanese, the rest he said in Mandarin.) Still going to bat for society's bad elements! Commit hari-kiri, that's what you should do. Why? Because you're letting down your voting public. Is that what I taught you? Don't give me that nonsense.

"Let me tell you what happened. I'm reporting in. Didn't you ask me to call from time to time and report on the progress of our great endeavor? Well, everything's moving along smoothly. Fifty *bar girls to be* have been selected and are getting *checkups* from Venereal Wang. That's right, that's what I was thinking. This is an international exchange, so we need *everything best*. Am I right? No need to thank me, Chief. When one is entrusted with a job, faithful duty is expected. I'm just carrying out my mission.

"Please, you'll make me blush—" His voice dropped suddenly, most likely out of embarrassment over Councilman Qian's compliments. His knees quaked so violently that the floor actually creaked, and he looked around, searching for a place where he could hang his utter glee. "Oh, right, Chief, have you contacted those two bartenders, the ones from Kaohsiung? What do you say to this? Hold on a second, Chief—" He took out the class schedule he and his four assistants had put together (actually, it was pretty much all his doing) late the previous night and spread it out in front of him. It was filled with corrections and changes, like a child's homework assignment in progress. As he scanned it, he said, "I've got them in class on Wednesday and Thursday afternoons, from two to three. How does that sound? Fine with you? Good, then I'll ask you to make sure they're on time. Two hours for the 'Art of mixing drinks' should be adequate. All we need to do is teach the *bar girls to be* the ABCs of foreign drinks—whiskey, martinis, cocktails, and gin-and-tonics (in fact, the Kaohsiung bartenders spent two hours instructing the girls on over thirty separate drinks, and all they could remember were 'monotony' [martini], 'risky' [whiskey], and goddamned 'cunnie act' [cognac]; the names of all the other drinks were returned unclaimed to their teachers). All right, I'll call again if anything else comes up."

Siwen hung up the phone, let his knees quake happily a while longer, then picked up his pen and put a check mark alongside "Art of mixing drinks" to signify *OK*. He did the same for dance lessons—*OK*—and since he was the instructor for "English" and "Introduction to American Culture," naturally he *OK*ed them too. He studied the heavily edited class schedule, discovering two or three blank spots where he still hadn't figured out what should be taught, but he'd leave those unchecked for the time being. What concerned him now was the "personal hygiene" class he'd scheduled, since he still didn't know who would teach it. Ah! Venereal Wang was his first choice, but he was supposed to go to Taipei for some kind of syphilis symposium. It had to be someone else. But who? Yun Songzhu would be perfect, but, *damn*, asking a busy man like him is a waste of time. So who? Siwen gnawed on his nails, but that didn't supply the answer he sought. Maybe Yun Songzhu could do it, after all. He turned back to his class schedule. "If I move the personal hygiene class to the morning, from seven to eight. . . . No, that won't work. He's at home seeing patients then. Sometime between eight and twelve? No, that won't work either. He's on call at the provincial hospital. Noon? No good. He's back home seeing patients. In the afternoons he sees drop-ins at the public health clinic. Evenings? No chance. More private patients at home. On Sundays he spends the whole day mixing medicine and elixirs. So now what?"

Siwen tossed down the class schedule and gazed up at the pink ceiling, concluding that he would have to cancel the class. But that decision was itself quickly canceled by the conviction that this class schedule, a stroke of genius, could not be abandoned. Besides, hygiene was one of the most tantalizing parts of the training course. He was intent on teaching his *bar girls to be* all about the Americans' sex lives—physically and psychologically—and dispensing information on their sexual habits and propensities. This knowledge would assure compatibility and help avoid culture shock (in terms of sex)! Abandon the class? Never! Once more he gazed at the pink ceiling, as if seeking guidance. Ah! That's it! Six A.M., six to seven. He can still get back in time to see his patients. That's it, that's how we'll do it! *Damn*!

He looked at his watch. Not quite noon. Assuming that Dr. Yun Songzhu would not be home, he decided to go downstairs for some lunch before walking the short distance to Dr. Yun's place on Linsen Road, next to Mingyi Elementary School, no more than a seven- or eight-minute walk from the hotel. During lunch he had another stroke of genius. The mission he was undertaking today, and the role he was playing—Ah ah! How important they are, ah! It was essential that he not let exhaustion or illness claim him. Abundant strength would be his defense against both. And abundant strength required abundant nutrition, which came from rich, sumptuous food and drink. So he supplemented his class-A fast-food lunch with a fried egg, a plate of Jiayi pig's feet, and a glass of fresh milk.

Dr. Yun lived in a brand-new two-story house with a separate entrance and its own yard, surrounded by a stone wall three times a man's height with iron spikes every three feet, strung with barbed wire. The Berlin Wall could boast no finer. Dong Siwen shook his head and belched. It's a damned prison, not a hospital. And the plaque on the door proclaimed not a hospital or a clinic, but the Mercy Hall Pharmacy (the license for pharmaceuticals was registered in the name of Yun's wife, a pharmacist).

Siwen recalled that when the couple started out, they set up their practice in a little rented frame house on Shanghai Road. Then they moved into a more modern building with a storefront on Chiang Kai-shek Avenue, and now they'd built a home on their own land. Rags to riches in only a couple of years. Dong Siwen belched again, thanks to that extra egg. *Damn*! I can't fart as easily as a doctor rakes in money. Had Yun Songzhu been joking when he said that the practice of medicine was like a license to print money? All you needed was the formula of mixing effective, low-cost medicine with controlled substances like cortisone and everything was *OK*. Money, money, money. He laughed. This formula's easier than $A + B$ squared equals $A^2 + 2AB + B^2$, wouldn't you say?

Is it? Siwen shrugged his shoulders and belched.

The red iron gates of the Mercy Hall Pharmacy opened wide. Siwen walked in, and the first thing he saw was a crowd milling around the yard waiting to see the doctor. But even that didn't prepare him for the mass of humanity inside. Shock registered. How could Songzhu's business be this good? And how could so many people be sick all at the same time? He spotted Dr. Yun's wife busily preparing and packaging prescriptions behind a dispensing window, where a woman in a lavender smock was taking money and giving change and telling patients to take the medicine a half hour before or after meals, and how many pills to take each time. Nurses carrying syringes or drips were running up and down the corridor, busy as bees, as though they were in an emergency room in the aftermath of a horrible accident.

The walls were painted white. Hanging from the west wall were famous gems from the Bible: "He suffered for our sins, and by His wounds we are healed." "He who forgives your sins heals your diseases." "For I am the Lord, who heals you." The bench beneath them was fully occupied. A man in his fifties, who was coughing so hard his face was beet red, stood beside the bench. Women were yelling at their children to sit down and stop running around and stop touching everything and stop. . . . Others were leaning against the back of the bench fast asleep. A little two- or three-year-old boy waddled up next to Siwen, tugged his pant leg, and giggled:

"Shi Song, hee hee, Shi Song, hee hee . . ."

People turned to look, embarrassing Siwen, who made a face at the little boy, then turned and walked toward one of the examination rooms. The door abruptly swung open, and out stepped a handsome young man in his twenties, buttoning up his shirt with one hand and smoothing his hair with the other. Wow, look at that red face! Even a spiking fever doesn't make a face *that* red. More like someone mortified by being caught masturbating. He was followed out the door by a woman in a date-red sweater and a white nurse's cap. She glanced at the patients waiting on the bench.

"Number thirteen, Miss Lin." No response. "Number thirteen, Miss Lin," she repeated.

Still no response. She raised her voice and tried again. "Number thirteen, Miss Lin!"

A shout came from outside: "Coming! Coming!" It was a raspy man's voice. "Coming! Coming! Coming!" A wave of excitement swept the waiting room as every eye turned to the doorway, including those of the people who had dozed off.

"Coming! Coming!" A bald-headed, toothless old man in a T-shirt, shorts, and open-toed sandals burst through the door, yelling "Coming! Coming!" and ran up to the nurse. "I couldn't hear you out there," he said breathlessly. "Sorry, I'm really sorry!"

"Coming?" The nurse, by now wide-eyed, peered around the old man to see who else was there. "Where is she?"

The old man, his T-shirt faded yellow, scratched his head. "Where's who?"

"Where's Miss Lin? The doctor's waiting." The nurse's impatience was beginning to show.

The old man pointed to his chest with his leathery hand. "I'm Miss Lin! Isn't it number thirteen's turn? Miss Lin? That's me. See this registration slip? It says number thirteen."

People on the bench and near the dispensing window giggled. Dong Siwen nearly laughed out loud. The young man who had just been seen by the doctor stood off to the side snickering, his face far less red than it had been a moment ago. Even the old guy standing by the bench stopped hacking.

The nurse struggled to keep a straight face as she pointed a quaking finger at the bald old man and said, "You are—" She couldn't go on, so with a grin, she waved Mr. Miss Lin into the examining room.

Two minutes, that's all it took, before "Miss Lin" had seen the doctor and was striding back into the waiting room. Siwen laughed as he glanced over at Mr. Miss Lin, then strode into the examining room. The nurse froze momentarily when she saw him, but then turned businesslike and asked: "Are you number fourteen, Chen Xiaoyan, sir?"

"Chen Xiaoyan?" Dong Siwen had to laugh at that. The poor woman must have lost her bearings over the Miss Lin affair. "Haven't you got that wrong, Miss? I'm a man, in case you hadn't noticed, and about as fat as a pig." The nurse lowered her head to hide a smile. "Do you think it's likely that I'd have a cute name like Little Swallow?"

The nurse looked up at him, then shrugged her shoulders and lowered her eyes. "Beats me." Her voice was soft, as if she were talking to herself. Then she looked up at Siwen again and said in a slightly louder voice, "Then what number are you, sir?"

"I need to talk to Dr. Yun about something. We were schoolmates. It'll only take a minute." Without giving her time to react, he spun his portly body around like an old horse that knows the way and went behind the white screen, the date-red-sweatered nurse's shout ringing in his ears: "Number fourteen, Chen Xiaoyan!"

The examining room walls were white and spotless, reminding Siwen of a description from a classical novel: a snow cave. Yun Songzhu wasn't there—probably next door with a patient's records, prescribing medication. So Siwen sat down on the patient's stool, crossed his arms, and put his feet up on the table, making himself right at home.

"Hey, it's you, my favorite numbskull!" Yun Songzhu was standing in front of Siwen when he spun around. Two hands were suddenly stroking and kneading his soft, jiggly breasts. Yun Songzhu did this every time they met, a goofy way to say hello. "Oh ho ho! Getting kind of fat, aren't we? The fatter we get, the closer death creeps!" Seeing that Siwen was about to say something, Songzhu took his hands off the breasts and put them over Siwen's mouth. He kept them there until Siwen began to choke. "I can't breathe!" he gasped.

Songzhu giggled. "What's up? Ever hear of the telephone?"

"On the contrary." Siwen took a hard swipe at his mouth with his meaty hand, as if to obliterate the smell of Songzhu sticking to it. "Me, dare to contact *you* by phone? *The Doctor* Yun? You agreed to examine the girls on the phone this morning, *Doctor* Yun, did you not? That's what you said, isn't it? *OK*, then let me ask you this, *Doctor* Yun. When the girls showed up at your office, on time, I might add, why did you give them a *Big No*? The trustworthiness of your agreement over the phone deserves a great big question mark, *Doctor* Yun."

"A little less pedantry, if you don't mind. Numbskull! If you've got something to say, out with it, and keep it short. I'm busy as—" Dr. Yun shot a sideward glance at the nurse in the date-red sweater, who was leading a woman in past the screen. He broke off in mid-sentence and greeted her with a smile. "Ah, Chen Xiaoyan, it's you! I'll just pass on what I was about to say."

"What were you about to say?" Chen Xiaoyan asked with a modest little cough, the look on her face showing considerable interest.

Dr. Yun greeted her question with a foolish grin. "Long time no see, Miss Chen." He paused. Then: "Me, I save lives, not ruin them. Feel free to drop by anytime."

Miss Chen batted her eyes and smiled. Dong Siwen laughed along with her, until his chunky legs were jiggling. The nurse stood nearby straightening some medical records; she did not laugh, probably because she was out of earshot.

"What's the problem, Miss Chen?" Dr. Yun asked.

"I—" Miss Chen looked up at Siwen, then lowered her head shyly.

"Get up!" Dr. Yun patted Siwen's meaty shoulder. "Outside with you. I'll send *Miss* Yang for you in a minute," he said with a wave to the nurse in the date-red sweater.

"Let me say something. I'll keep it short."

"In a minute. Wait outside." Songzhu patted his shoulder again and flashed a smile. "That little bit of time shouldn't interfere with your great enterprise."

As luck would have it, there was an empty spot on the waiting room bench, probably vacated by Chen Xiaoyan. Siwen ambled over and sat down, squeezing his ample body into the expanding space as people on either side were pushed outward. The old man standing nearby was still coughing. "Miss Lin," prescription in hand, strode purposefully out the door.

Dr. Yun saw one patient every minute or so, and after five, then six, still Miss Yang hadn't called Siwen. His patience wearing thin, he stood up and walked to the door to see what was going on. He tried the handle. What? Locked! Back to the bench. Now even the cough-master had gotten his prescription and left. What about me? I've got urgent and important business to take care of at Big-Nose Lion's place. Where's Miss Yang? "Little bit of time, no interference!" *Damn*!

A chatty young woman sitting on the far edge of the bench abruptly stood up and ran to the door after the little boy who had mistaken Siwen for Shi Song a while before. Controlling her voice as much as possible, she hissed, "Where do you think you're going, Xiaomao, get back here!" The little boy waddled toward the door, but his mother was too fast for him; she grabbed him like a hawk snatching its prey. "Naughty little Xiaomao, you need a spanking, a good spanking." Which is what he got, as she patted his bottom, sending a gold bracelet sliding up and down her arm. "If you don't behave yourself, I'll have the nurse give you a shot with a long needle."

The child fought and squirmed, but his mother held him too tightly to get away, and his screeches and cries filled the waiting room. Siwen was enjoying the spectacle as Miss Yang came through the door.

"He'll see you now, Mr. Dong."

Siwen had barely risen off the bench when his neighbors slid sideways to fill the vacuum, their faces stamped with looks of relief, as of laying down a heavy burden.

A scant few sentences into his conversation with Dr. Yun, Siwen spotted Miss Yang bringing a young (male) patient into the room. He gave up his seat to the newcomer as he blurted out the gist of what he had come to say, ending it with an *OK?*

Dr. Yun, who was staring at the young patient so intently his long eyelashes scarcely moved, obviously hadn't heard a word.

OK? Siwen tapped the doctor on the shoulder. "We'll hold class between six and seven A.M., for your convenience. Just get up a little early, that's all. So, it's settled then?"

Dr. Yun reluctantly shifted his gaze from the young man to Siwen. "I play golf on Saturday mornings from six to seven. I'll think it over and let you know."

"I need your answer now. I have things to take care of."

"I said, let me think it over." Dr. Yun patted the fair skin of his brow. "I'll let you know the minute I make up my mind."

"I'll wait outside."

"No need for that, you can wait right here."

"You want me to stand here while you're thinking?"

"What's wrong with standing? It won't make you any fatter."

The young newcomer laughed, displaying the cornrows that were his teeth. Even Miss Yang smiled.

"What I meant was won't—won't I, won't I be in the way—" Siwen clutched his sagging jowls. "I mean, won't it be awkward for me to hang around while you're seeing a patient?"

"Why's that? You and he—" Dr. Yun smiled knowingly and pointed to the young man. "You're not *that* different."

"Not different?" Siwen said, clutching his jowls even harder.

With a mysterious grin, Dr. Yun reached down with his hairy hand and patted the surprised young patient on the crotch, once, twice, three times; then he shot a sideward glance at Siwen. "You're no different down here, are you?" He patted the area again with his hairy hand, and a second time, then lowered his voice. "You've got a hot dog just like it in your pants, haven't you?"

The mortified young patient turned bright red.

Muttering Fuck you! under his breath, Siwen clenched his teeth and glared wide-eyed at Songzhu, then turned to look at Miss Yang, who had moved over to the screen to straighten up some things. She wasn't smiling, in fact wore no discernible expression at all. She probably hadn't observed Dr. Yun's antics.

When Dr. Yun asked his patient, "Your name is Li Fayu [well-developed Li]? You're eighteen years old?" Siwen moved self-consciously to the side, giving way to Miss Yang, in her date-red sweater, who walked up beside Dr. Yun. With nowhere to sit, Siwen stood at the door with his hands in his pockets, where all he could see were backs. But in the boxy little examining room, he could only have avoided eavesdropping by stuffing cotton in his ears.

"Are you still in school?"

"I graduated."

"What are you doing now?"

"I'm a dockworker."

"What seems to be the problem?" The tone of Dr. Yun's voice was fatherly.

"I've got no appetite, but I don't feel hungry. Sometimes I can't even force food down—I hurt here, and get pains here, not real sharp ones, but they bother me a lot—and my head—feels all stuffy, like right now—and—" Li Fayu's complaints, in a mixture of Mandarin and Taiwanese, poured out in a loud, clear voice, strong and unwavering, not what you might expect from a youngster who was really ill. "And my chest, it hurts when I take deep breaths, and I get backaches way down low."

"Anything else?" Dr. Yun asked after a momentary silence.

"That's it."

"Now why would a well-developed [fayu] kid like you have so many physical complaints?"

"You don't think I'm—?" The young man's voice softened abruptly, and Siwen didn't hear the rest.

Nor did Dr. Yun. "What did you say?"

"Potency problems," the embarrassed young man said.

"Oh! Potency problems, eh!" Dr. Yun was grinning. "Are you married?"

"Not yet."

"They how do you qualify for potency problems?"

"Huh?"

"Take off your shirt."

Yun Songzhu turned to whisper something to Miss Yang, in what could have been American or some aboriginal tongue, for all Siwen knew. "Oh!" was her reply. She turned and went into an adjoining room, closing the door behind her.

"*Wow!*" Yun Songzhu exclaimed excitedly, as if he had discovered a rare treasure. "*Wow!* (By 1982 he had replaced *wow* with the new term, *wasai*.) You're actually wearing an undershirt! Young people these days don't seem to wear them much."

This excited outburst turned Siwen's head, and what he saw was the scantily covered torso of the young man, who was sitting up straight, his muscular build—upper arms and back—that of a weightlifter. His shoulders and neck were tanned bronze. Siwen found it hard to believe that a strapping young man like that could have any physical problems.

Modesty, most likely, kept the young Li Fayu's head down. The fair-skinned Songzhu was grinning so broadly his nose was twisted out of joint.

"Today's youngsters can't be bothered with putting on undershirts. Did you know that some don't even wear underpants? You're obviously a clean-cut kid, wearing an undershirt and all. Look at me, I'm not wearing one, and I'm a generation older than you! See there?" He undid the top buttons of his shirt to reveal the fair skin of his chest. Hey, there's a triangular patch of dark hair right above the breastbone, like a woman's mound of Venus! The next thing Siwen saw was Songzhu grabbing the young man's smooth hand with his own hairy one, lightning-quick, and placing it on his patch of chest hair. "See, I'm not wearing one, am I?" Songzhu had excitement written all over his face; the young man, on the other hand, dropped his head as low as he could. "A real clean-cut kid!" Songzhu released the young man's hand and tugged on his undershirt. "Take this off, off with it. The more you wear, the sicker you get!"

The young man did as he was told, reaching down to remove his undershirt, which he tossed, together with his outer shirt, onto the examining table.

"Now isn't that better?" Songzhu scrutinized the young man's bare torso like a connoisseur viewing a work of art, eyes wide, long lashes dancing.

The young man's chin was touching his chest, and Siwen couldn't hear his answer, if there was one.

Songzhu laughed complacently. Picking a stethoscope up off the table, he put the ends into his ears and said genially, "Come here, sit closer. I need a good kissin.' "

What kind of talk is that? Siwen nearly blurted out.

"Doctor, did you just say you need a good kissin'?" The young man's head shot up, and he must have been staring at Dr. Yun with fright in his eyes, or so Siwen figured.

Dr. Yun took the stethoscope ends out of his ears. He giggled, then softly tapped the young man's bare shoulder. "Do you have trouble hearing? What made you think I need a good kissin'? I clearly said I need a good listen, didn't I? Don't tell me my Mandarin's so bad you can't tell the difference between *kissin'* and *listen*."

The young man's head drooped; he didn't dare respond.

Abruptly Songzhu's nose twisted out of shape as he grinned again. "You're not a girl, after all, so why would I want to give you a good kissin'? What were you thinking?" Another tender pat on a bare shoulder. The young man's chin was touching his chest again; he wrung his hands and didn't make a sound.

"Scoot over here so I can listen. You heard me right this time, I hope."

The chin pressed deeper into the chest, and still not a sound.

As a grunt of disgust escaped from Siwen, he turned and saw Miss Yang open the door of the adjoining room and enter with a clean white sheet; she smiled and walked past the screen into the outer room. Before long, she returned empty-handed.

"You're fine, like a brand-new car, trouble-free. How could you possibly ache all over? Now that's a puzzle—um! Let's do this—*Miss* Yang—"

Miss Yang scurried up to Songzhu, who whispered something to her, either in American or in some aboriginal tongue. Siwen watched Miss Yang scurry around the screen and out of the room.

"I'll give you a complete checkup. Come with me. Leave your clothes there on the table, you won't need them."

Siwen looked over at Songzhu, who buttoned up his shirt and tucked the young man's arm under his own, leading him gaily into the adjoining room. Siwen stared at the young man as he passed by. He was a towering tree standing before the wind, at least half a head taller than the five-foot-eight-inch Songzhu. An oval face you couldn't help but like, with bronzed, glistening skin that made Songzhu's fair complexion look downright pale; big eyes and bushy eyebrows, a straight nose and full, handsome lips; he seemed made for the camera. As he passed by, bare-chested and bashful, Siwen got a whiff of a subtle odor that was a mixture of dried plums and sour root.

Just before the two of them went into the adjoining room, Siwen rushed up behind Songzhu and asked, "Well, what do you say?"

"I haven't had time to think!" He stopped, turned, and waved at Siwen. "Come in while you're waiting." With Li Fayu's arm still tucked under his own, he walked through the door.

All the milk Siwen had consumed and all the pig's feet he had wolfed down suddenly began to grumble in his stomach. No time to worry about that now, so he tagged along behind the two men. *Miss* Yang brought up the rear, holding a pair of rubber gloves in a transparent bag, which she laid down on a wooden stand. Then she closed the door.

What to call this place? An examining room? An observation room? A treatment room? It had the feel of all three, yet there was more to it than that. It was half the size of the outer room, with the same whitewashed walls except that the one opposite the door, like its counterpart in the waiting room, was adorned with godly sayings: "For I am the Lord, who heals you." "He suffered for our sins, and by His wounds we are healed." "He who forgives your sins heals your diseases." An adjustable examining table occupied the center of the room, on which *Miss* Yang had just changed the sheet and pillowcase; white as snow, they still smelled of the hot iron that had smoothed them out. Against the inside wall stood a plywood closet, also snowy white, next to the toilet, the door of which appeared to be carved out of salt. A cabinet beside the door was also painted white. An assortment of bottles containing surgical pharmaceuticals lay scattered on top of it—iodine, mercurochrome, merthiolate, hydrogen peroxide, etc.—as well as stacks of gauze, cotton, adhesive tape, and the like. Siwen sighed in admiration: controlled substances plus cortisone, internal medicine and surgery, what a goddamned deal he has going here!

No sooner had Siwen entered the examining room than his legs began to ache from all that standing, and the abundance of nutrients he had ingested began shifting in his stomach, making it imperative that he sit down and get a load off. A quick search of the room yielded an empty chair in one of corners, which he hastily occupied before anyone else beat him to it. A silent fart greeted the chair as he sat down, releasing the grumblings from his stomach.

"Mr. Li," *Miss* Yang said to the young man as she pointed to the table, "lie down, please."

"Oh!" With a bright, wide-eyed glance at Songzhu, he slowly, politely extracted his arm, then walked over and hopped up onto the snow-white table.

"Take off your shoes, please," *Miss* Yang quickly reminded him, with the precision timing of a rehearsed scene. When the young man responded with a soft "Yes, ma'am," she continued: "And your clothes, please."

"Whaat?" The young man's red lips parted to reveal two rows of ivorylike teeth. He grabbed his chin with one hand.

"There are slippers on the floor. Put them on, then take off your clothes, hang them on the hook on the wall, then lie down on your back." These brief instructions by *Miss* Yang seemed not so much spoken as simply materializing, like a flight attendant's intercom instructions to fasten your seat belt and refrain from smoking prior to takeoff.

"All of them?" The red-lipped, ivory-toothed mouth remained wide open, as if the shock were too great for him to get it closed again.

Miss Yang nodded, stone-faced.

From beneath his long eyelashes, Songzhu glanced tenderly at the young man, then walked over to the closet and took down a white hospital smock; as he slipped it on he walked up to the patient, who stood there reluctant to take off his pants, and laid his hand on his bare back. "Speed it up. There's a whole waiting room full of people I have to see."

With an embarrassed "Oh," the red-faced young man bent down to remove his shoes, his thick, glossy hair tumbling down over his face as if poured from a bucket. His legs were long and straight, his waist narrow and smooth; not an ounce of fat anywhere. His back was smooth and shiny, like a biscuit right out of the oven. A strapping young fellow, Siwen was thinking, like a decathalon champion, not someone with all sorts of physical ailments.

After easing his feet into the slippers, the young man stood up and threw his head back, sending the hair up into the air like water from a fountain that then settled back into place. "Socks too?" His voice was tentative, plaintive.

Songzhu smiled and nodded, never taking his eyes off the young man's glossy skin.

Miss Yang took the rubber gloves from the stand and laid them on the table, then walked out, closing the door behind her. Siwen stood up.

"I'll wait outside, Songzhu, but please don't be long. I have lots to do."

"Don't leave. I'll be thinking if there are other obligations while I'm examining him. If not, I'll do what you ask."

"I'll phone you this evening, you can tell me then."

"I said don't leave, and that's what I meant, you blathering numbskull! Tell you this evening? You, you're something. Who's got the Yankee leisure time?" Songzhu gave Siwen a hard stare—the first time the eyes beneath those long lashes had left the young man's body. "Now, sit down!" Like a military command.

Siwen shrugged his shoulders and made a feeble gesture before sitting down as he was told. But as soon as his hindquarters found the respite they sought, they yearned to protest. Incorrigible! Siwen upbraided himself as he took a deep breath and squeezed shut the offending aperture.

"All right." Songzhu returned his attention to the young man's body, his eyes opened wide, not daring to blink for fear that the breathtaking scene before him would vanish. "All right, onto the table." If you listened hard enough, you could detect a slight quake in his voice, as if he could scarcely believe that such joy had dropped from the heavens.

As he removed his black cotton shorts, the young man exposed that part of his body that never saw the light of day—not a single mole, not the trace of a scar, marred the sculpted beauty of his buttocks. After hanging his trousers and shorts on the wall hook, he turned his head around slowly. Wow! His cheeks looked like they were rouged; his glistening eyes were glued to the floor, like a man walking through a minefield; his hands were cupped around the family jewels, as if to protect them from a lurking sneak thief. The flag must be going up the pole, Siwen thought to himself. Otherwise, why would he crouch over like that when he walked, as if locked in a perpetual bow?

The naked young man climbed onto the table and lay face up, his hands cupping the hot dog like a bun; not daring to let his eyeballs stray in any direction, nor to shut them, he stared at the wall in front of him—"For I am the Lord, who heals you."

Songzhu straightened his smock before walking up to the table and, in an exaggerated motion, thrusting his arms out wide. "Stick your arms out, like this."

Li Fayu [well-developed Li] spread out his arms, revealing hairy armpits. Like Jesus on the cross. Siwen barely kept from saying it.

"You're quite well developed—" Songzhu finally broke the silence, followed quickly by a soft, half-hearted "Yes" from the young man. Songzhu laughed. "What's wrong with you? I'm not taking roll here. What I was about to say is you're quite well developed. Very well developed. Especially here—" He reached out and touched, rather forcefully, Li Fayu's robust penis. "Heh heh heh, this would stand up well against one of our Pingtung bananas!" The young man's face was as red as a drunken groom at his own wedding banquet. In a voice oozing sympathy, Songzhu clicked his tongue and said, "If only the foreskin weren't so long. It covers the entire head. That won't do, it keeps all the gunk in, know what I mean? That could affect your sex life someday, might even cause cervical cancer in your wife. If you can't pull it back with your fingers, surgery is your best option. Of course, that would require a hospital stay. And if something went wrong (here he switched to Mandarin) and nerves were cut, well, you can forget about ever seeing it stand this proud again!"

Songzhu bent down to examine the young man's testicles. "Very good, no sexually transmitted diseases." The hairy hand then moved up to Li Fayu's chest, pressing here and thumping there, then an ear pressed up against the heart, where the doctor listened intently. He nodded to show he heard nothing abnormal, then jammed his face into one of Li Fayu's hairy armpits, sniffing around for the longest time.

"How many days since you bathed?" he asked in a serious, almost accusatory tone after emerging from the armpit.

"I bathe every day."

"Honest?"

"Honest." In a move to underscore his candor, the young man added in Mandarin, "That's the truth."

"You're lying!" Songzhu fired back in Mandarin.

"Honest, I shower yearly." The young man's face was bright red, the color of the God of War in Peking opera.

"Yearly?"

"I mean daily! Honest, I bathe every day."

"You're still lying!" Songzhu frowned and shook his head. He reached out and slapped the young man lightly, then thrust his hand into the armpit, grabbed a fistful of hair, and yanked. The young man winced in pain. "You stink like hell! I mean, really stink! In my opinion— " Once again he buried his face in an armpit and sniffed hard, then looked up with a scowl.

"In my opinion, you haven't bathed in at least three days, am I right? Tell me, am I right? It's only reasonable to assume that if you bathed every day, you wouldn't stink like that, am I right?" The young man, his forehead getting feverishly sweaty, rolled his eyes and let his mouth hang slack; he couldn't say a word. "You're still lying to me!" Another slap across the face, more like a love tap.

With all the pressure building up inside, Siwen could no longer hold back the fart (a noisy one) demanding to get out. His gut felt better immediately.

Songzhu heard the noise—he couldn't *not* have heard it—and spun around, throwing a fright into Siwen that turned his cheeks hot.

"That stuff they call *deodorant*, what do we say in Chinese, antiperspirant, or something like that?"

Siwen, who hadn't understood the question, turned red.

"You know, American *deodorants*, like *Ban* and *Right Guard*, those *deodorants* the Americans use down here." Songzhu gestured toward the young man's armpit.

"Oh! That's what they, uh, what they call— " With a roll of his eyes, he said the first thing that popped into his head. "It's something like anti-b.o. cologne."

"Hogwash! Who in his right mind would buy anything with a name like that?" Songzhu's eyes flashed beneath his long lashes. "Hey, why not call it fragrant pits cologne? That's the ticket! Fragrant pits cologne, a perfect name. I thought a literature major could come up with a better name than anti-b.o. cologne." With this inspiration, he turned his fair-skinned face back to the young man with an ardent gleam in his eyes.

"You go out and buy a bottle of fragrant pits cologne and rub it in. It's not perfume, virtually odorless, rub it in here— " His hand snaked its way back into the young man's hairy armpit. "It'll keep you from stinking even when you sweat, so go buy some and rub it in. You don't want to smell bad around people. Folks like you, who hate to bathe, need it worse than anyone. It doesn't cost much. You can get it anywhere they sell American products. Ah—I've got it! I'll buy a bottle for you!"

"No, I'll buy it." A smile appeared on the young man's face for the first time, but it vanished almost at once, like a sand castle at high tide.

"I'll order a bottle for you. Come back next week, same time, to pick it up."

"Thank you very much." The young man seemed genuinely moved.

As Songzhu's hand moved down to his patient's abdomen and began fondling him, the young man quickly folded his arms across his chest, as if to avoid offending Songzhu with the sweaty odor of his armpits.

"You're in great shape! No trace of Saigon Rose, that v.d. strain that's almost impossible to cure, so how come you have aches and pains all over your body? Try switching positions," Songzhu said, flipping his hand over to illustrate. "Roll over and lie face down."

Given his state of arousal, the young man had trouble carrying out the order, and when he finally managed to roll over, his rear end was sticking up in the air, and he had to curl his legs to even get that far. The sight instilled in Siwen a desire to laugh, and to fart.

With a loud smack on the young man's rump, which never saw the light of day, Songzhu laughed lustily. "Flatten out! With your rump sticking up like that, you're just asking for a good humping." He smacked him again, harder this time, and in no time two reddish handprints decorated the young man's lily-white hindquarters.

The young man tried again, the poor devil! A prone position was out of the question. His legs stayed curled, his rump stuck up in the air; he swiveled his head around to look at Songzhu, a look of utter supplication on his face.

"All right, forget it, if that's the best you can do!" With one last smack on the young man's rump, Songzhu began to pinch and thump and *massage* his hips and lower back and thighs and rump, then picked up the rubber gloves and walked over to the white stand for a flashlight, with which he checked out the young man's anus. Whatever examination method he was using had Li Fayu yelping out loud.

"I'm almost finished, just be patient."

The agony continued for a while longer. "All right!" Songzhu all but yelled. "All right! You can roll over now."

Once the young man was on his back again, his brow was beaded with perspiration, most likely squeezed out by the pain. As for his pride and joy, which had stood up so proudly for so long, it was now like the wick of a burning candle: wilted.

"Nine out of ten men have piles, but not you. You're in perfect condition. In my opinion—" As he tossed his flashlight and rubber gloves onto the stand, Songzhu gazed up at the ceiling through his long, lush eyelashes, as if lost in thought. To a casual observer he appeared to be trying to guess the ceiling's age or learn its history. That went on for a while before he let his gaze fall back to the young man. "Your problem stems from an unwillingness to bathe and the excessive length of your foreskin. No problem, that's just what I figured! You say your belly often gets bloated—" Back to the ceiling, and further investigation into its history. A pregnant pause, then he completed his thought. "Here's what we'll do!" He picked a specimen bottle up off the stand and handed it to the young man. "Take this into the toilet and get me a sperm specimen—you'll have to do it by hand. I'll check out the color and its odor (it was all Siwen could do from saying, 'How about the taste?'), and that should tell me whether or not you've got a stomach disorder."

"You want me to do zat?" In his panic, the young man's th's turned into z's.

"It's the latest diagnostic technique."

"Zat is?"

Ah ah! Has medicine really progressed to this point? Siwen was so startled by the news that he released two farts, one noisy, the other silent; not only that, he felt stirrings down there at the other extreme. (This *is* an actual diagnostic technique; ask your health care provider if you don't believe me.)

"Go on," Songzhu pressed the young man, "into the toilet with you."

The young man's handsome face abruptly transformed into the God of War again; he rubbed it with his bare hands and muttered incoherently for a long time before admitting in a low voice, "I—I—don't know how to do it by hand."

"You don't know *how*?" Hearing no response from the lowered head, Songzhu repeated the question: "You don't know how?"

The young man shook his head without looking up.

"You really don't?"

More head shaking, but this time he gazed apologetically into Songzhu's eyes.

Songzhu gave the young man another love tap. "There you go, lying to me again!" he said. Yet another love tap. "I know you are. Heh heh heh," he laughed with a tight smile. "Nine out of ten young men fire their own pistols, and you don't know how?" Heh heh heh, another tight smile. He snatched the specimen bottle out of the young man's hand.

"OK, since you can't do it yourself, I'll give you a hand!"

With one hand protecting his pride and joy, the young man quickly sat up. "That's too much trouble, I'll do it—" He grabbed the specimen bottle. "Where's the toilet?"

Songzhu smiled and pointed it out for the young man, who climbed down off the table, bare-ass naked, specimen bottle in hand, stepped into the slippers, and headed dispiritedly off to the toilet.

"Do—you—know—how?" Songzhu asked sarcastically.

"I'll try," came the dejected reply.

At that moment—at that very moment—Siwen had a stroke of genius. If, he was thinking, just *if* he could hire a few strapping young men like Li Fayu for his bar, and get them to entertain the *homo cases* among the GIs, that would make everything perfect.

Well, wouldn't it? Siwen gulped down a mouthful of saliva and stared into space, as if sizing up a sumptuous gastronomical spread.

After the young man closed the toilet door behind him, Songzhu walked up and pinched Siwen on the nipple, forcing a yelp out of him. "All right, I'll pass up my golf game this Saturday morning."

"You're *OK* with that?"

"But if there's an emergency, my hands are tied."

"All I ask is one hour of class time."

"All right, all right! Anything for an old school buddy."

"That's wonderful!" Like a celebrant or a welcoming committee, Siwen released a melodic fart. Songzhu's brow crinkled and his nose twisted to one side, as if this might help him avoid the odor. "You know what I've been thinking? We could use a few, just a few, mind you, handsome young fellows like that one to work at the bar. I'm sure some of those GIs will need that kind of *service*, know what I mean? What do *you* think?"

Songzhu stood there wide-eyed, as if he couldn't believe his ears.

"No good?"

"It's brilliant!" Ecstatic, Songzhu reached out and pinched both of Siwen's nipples; Siwen forced back the yelps aching to get out through his open mouth. "If you manage that, you can put me down for two hours, eight to ten, any morning. I won't be late, you can count on it."

"You mean it?" He pushed Songzhu's hands away before they could make their next assault (after 1983, this is the way it would have been said: He pushed away the hands that were about to sexually harass him) and stuck his finger under Songzhu's nose. "I always knew you had this problem. One helluva of a great cover for something so seamy."

"Horseshit!" Songzhu slapped Siwen across the face. "Where'd you get that idea? I'm a doctor, I've got a wife and kids!"

"I was just joking!" Siwen rubbed his cheek.

"That kind of joking has no place here! What the hell did you mean by 'a great cover for something so seamy'? Up your old lady, up your old granny!" Then Songzhu softened his expression. "Where will you find them?"

"I'll get the whoremasters and madams to do it."

"Think they can?"

"I don't see any problem."

"Say!" Songzhu laughed out loud. "We've got one already. I'll recommend him."

"Li Fayu?" Siwen pointed to the toilet.

"No." He really laughed now. "I'm talking about Chief Qian! Isn't he big on taking off his pants?"

"Fuck!" Siwen stood up and took Songzhu's hairy hand in his. "We'll do it! No backing out! If Chief Qian takes my advice, I'll arrange the time for you, all right?" Songzhu nodded gravely. "It's a deal, then!" He waited for Songzhu to nod again, then, with a mischievous laugh, said, "Well, thank you then, my dear Dr. Yun!"

"Screw you!" Songzhu punched Siwen on his meaty shoulder. "It's not enough that I have to help you out *and* endure your farts, but I have to listen to your abuse as well! Screw you!"

"*Bye!*" With a parting wave, Siwen opened the door, a look of satisfaction over a job well done prominently displayed on his face, and was on his way out when he heard Songzhu say to Li Fayu, the young man "trying" in the toilet, "Speed it up in there, will you? Be quick about it. That's no bedroom, and there's no woman in there requiring foreplay!"

Chapter Nine

As he emerged from the Mercy Hall Pharmacy, Siwen clapped his meaty hands loudly. What a terrific idea, a stroke of genius if ever he'd had one! No time to waste. *Right*, get things started now, before making a patrol over to Big-Nose Lion's.

The first thing Siwen did upon his return to the hotel was go to the second floor to check on the preparations; when he saw that his assistants weren't back yet, he left a note telling them to stay put in the *office* and await his *instructions*. He then went to his pink suite on the third floor, where he placed a phone call to Chief Qian, who wasn't in. He was having lunch at the Aristocrat. So Siwen called the Aristocrat where, after being put on hold for far too long, he was told that Chief Qian had driven off to the Legislative Assembly. So he phoned the Meilun County Assembly offices, where his call was transferred from one office to the other until, finally, he had Chief Qian on the line.

He no sooner blurted his idea out than Chief Qian lodged an immediate objection: Who ever heard of *that* kind of bar—where boys, and not girls, did the entertaining? That sort of corruption of public morals would really get people talking.

Siwen, who had been sitting down, stood up, as if he needed to be vertical to show he was serious about this. "We don't have to do what other people do. We dare to do what others won't, and that puts us head and shoulders above the crowd. We set the standards, ah!"

He stood straight as a soldier in formation, the telephone cord stretched so taut it nearly lifted the phone up into the air; he was looking more and more content by the minute, and that blossoming smugness led to an increasingly voluble discourse: statistics published in an authoritative American magazine showed that one out of every four adult males was a *homo case*. One out of four! He urged the Chief not to take that number lightly. "A hundred one-out-of-fours is twenty-five. Three hundred *quarters* is seventy-five. Which means that for every three hundred GIs who come to Hualien on R & R, at least, *at least* seventy-five will be *homos*. I'm sure it will be more than that. They're *GIs*! From a war zone. It's a natural phenomenon. If we include these *homos* (it would be several years before they were called *crystal boys*) in our business plans, that will automatically increase our income, won't it?" He tirelessly underscored this point in his analysis, determined to show the Chief that there was a pot of gold at the end of this particular rainbow. If, in the service of these seventy-five or more *homos*, they could locate a few, just a few, clean, handsome young men as personal hosts, the profits generated by those seventy-five individuals were theirs for the taking. If, on average, each GI spent a hundred U.S. dollars in the bar—in fact, that was a conservative estimate—"then we're talking about seventy-five times a hundred. How much is that? It's seventy-five hundred dollars! *My, my!* Seventy-five hundred U.S. is three hundred thousand New Taiwan dollars! All the Big 4 have to do is invest a little more to bring in an additional three hundred thousand! Not thirty thousand, three hundred thousand! Enough to build two new houses. I don't mean we make this our prime business, and it doesn't have to interfere with our *normal* functions. Bad money can't drive away the good, so we'll just work these transactions on the sly—no flagrant displays of *homos*, no street parades, no corruption of public morals." (At the time, no one knew that gay American men were capable of transmitting a frightening disease called *AIDS—Acquired Immune Deficiency Syndrome*—which lowered one's immunities against a host of diseases. This disease is so frightening that even mortuary workers refuse to prepare its victims for burial. If Siwen had known about *AIDS* at the time, would he have made a similar proposal to Chief Qian? An interesting question, wouldn't you say?)

Siwen's gold speech had the desired effect on Chief Qian, so bewitching him that he said, and not just once: "Do what you think is right. Whatever you think is right."

After hanging up, Siwen couldn't choose between sitting down and lying down, so he prowled the room like a bloated, and very happy, serpent. That went on for a while, until it suddenly dawned on him that he hadn't touched so much as a drop of water all day. That'll never do! I don't want kidney stones! He picked up his vacuum bottle and poured a glass of hot water, added some ice water from the refrigerator, and, as he was taking a big drink, was reminded that he had neglected his vitamin C regimen today. He quickly located the bottle, dumped out two tablets, popped them into his mouth, and swallowed them with some water. After that he sighed contentedly and spread out across the sofa to stare at the pink ceiling. Ah ah! The color pink! It sure is intoxicating. A new idea shot into his head before the last "ah" had died out. Another perfect idea, another stroke of genius. Another— He put down his glass like a hot potato, jumped up, and ran downstairs, whistling out of tune the whole way.

It was quiet outside, nothing but layers of sunbeams; no sound emerged from the Heaven's Omens Theater across the street. Everyone was probably napping. The few pedestrians out on the street and the occasional passing automobile all seemed wrapped in a dream, like a silent movie. The entire block was taking a nap. That included a pedicab driver, who was fast asleep. Siwen let out three or four loud whoops, waking the man from his fantastic dream. "Where to?" he asked, rubbing his sleepy eyes.

"To Ditch-end!" came the answer.

(If you ever vacation in Hualien and just happen to have an itch, but don't know where to go to scratch it and aren't sure how to ask, here's how you make your inquiry [do not, under any circumstances, ask a local woman]: Excuse me, can you tell me how to get to Ditch-end? This is my first visit to Hualien, a lovely place with its bright hills and clear waters, a soulful place with such wonderful people. Excuse me, one more thing. How much is a pedicab ride to Ditch-end? [These days, of course, you would change that to "How much is the cab fare?"] Do that, and you're assured of finding Ditch-end with no trouble, and there you can take care of your bodily urges.)

When the pedicab driver heard Siwen's request, he thought he had heard wrong; he asked—twice—just to be sure: "You want to go to Ditch-end?"

After Siwen nodded his affirmative reply, the man laughed gleefully, as if the person going to seek his pleasure there were not his customer but he himself.

"Isn't a little early to be going to Ditch-end?"

"Just what are you thinking?" Unfortunately, Siwen was in such a happy state that he failed miserably at acting angry, and all he managed was to raise his finger and point to his slightly elevated nose. "I'm a high school teacher! I have personal business in Ditch-end!" He stepped into the pedicab and sat down hard.

The driver climbed up onto the seat in front. "Of course you've got personal business!" he muttered. "You wouldn't be going there to take care of public business, now would you?"

On the way, the driver cautioned him that the girls would be napping, recharging their batteries, as it were, and not many would get up to greet a customer. "They don't start coming out until five or six in the evening. After nightfall, especially around eight or nine, hell, it really starts to rock then! By then there are girls on every street, standing shoulder to shoulder in long columns. Did you know that? By that time, the streets are crawling with people, packed solid, like local temples around New Year's, like the temple grounds when crowds of people watch puppet plays. Visitors strolling the streets sometimes turn nasty and taunt the whores; the really bold ones actually walk up and start touching and groping, until the girls screech like chickens getting plucked. Girls just line the streets—you ever watch TV? I knew it, at first glance I thought you were that numbskull Shi Song! You know, the guy on TV. If you hadn't said you were a high school teacher, I'd have thought that Shi Song had come to taste the forbidden pleasures of Hualien–girls line the streets, like on TV, you know, at the Miss World pageant!

"Those girls sure know how to drag in the customers, know what I'm saying? No one gets past them. Up and down the street, all you hear is, 'Come on, come on, come on, it's time to party.' 'Go on, go on, go on, go buy an admission ticket!' 'Come on, come on, come on, it's time to party.' 'Go on, go on, go on, go buy an admission ticket!' Hell, the noise'll drive you crazy! And when the Japanese customers show up, the whores announce, '*Irashaimase*, welcome to our establishment,' before grabbing a handful of clothing and refusing to let go until the guy buys a ticket and goes inside to party. Hell, I tell you, some of those girls are so shameful they grab the men's balls, for crying out loud, and all you hear is 'Ouch! *Itai*! That hurts!' "

All that talk frightened Siwen, who had cold sweat all up and down his spine as if he'd rubbed up against a block of ice. If his trainees put on an unseemly show like that, it'd mess up all his carefully worked-out plans! If they treated the GIs that badly, if they came on to them like that, it could absolutely ruin relations between the two countries. He bit his lip. How could he tolerate something like that? He clapped his hands. Right, that's a *spot*, a big, dirty *spot*, a frightening and very serious *spot* he'd have to guard against and not give a chance to make an appearance in his endeavor. So he took out his pen and notebook and scribbled a note to himself: "Arrange for a crash course in global etiquette." He drew three lines beneath it to underscore its importance, like adding *est* to an English adjective. After putting away his pen and notebook, he said to himself: We've got to have that course, and there ought to be some empty slots in the curriculum where it will fit in. We've got to have it. Now, who will teach it? Ah! I'll ask Mao Two, the dean of students. That's it! He's the one, no doubt about it! That's settled. He stroked his jowls and let out another contented sigh. Once again the pedicab driver's tales of "yellow peril" floated back to him.

"It's true, I'm not just making it up. After nightfall, every road and street corner is packed with people, packed like sardines, and noisy as hell. I'm telling you, if you want to see a lively scene, you have to come back at night. You're a schoolteacher, how come your pants are on fire? Can't you wait till after dark?"

On and on he prattled, and before long the pedicab began to slow down. He turned his head back. "We're here, this is Ditch-end. As you can see, it's much too early in the day, wouldn't you say?"

Siwen sat there wide-eyed, the expression on his face an exact replica of the one he would wear years later on a trip to Disneyland in the company of TV actors—unadulterated rapture. His first glimpse of the place, and he was so ecstatic he felt like jumping up and down! Which is why he preceded his next comment with a pair of "ah"s and ended it with another.

"Ah ah! So this is Ditch-end, ah!"

"This is it. See there." The driver pointed to a ditch with filthy water on the side of the road. "It's located at the end of that ditch, which is why they call the district Ditch-end."

"Oh."

"Where do you want me to let you off?"

Siwen took a look around. "Do you know where the Rouge Tower is?" he asked the driver.

"Wow!" The driver turned his head again, his grin exposing two lines of yellowed teeth. "The Rouge Tower is a high-class whorehouse. Expensive as hell. But their girls aren't any better looking than other places, and the house is just as run down. I'm telling you, if you want to take care of business, don't go to a place like that. It'll really cost you! I'm telling you, teacher, go over to the place run by A-lan, Night Fragrance. It's more affordable, and friendlier . . ."

But Siwen wasn't listening. Out came his pen and notebook, which he flipped through until he found the addresses and phone numbers of the Big 4. He waited for the driver to stop talking. "Where's Filial Piety Street?"

"Go down Loyalty Avenue, the one we're on now, and turn left at the end. The Rouge Tower is at the far end of the first lane on Filial Piety Street."

"I'll get off here, then." He put away his notebook and took some five-yuan notes out of a hidden pocket sewn into his waistband.

The pedicab came to a stop. The driver took the money, counted it, and reached into his pocket. "Keep the change," Siwen said with a shake of his head.

"Thank you," the driver said, more than once, from behind him, then added sympathetically, "So you've got your heart set on the Rouge Tower, have you? It'll really cost you. That place is notorious for fleecing its customers!"

It was indeed too early. The streets and lanes of Ditch-end were deserted, unenlivened even by the shadow of a stray dog. It looked like an air raid drill in progress.

Anxiety gripped Siwen as he turned into the lane at Filial Piety Street, suddenly concerned by the remote prospect of being seen by one of the other teachers or by a student. He stopped in his tracks and took a good look around, resuming his walk only after he was sure there was no one in sight. He had walked only a few steps when he said to himself: If I don't enter hell, then who will? The mind thus settled, what, pray is there to fear?

It was a very narrow lane, no more than ten feet wide. The smell of fresh tar on the recently paved ground seemed to hang in the air. Frame houses faced one another across the lane, most of them single-story, with an occasional two-story building here and there. Turned dark by the sun's rays, they were old and dilapidated, like the shacks of early pioneers. The signs hanging from the eaves gave them a sort of "modern" feel; all the names had links to flowers–Night Fragrance, Flower of the Night, Seven-Mile Bouquet, Orchid Valley, Peony Pavilion, Rose Villa, Peach Blossom River . . . making you feel as if you'd stumbled into a garden where there were no visible flowers, just an array of markers indicating what was planted where. What really caught his eye were white plastic signs nailed to posts at each house; roughly eight-by-ten in size, they displayed in vigorous terseness: "First-class Brothel" or "Second-class Brothel." Most were of the second-class variety; only a few could boast first-class status. A close examination revealed to Siwen a total lack of third- or fourth-class operations. *Boy!* Obtaining a license for a brothel was like a graduate school exam, where anything under a B was a failing grade.

Every door was ajar, and there didn't seem to be anyone inside, not even a doorman. He had truly entered a utopian world where doors stood open the day long. The pedicab driver must have been right when he said that the girls were recharging their batteries for the boudoir battles ahead. Every now and then he caught a glimpse of a girl sprawled across a chair watching TV and nibbling melon seeds or munching rice cakes. Ah! Siwen exclaimed, as if he had spotted a precious gem. He repeated himself twice more, for he caught sight, actually saw with his own two eyes, one of the girls perched upon a low stool as an old woman plucked fine hairs from her powdered face. As a child, he had seen people do the same thing for his mother, but that was the last time he had observed this sort of facial treatment—until now. Seeing it again today made him ecstatic. Ah ah! That's it! Decorum lost in the city can be sought in the wilds.

The Rouge Tower was at the end of the lane, just where it was supposed to be. It too was a frame building, also old and dilapidated; but, true to its name, it sported a squat tower. As Siwen stood there sizing the place up, he noted that, with the exceptions of a somewhat wider porch and a slightly newer brothel sign, there were no obvious signs of its premier status; in fact, the red paint on the fence was so mottled it looked like a beat-up old five-yuan note. He thumped himself on his meaty chest. Right, ah! I should have gone over to check out the bar. If it looks anything like one of these *slum* buildings, it'll be a great loss of face for the nation, and a miracle if the *GIs* don't go back talking about how backward we are! I really ought to go take a look before *everything too late*.

The door was wide open, just like the others, and just as quiet—not a soul in sight. Siwen paused long enough to take a look around, and when he spotted someone out of the corner of his eye, he nervously turned to get a better look: it was a blind man in a gray cotton robe and sunglasses, tap-tap-tapping his way from the entrance to the lane. Siwen heaved a sigh of relief, then, like a job seeker, straightened his clothes, smoothed out his hair, and stepped tentatively through the open door.

Chapter Ten

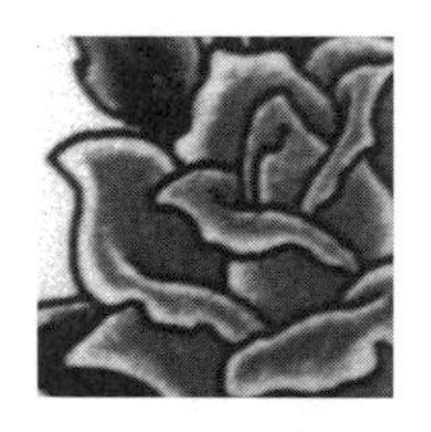

A-hen was sprawled across the sofa, feet up on a tea table; the room's only occupant, she was wearing a light purple bathrobe made of Thai silk and a pair of pink panties. She was scratching the toes of one foot with the heel of the other, then switching them around to do the same thing again, over and over, with obvious pleasure. She nibbled white-shelled melon seeds from a plate on the sofa as she watched TV, spitting the shells onto the floor. She was engrossed in an episode from the Taiwanese drama *The Seven Swordsmen of Xilo* (somewhere along the line they became known as Fukienese dramas). She never missed an episode, nightly from 8:30 to 9. (Back then the Fukienese dramas were broadcast at almost any hour, free of all laws and regulations. But by the time Siwen went to work for the Taipei TV station, for some reason the Ministry of Information required that all TV stations broadcast their Fukienese dramas between 6:30 and 7:30 at night, and for no more than thirty minutes. In other words, each station was restricted to half an hour of Fukienese programming, which had to be completed before the evening news at 7:30. All three stations were free to broadcast news and weather whenever they pleased: Central TV went on at six o'clock, Taiwan TV at 6:30. Once Siwen was in the TV business, the Electronic Media Office made it mandatory that all stations air the news and weather at exactly 7:30. I wonder why.)

Every time she watched an episode of *The Seven Swordsmen of Xilo* A-hen railed at the TV set for running so many commercials—one damned commercial after another. A thirty-minute episode was interrupted by seventeen or eighteen, sometimes as many as twenty, minutes of commercial advertising, which left about ten minutes of viewing, a mere smidgin of actual entertainment. She'd sit there giving the TV set hell—Drop dead, damn you! It wasn't until Siwen went to work at the TV station that the Ministry of Information intervened to restrict the amount of TV advertising to five minutes per thirty-minute broadcast, or a maximum of 600 seconds per hour of broadcasting. Even one second more resulted in heavy fines. Finally, television got on track, became peaceful and orderly. And yet, and yet, even that didn't stop her from roaring at the TV as always, except that now she included the quality of the dramas themselves in her vitriolic outbursts.

A-hen naively thought that after the ads for cold medicines, antacids, acne ointment, lactates, Chang Guozhou's Stomach Tonic, Triumph Brassieres, hemorrhoid creams, vitamin supplements, and Sanyo Washing Machines, she could learn whether or not the hero would be saved from the forces of evil, but, but what followed close on the heels of the others were ads for Datong appliances, which included not only booming background music but also jingles: "Datong, Datong, China's best buy, on Datong products we all rely, Datong fridges, styles brand new, right for families, my oh my, first-rate goods, the ratings high, Datong, Datong, our service is tops . . ."

"Drop dead! Now top that!" She flung a handful of melon seeds at the screen. "You can just go to hell! Won't this commercial ever end? I bought a TV to watch TV programs, not your damned commercials, do you understand that? Do you . . ."

She was just getting started when the telephone rang. So she took her feet off the table, stood up, and grabbed the receiver, assuming the call was from Big-Nose Lion. "Hello, Ani—" But it wasn't Aniki, it was her father.

"Oh! It's YOUUU!" There was disappointment and anger in her voice. "What do you want? Nothing? Then why are you calling me? I'm watching TV. T—V, got that? No mahjong for me, Aniki's coming by tonight. If you've got something on your mind, Pa, spit it out, OK? Out with it. Quit beating around the bush—what's that, you need money again? I gave you two thousand Taiwan dollars just last week! I said dollars, not hollers! You drank it all up, for crying out loud!" Her almond-shaped eyes arched up angrily. "You went through two thousand dollars in less than a week! Dollars, not hollers! An ordinary public servant doesn't make that in a month, for crying out loud!" Out of respect for an elder, she forced back the words "Drop dead!" "That's enough, Pa. I don't have any money, and that's the truth. Aniki only gives me two thousand a month, and I gave every bit of it to you. That's all there is. Things are different these days, Pa. Your daughter's out of the business now, she has to rely on someone else to get by. I'm only able to give you two thousand a month by tightening my belt and going without. I've got nothing else to give. Pa, nothing else means exactly that. Sick? Who's sick? Is it Ma? Oh, it's you, Pa." Her glossy red lips twisted into a sneer. "Where did you find the time to get sick, Pa? Did you burn your foot with ice water? Oh, you've got the flu! Oh, your head aches! Hmph! Well, if it aches, you can—" Again the filial daughter swallowed the words "drop dead." "Don't try to put one over on me, Pa. You gambled it away, didn't you? I keep telling you you're bound to lose nine times out of ten, but you won't listen. You didn't gamble? Honest? You didn't yesterday, but you did today, right? For crying out loud, Pa! I don't have it! I haven't got a red cent on me. You'll just have to wait till next month. Next month, hear me? The flu's no big deal. Stay home and get some rest, Pa, and drink plenty of fluids, and don't go running around like an idiot. You don't need to see a doctor. You'll be fine, all right? You're wasting your breath, it won't do you any good to keep talking, since I don't have it to give you." She glanced down at the TV screen, just as the hero made an appearance. "Wait till next month, I said!" she shouted into the receiver. "Got that? My program's on, OK? I don't have time to talk to you. My program's on, do you hear me?"

She slammed down the receiver, sat down, and put her feet back on the table. Quickly caught up in the drama, she turned back to the melon seeds, spitting the husks onto the floor.

The episode of *The Seven Swordsmen of Xilo* ended, the words "Tune in same time tomorrow" flashed on the screen, and still Aniki wasn't back. The braised pig's feet had turned cold, and still no Aniki. The damned pig's feet are cold! She was tempted to give him another call, but she didn't want to go through all the hassle if he blew up at her.

That evening she had already phoned him twice, the first time to report that she'd gone to Venereal Wang's clinic for a checkup, as he'd told her to. From there she'd gone to the home of Mrs. Zhu, the bank manager's wife, for a few games of mahjong. The results of her checkup? Couldn't be better! No v.d., clean as a whistle, perfectly qualified to replace any girl who failed the physical to *service* the GIs. What could be better? Then she asked him somewhat breathlessly when he was coming home. She phoned a second time to tell him that while they were playing mahjong, Mrs. Zhu had taught her a few social phrases in English, and she'd picked them up with no trouble at all. Mrs. Zhu had even praised her as smarter than most people! Once more she asked solicitously when he was coming home. The braised pig's feet were waiting for him.

Both times Big-Nose Lion had replied impatiently, "I'm busy, really busy! You go ahead and eat. I'll be over as soon as I'm finished." The second time she called, he added, "And don't call me again, you hear me?"

It must be that bar that's keeping him so busy. She yawned as she slipped on her red wooden clogs and stood up, then clomped noisily over to the dining table, where she lifted the protective cover off the food and sat down. Arrayed on the table were braised pig's feet, pan-fried bean sprouts, sliced raw turnips, steamed pomfret, sliced pork stomach, and a soup, plus a bottle of aged Shaoxing rice wine, two sets of chopsticks, and a pair of Japanese crystal goblets. She sat there for a few minutes before putting the cover back over the food, standing up, and clomping noisily to the tiny bathroom in back. The wooden Japanese tub looked like a big vat. She tested the water with her hand—barely warm. So she ran out back, opened the trap door, and tossed in two spadefuls of wood shavings; bright flames shot up and began to crackle. After closing the door she decided to take a bath, but then had second thoughts: she didn't want to dirty the water before Aniki had his bath. So she turned and went back into the living room, where she sat down on the sofa, put her feet up on the tea table, and recommenced scratching the toes of one with the heel of the other. She lit an American menthol cigarette. An English-language sitcom was on TV, and though she usually shied away from foreign programs, this one she watched with rapt attention, waiting for the actors to say *Hey* [hai—mess up] or *Morning* [mo-ning—cop a feel], so she could "Hey" and "Morning" right along with them. That afternoon, Mrs. Zhu had told her that Americans greeted one another with "Hey," except in the morning, when they said "Morning," drawing the "Mooorn" out to show they meant it. Mrs. Zhu made a special point of telling her that "Hey" and "Morning" could be used together—"Hey, mooorn—ing." A-hen paid no attention to what the sitcom was all about, concentrating instead, like a real linguist, on catching all the "Hey"s and "Morning"s on the screen, and listening to see if they "Hey"ed just right and if they seemed to mean it when they "Morning"ed.

She kept at it for quite a while, but didn't hear a single "Morning" or "Hey, mooorn—ing," and grumbled as she puffed on her cigarette: "What kind of sitcom is this, where the characters don't even 'Morning' each other when they meet? What happened to common sense?" She was about to exhale a grunt of disdain in a cloud of smoke when the telephone rang. This time she was in no hurry to answer it, so she waited until the seventh or eighth ring before lazily picking up the receiver and putting it on the tea table instead of up to her ear, so she could keep puffing away. Whoever was on the other end anxiously, even angrily, shouted, "Hello—hello—hello—" After a couple of final drags, she flipped the cigarette into the wastebasket at the base of the wall and picked up the receiver, pressed it up against her mouth, and roared angrily, "Why are you calling me again didn't I tell you didn't I that I don't have any money and you'll have to wait till next month Pa for crying out loud—Ahhh—" Anger turned to exteme penitence. "Oh! A—ni—ki—it's you!" Her voice took on the softest tone she could manage. "I thought it was—"

"All right, all right, enough of that bullshit! I want you to drop everything and do as I say. Exactly as I say, you hear me?" Big-Nose Lion sounded like a military commander.

"OK, but when are you coming home? The braised pig's feet are cooked and ready."

"I said no bullshit, didn't I? I don't have the Yankee leisure time to discuss food with you. Pack a bag, and make it simple, just a few things, a change of clothes and a couple of sets of underwear will do it. Then get your ass over to the Flying Happiness Hotel."

"What's wrong with my place? I just changed the sheets. And the bath water's ready. Why spend good money on some hotel?" Just like the ideal wife and mother, gentle and considerate.

Big-Nose Lion lowered his voice and said, "What are you thinking? I'm not asking you to move into a hotel so we can have a romp. What are you thinking?"

"Then—"

"No more questions. You'll know when you get here."

"What's this all about?"

"I said no more questions, do you hear me? Pack your bag, call a pedicab, and come straight to the Flying Happiness Hotel. It's in the lane behind Mercy Chapel."

"I asked you what this is all about." She swung her left hand as if pounding someone on the shoulder—hard.

"No guessing, I said. Now pack your bag and get over here. I'll be waiting at the hotel. I want you here in half an hour, not a minute later. And don't forget your ID card."

Chapter Eleven

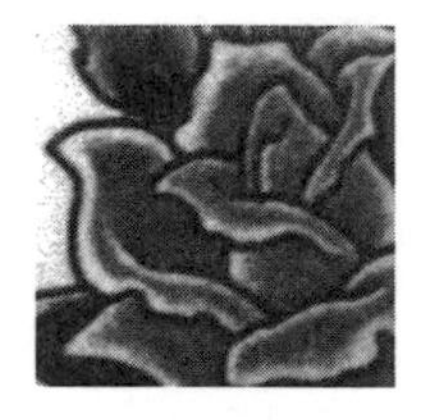

A-hen reached under her bed and slid out a small white leather suitcase she'd bought on Taipei's Bright Skies Road; she dumped out the winter clothes she'd stored in it and replaced them with clothes and other sundry items to take to the Flying Happiness Hotel. That Aniki, he's so mysterious. If he wants to meet me in a hotel room, why deny it? We're the same as married, for crying out loud! So why a hotel, when we've got our own place? She smiled and shrugged her shoulders. If anyone heard about it, they'd die laughing. What could be comfier than home? It's got everything we need, it's clean and convenient, and it's quiet. You're just asking for chaos at a hotel. You feel like you're holding your heart in the palm of your hand, worrying about prying eyes. It's a bad deal all the way around.

She tossed her rose-colored panties into the suitcase. The training program starts tomorrow morning, so I'll have to rush home to change for the ceremonies at the church. All that running back forth is a waste of time and energy. That Aniki! Now he wants me to take a room in some hotel! She packed a new Japanese toothbrush into a secret compartment in the suitcase. A waste of time and energy, for crying out loud!

Her bag was soon packed as simply as she could manage, just as Big-Nose Lion had instructed. After closing the half-filled suitcase she reflected upon how Big-Nose Lion had told her he was going to stay over a few days. Which reminded her how important it was to serve his every need, from good wine to good food. It didn't look like she'd have time to go grocery shopping tomorrow. If only the obasan had a phone, she could have her buy the food, and she'd pay her back. Of course! She looked at her wristwatch—plenty of time. Back to the living room, where she picked her address book up off the tea table. She looked up a number, laid down the address book, and dialed.

"Hel—lo! Boss Zhang? I need a few things. Send over a catty of shrimp tomorrow, no, make it two catties. Plus some sashimi—no bones, real tender, you know, raw fish. Two catties of that, too. Aiyo! Aren't you the one! Who am I? Now you ask? You don't even know who I am? Miss Wang, the Miss Wang who shops with you every day. A foreigner? What are you talking about? No need to butter me up. Yes, that's right! Aniki is staying with me these days. You sure have your ear to the ground, don't you? That's right! And I want a pomfret. Not too big. OK, and a whitefish. A catty of shrimp, a pomfret, what? Oh! No, I don't. Some raw fish for sashimi, two catties of that, the tenderest you've got. To put in an herbal tonic. You heard me, didn't you? The tenderest you've got. I want to make an herbal tonic for Aniki—what's that? To enhance his virility? Go enhance your own corpse! Oh, right, and one more thing. When you go to the market tomorrow, drop by Li's stall across the way and get me two catties of pig's feet. From dark-bristled pigs. And some pork stomach. Are you writing this down? Two catties of dark-bristled pig's feet, and some pork stomach. Got that? Deliver it first thing tomorrow. If I'm not home, just give it to the obasan. Tell me how much I owe you. Money's not important? Really? It's not important? OK, then I won't pay you. Ha ha ha. I never thought you were so generous. Ha ha ha! OK OK, write it down. Don't forget. You'll deliver the meat and fish tomorrow morning. *Gu-de-bai, bai-bai*, that's American. *Gu-de-bai, bai-bai*, that means good-bye. Did you know that?"

She locked the suitcase, hid the key in her alligator handbag, then turned off the bedroom light and walked into the living room with her suitcase and handbag, suddenly recalling that she'd left the furnace on under the bathtub. Quickly laying down the bags, she rushed out back, squatted down to open the furnace door and pick up the tongs, then started poking out the fire. It took quite a while for the flames to die down. She scooped up a ladleful of water and dumped it on the cinders, which crackled and sent a little cloud of white smoke curling into the air. With one hand over her mouth and nose, she picked up the tongs and stirred the ashes until she was sure the fire was completely out; the smoke limped skyward like an invalid, then expired. She got up, washed and dried her hands, and went into the kitchen, where she put the dinner into the refrigerator, plate by plate. Then she turned off the light and walked back to the living room, where she gasped in shock at the sight of someone on the sofa.

"Take it easy," the person said, standing up and turning to face her. "It's only me, what are you scared of?"

"Oh, it's you!" A sigh of relief, a little laughter. "I thought it was a thief or something. You scared the pants off me!" She looked at him out of the corner of her eye and said slowly, "*Mo—ning* [cop a feel], Aniki, hai, mo-ning."

"What?" Big-Nose Lion's brow furrowed. "I'm dead on my feet, and you want me to cop a feel? For crying out loud. Let's hold off on that till we're in bed. Who's got the fucking strength?"

"Aiyo, is something wrong with your hearing? I was just greeting you in American."

"Who'd have thought the fucking Americans were *that* crude!" Big-Nose Lion, his hair glossy as ever, yawned grandly and tossed the front-door key down on the table, then stretched out on the sofa, pillowing his head in his hands. He closed his eyes, too tired to keep the conversation going.

"I'm glad you came to your senses," A-hen said as she sat down on the arm of the sofa next to his reclining head, a smile on her face. She twirled strands of his glossy hair on her finger. "Home, sweet home, isn't that right? What's so great about a hotel?"

He answered her, but only after a long silence, and without so much as opening his eyes. "Don't bug me. Forget the hotel!"

"Why didn't you say so earlier?" She pointed to the little white suitcase on the table. "Before I wasted all that time packing."

"Ya–wn ya–wn." Big-Nose Lion's eyes watered. "Dead on my feet," he muttered, "absolutely dead on my feet! Our dear schoolteacher Dong, for crying out loud, ya–wn ya–wn, he'll be the death of me yet . . ."

"How could anybody be *that* tired?" She bent down to study his face and stroke his cheek. "Have you had anything to eat?"

"Eat?" Big-Nose Lion's eyes snapped wide open and emitted a fiery glare. "I went all fucking morning without so much as a sip of water. And you ask if I've eaten?"

"I'll go warm up the food."

"Not so fast." He held her arm. "I'm past being hungry. I don't feel like eating. What I need is a bath, a good soak in hot water." Another yawn, arms spread, then a huge yawn. "Shit! I'm fucking drop-dead worn out, for crying out loud."

She jumped up and ran out back, where she lifted up the tub's wooden lid to test the water. Tepid, maybe a little warmer. She told Big-Nose Lion to get in and soak while she went out to heat up some more water.

It was a struggle, but she finally got the fire going again, and as she added kindling, she asked Big-Nose Lion if the bath was heating up at all. As soon as she heard his yes, she turned and went into the bedroom to get him a set of underwear and a kimonolike bathrobe, which she folded neatly and carried into the bathroom. From there she went into the kitchen and took out the braised pig's feet, the beansprouts . . . all the food she'd just put into the refrigerator, carried it to the stove, and heated it over a sizzling gas flame.

Chapter Twelve

After finishing his bath and polishing off two helpings of braised pig's feet, along with several cups of aged rice wine, Big-Nose Lion felt reinvigorated, no longer as spent as a man who's just performed heroically in bed. And his gift of gab returned with a vengeance.

"Do you realize, A-hen, that all the girls undergoing training are supposed to move into the hotel? Ah, now you get it, finally. When I told you to go to the hotel, it wasn't for a romp, but to report for duty, more or less. Why? You ask why? Forget the whys for a minute. The bottom line is that all trainees are to check into the hotel. Hell, just one more opportunity to separate us from our money, you know what I mean? Trainees? Trainees are the lucky individuals who will be bar girls. That's what our dear English teacher, Mr. Dong, calls them. He says it sounds bad to just call them 'girls,' that 'trainees' is more refined, more formal.

"If that foster daughter of Sister Red Hair, actually her husband's foster daughter, hadn't come over from Ruisui, you'd have been a bona fide trainee yourself. We all figured she lived so far away she couldn't make it in time. Yeah, they phoned her, but she lives so far away, and we have to move fast on this, so you were chosen to replace any girl who didn't pass the physical. Nobody thought she'd actually come this far, but since she's his foster daughter and she passed the physical, and she isn't having her period, well, I went ahead and told Sister Red Hair that you'd let her have it. 'We couldn't, we simply couldn't,' Sister Red Hair said. But I just said, 'Why not?' Don't be disappointed, A-hen. You're not? Really? Don't try to fool me, now, I can tell. This was a once-in-a-lifetime opportunity! OK, OK, I'll shut up. I'll stop. But I mean it, don't be disappointed, you're still a reserve. If anything happens to one of the others, you're first backup. You don't care? You really don't?

"Come on, drink up. Here's to you. No need to be polite. Here's to you! Sit down, I said, sit down, I don't want you to stand. We're like husband and wife, after all, so to hell with formalities. If anybody saw you do that, they'd pee their pants laughing. Come on, bottoms up! That's better. I never knew you could drink like that, A-hen. Everything will turn out fine. If you get the chance to move up, you'll become an ace bar girl! Come on, fill me up again. You too.

"Wow, these shrimp are delicious! They melt in your mouth. And these bean sprouts, I've never eaten any this tender! In the week or so since I was last here, you've turned into a great cook. This is *ke-kou ke-le* [mouth-watering good], you know, like that American soft drink, Coca-Cola. Heh heh heh, get that? Mouth-watering good. From now on I'm going to be a regular at your Coca-Cola cookouts. I'm always welcome? Really? Great, that's just great. Come on, fill me up again. Mm, these pig's feet are good, real stomach pleasers. I mean it, they're delicious.

"Forget it! There's no need for you to attend the opening ceremony. Stay home and take it easy. It's just going to be some boring speeches anyway.

"What? You still don't understand what I've been saying? Look, if you were a trainee, not a reserve, of course you'd check into the hotel. All the trainees, every girl being trained to service the GIs, has to stay in the hotel, every one of them, without exception.

"Who thought that up? Who else? That's right, that numbskull teacher. Fuck him! That guy says whatever pops into his head, and does things on the spur of the moment, without any thought. And he's got no sense of shame. It's always, 'I've got an inspiration, a stroke of genius.' Fuck him! Every one of those inspirations has the four of us as busy as what the mainlanders call turtle spawn. I'd slap him silly if he wasn't so close to Councilman Qian and the fact that we stand to rake in all those U.S. dollars. Whenever the four of us see him wiggle that big ass of his and say, 'I've got an inspiration! A stroke of genius!' well, we just moan and groan. Fuck him! This is going to cost us more hard-earned money! You want to hear something funny? Whenever Sister Red Hair hears that idiot teacher say he's got an inspiration, she's off to the toilet! All afternoon I watched her make one trip after another. So damned funny! And Stumpy Courtesan? The minute she hears that comment, her face goes white as snow and she squeezes her eyes shut, like somebody was holding a knife to her throat.

"Some teacher! Fuck him!

"You've turned into a real pro, preparing sliced raw turnips like this. They go perfect with pig's feet. A drop-dead match. Try some. It's fattening, you say? No! Didn't anyone ever tell you that the best way to lose fat is to eat more fatty foods? Fat attacks fat. There's nothing fatter than pig's feet, and every one you eat takes off a pound! Of course it's true! Come on, eat one, try it. You won't know if it works until you try. Come on, give me your bowl. Just this little piece.

"I'm famished all of a sudden. Drop-dead hungry, for crying out loud! Like I could wolf down that whole plate of pig's feet. Why? Because from two o'clock this afternoon until after eleven, when I got here, nine whole hours, I didn't have a bite to eat, not a drink of water, for that matter, know what I mean? How come? Go ask that idiot teacher! First thing this morning he had us running all over the place, and we didn't get a break till after one o'clock. We were four tired and very hungry people, so we had the Aristocrat send over some food, figuring we could finally sit down for a decent meal and rebound from our exhaustion (at the time, the print and electronic media used the term "rebound from exhaustion" for "reinvigorate"). We weren't halfway through the meal when that idiot teacher came charging into the room.

"He came straight to the Rouge Tower! Now why would we tell him to come over? Who in his right mind would invite a high school teacher to a place like that? Ha ha ha, at first I thought it was someone looking for a little action, and who came around back when he couldn't find any girls out front. We were sure surprised to see *him*. We threw down our chopsticks and jumped up like schoolkids when the teacher enters the classroom. Just thinking about how we stood at attention like a bunch of soldiers floors me.

"That numbskull teacher walked in with a big grin on his face, and a giggle, and told us to sit down and keep eating. He was giggling like that numbskull on TV, Shi Song. Stumpy Courtesan ran over to get him a bowl and some chopsticks, but he said he'd eaten at the hotel already, and if he ate any more he'd be fat as a pig. Hell, he's already fat as a pig, for crying out loud! Ha ha ha, that's what happened, I'm not making it up. Then he said—still giggling, mind you, he's a teacher, after all, so he talks like a gentleman. Hell, it's because of the gentlemanly way he talks and his refined manners that we fell into his trap in the first place, and why we're suffering so much now.

"What did he say? Listen to this. First he asked around, starting with Stumpy Courtesan, then Sister Red Hair, then Black-Face Li, if the rooms in the place where they'd put up the trainees were any different than the rooms at the Rouge Tower. We didn't know what he was getting at, so we said they were the same. Delighted with the answer, our kind-hearted teacher told us that the first thing he did when he came in was go into the girls' rooms and have a look around. Some had left their doors open, and no one was here—I explained that they'd gone over to Mercy Hall to have their nether parts examined. What do you mean, nonsense? What do you expect them to have examined? Their dicks? OK OK, I'll stop talking like that! What happened? What happened was that he said, 'After seeing the girls' rooms, I had an inspiration, another fine idea, a stroke of genius. Want to hear it?' Naturally, we said we were all ears. But he didn't seem to be in any hurry, so Stumpy Courtesan urged him to speak up: 'Hold on, Teacher, don't be like that! Hurry up, tell us, please.' Well, as soon as she said that, he put on this well-if-you-say-so look, for crying out loud! Oh, he told us, all right. Just listen. 'The rooms where the girls entertain their customers are crude and unappealing,' he says. 'They're cramped, the air is stale, and all they have is a bed—a hard wooden bed at that. How do you expect a john to have a good time under those conditions?' That's what he said, I'm not making it up. He didn't stop there, either. 'No chairs and no bathroom. And the walls, they're nothing but plywood, with all sorts of gaps and holes. Anyone in the next room can see and hear every little bit of the action, from sticking it in to taking it out. Crude, unappealing rooms like that will never do for entertaining the American GIs. They'll go limp as a noodle if they're taken into an unsanitary room like that.' You understand what he was saying? What he meant was—You understand? You do? We laughed when he said that, and Stumpy Courtesan even congratulated our Mr. Dong. 'Oh, Teacher, I love the way you talk, you're so wise.'

"Mr. Dong stopped and stared at us, checking to see if we got his drift. Pretty soon a shit-eating grin creased his face and he asked, 'Do you think U.S. dollars will float out of their pockets in crummy rooms like that? I'll give it to you straight: On the contrary. What does that mean? You don't know? Where did you go to school? You don't even understand a simple Mandarin sentence like that? On the contrary means, it means—Ah! Now you get it! That's right, that's what it means.' How come he says it that way? You'll have to ask him that.

"On the contrary, on the contrary. By then our nerves were just about shot, and when he saw us all tongue-tied like that, he started talking in a mixture of Mandarin, Taiwanese, even some American. (Hell! He was holding class!) What did he say? He said the first principle of doing business is to have a clear understanding of what you're selling. Once you have that, you need to come up with a targeted clientele. Hear what I'm saying? What he means is you have to figure out who you want to sell to. Now do you understand? Well, he gave us a long spiel on production and marketing, our Teacher Refinement—that's his name, Refinement. That's the truth, I'm not making it up. A fat pig like that has the name Refinement! Just listen. He said, 'I have a question for all of you. What's the product we want to sell? Bar girls, right?' Bar girls are people, so how can they be products? That's a good question. But that's exactly the way our Teacher Refinement put it. Who cares if it makes sense or not? Then what did he say? Just hear me out. He said, 'OK, we all agree that bar girls are the product we want to sell. Now then, who are the clientele for our bar girls? American soldier boys, right? OK, now that we've identified our clientele, in other words, we've positioned our product'—right, our dear teacher peppered his speech with lots of American, but that fucking word is the only one I jotted down. Do you want to listen to me or don't you? OK, listen. It came out *po-li-xiang* [smashing ideals]. Isn't that a riot? 'Smashing ideals' (the English word is *position*, but to Big-Nose Lion it sounded like po-li-xiang. But you can't blame him, since *position* and po-li-xiang sound so much alike.) He might as well have said *mo-li-xiang* [no ideals]!

"Then what? Then he continued: 'OK, now that we've po-li-xiang-ed our product, we need to work on its manufacturing and packaging, to fit the desires of our clientele. In other words, the success of this business venture depends entirely on our ability to manufacture and package our product to fit the tastes of the American soldier boys. So, what are their tastes?' Our dear Teacher Refinement said: 'When Americans buy things, their first concern is hygiene. After that come quality and price. So if we're going to do business with the Americans, we have to look first at the matter of hygiene.' Hell, this last comment from that fat pig Teacher Refinement was directed right at me and Black-Face Li, like he was saying, 'Do you really expect the American GIs to *tomari* [spend the night] or even *QK* [quickie] in rooms that don't have bathrooms? (the term 'sanitary facilities' hadn't yet come into use; if it had, it's a sure bet that Siwen would have said, 'rooms that can't even boast the hint of a sanitary facility'). On the contrary, I tell you! I have no objection to entertaining our own countrymen in filthy rooms like this, since we Chinese have never been very picky about hygiene. Eat in garbage, get fat in garbage, sleep in garbage, thrive in garbage. It's no big deal to us if we have illicit dealings in a barn or a pig sty, but it *is* a big deal to Americans if you ask them to do so in unsanitary conditions. Besides, if we let the GIs *QK* or tomari in shabby, filthy rooms, the whole nation loses face. Am I right or aren't I? Well, am I?' That all came out of his mouth, but what would you expect from a teacher? Illicit dealings, that's the term he used. Is that refined enough for you? But that's not all he said. Hear me out, will you? 'If you ladies and gentlemen are entertaining the idea of making improvements in the rooms, heed my word, you don't have the time. We're not talking about something simple, like throwing together a piece of furniture.'

"All this did was make us even more jittery. Black-Face Li put down his chopsticks and bowl, stopped eating, and took out a handful of Shuangdong betel nuts, which he laid on the table in front of him and started chewing, one after another. His eyes were almost popping out of his head as he stared at me. Why? He wanted me, Aniki, to jump in and ask the teacher what we should do. What do we do? After all the money we've put into this, we can't write it off without taking in any U.S. dollars, can we? But before I could open my mouth, Sister Red Hair, who had been stuffing her face without a word, suddenly spoke up anxiously. 'Aiyo, Teacher, what do we do? There has to be something we can do! Teacher!'

"Our dear Teacher Refinement didn't answer her right away. He just sat there smiling. Now that I think back, it was one of those sinister grins. The lips were smiling, but not the face. That's what it was, for crying out loud. He just kept smiling at us. As they say in Mandarin, it was tantalizing. And so it went, till he finally opened his mouth and class was back in session. Actually, it was more like a sermon. Honest, that's what it was like. Lots of American, a whole bunch of 'on the contrary's—on the contrary this and on the contrary that—until my ears were about to burn up and ooze pus. What was his sermon about? He said, 'Now we know that our clientele are American GIs, and we've got a handle on what they like, which is sanitary conditions, hygiene above all, so we must make sure that our product is manufactured to those specifications. Tell me, am I right or aren't I? Well, am I or aren't I?' He used that 'am I or aren't I' a hundred times, it seemed, like he was singing a song.

"He kept pushing us with his 'am I or aren't I's until we managers of the Big 4 just sat there nodding our heads up and down. Yes, Teacher, you are. Like we were his students or something. From there he launched into a bunch of damned theory. Here's what he said: 'The product has to be sanitary, and that isn't limited to the materials and the tools of production. Even the place of production has to be clean and sanitary to avoid the possibility of polluting the product'—polluting, do you hear that? Everybody's using that word these days: air pollution, political pollution, and crap like that! It means making something dirty and filthy. Now do you understand?

"Hell, then the teacher got into a fucking pots-and-pans discussion of products and merchandise, and pretty soon I didn't know which end was up! Sister Red Hair was in the same boat. She kept looking over at me as if to say, What the hell's the teacher talking about? Stumpy Courtesan was listening intently, you know, holding a drumstick in her hand without taking a bite. I thought she was hanging on his every word, thrilled by what he was saying. How was I supposed to know she'd be the first one to tell him she didn't understand what he was talking about? She's got one of those shrill voices, like an opera singer. I'll see if I can imitate her. 'Hold on, Teacher, what are you talking about? How come I can't understand a word you're saying? You aren't talking American, are you?' Ha ha, not a bad impression, wouldn't you say? You think so, really? Ha ha.

"That's when Black-Face Li stopped chewing his betel nuts and spoke up. Hell, that Black-Face Li is as unsanitary as you can get, for crying out loud. Right in front of the teacher he sprayed the area with betel-nut juice and turned our dining table into a slaughterhouse floor, with bloody red streaks all over the place. He's a real slob, for crying out loud! He seconded Stumpy Courtesan's complaint: 'Teacher, don't keep talking over our heads!' Teacher

Refinement just frowned when he heard that, but not like he was unhappy or anything. He pinched his fatty cheeks and nodded, then started laughing: 'I'll make it simple,' he said, 'maybe you can follow me then. We've already got the ball rolling on a training course for the girls. You can envision this training course as a factory where the product is manufactured. Now those two might not sound like the same thing to you, but in essence they are.' No, he said 'essence,' not 'as is.' Because I asked him, that's how. He even spelled it out for me: e-s-s-e-n-c-e. In fact, *as is* and *essence* mean about the same thing. But teachers like to show everybody how learned they are. And can you blame them?

"First he had us see the 'training course for bar girls' as a 'factory,' then he wanted us to see this picture: 'The girls selected for training are the raw material, which is why I was so strict in the selection process. To prove beyond doubt that the girls who made the cut were absolutely sanitary, we sent them to the Meilun V.D. Clinic for Venereal Wang to check them out. Those who passed were retained, those who didn't were eliminated. Qualified trainees are the raw material for our product.' See there, our dear teacher was talking in circles again, and it was too much for me to take down to tell you all the details. But what he meant was, we now had acceptable raw material, and our next job was to make sure we had machinery that met all the sanitation standards. He said he'd just about taken care of this second step—hold your questions till I finish, and you'll understand. He said that for this second step, the procurement of up-to-standard production machinery, he had invited excellent teachers to hold class, and that local dignitaries—some doctor and some lawyer—had agreed to help out. He'd scheduled classes in English, dancing, singing, global etiquette, beauty, and makeup, plus an introduction to American culture, an outline of Chinese civilization, personal hygiene, points of law, the art of tending bar, and Christian prayers, just about everything you could think of. What are you laughing at? Heh heh heh, it's a good thing you weren't chosen, or you'd be a wreck from all that classwork. That's right, I asked him that myself. I thought we were only going to teach the trainees how to speak a little American, so how come they have to learn about Chinese civilization, Western cultures, and Christian prayers?

"What was his answer? Just listen to this. Stop gnawing on those chicken feet for a minute, and listen! Just listen to his answer. He said, 'My ideal bar girl is like one of those Japanese geishas, who can do it all: sing, dance, write poetry, whatever. Which is why I scheduled classes that will elevate the trainees' cultural tastes (actually, what Dong Siwen said was 'cultural level') and open the eyes of those big-nosed customers, something they'll never forget.' He told me not to forget that contact between the bar girls we train and the American GIs can be viewed as diplomatic activity—*nei-xin* [heart] to nei-xin and *pi-gu* [buttocks] to pi-gu. That's what he said. Who the hell knows what nei-xin to nei-xin and pi-gu to pi-gu means? (What Siwen actually said, in English, was *Nation to Nation and People to People*.) Why learn Christian prayers? Hell, he said that all GIs are Christians, and since they're coming from a place where they could be killed in the blink of an eye, they'll probably need plenty of comforting. They'll feel right at home if the girls come out with an Amen every once in a while. Hell, I think a couple of Amita Buddhas would be better than a bunch of Amens! But our dear teacher hadn't finished talking when he was interrupted by Stumpy Courtesan, who thinks money's as important as life itself! She was still holding that uneaten drumstick in her hand. 'Teacher,' she said, 'won't it cost a lot to get so many teachers?' Teacher Dong frowned when he heard this—he seemed a little unhappy to me this time—and he looked long and hard at all of us. That fucking smile of his disappeared down his pants somewhere before he said anything (Hell, you should have seen his fucking expression! You could tell he didn't have much use for us, not for a bunch of entrepreneurs who don't know anything but money money money!). He said, 'Have any of you ever heard what Fran-something-lin said?' That's the best I could make of it—probably some American guy. Some foreigner, I know that. He said this Fran-something-lin had a famous saying that it takes money to make money! You don't know what that means? I'll be damned! It means you need to spend money to earn money, and the more you spend, the more comes back to you. Is that true? Who knows? But since he said this was a famous saying by some foreign guy, there must be something to it. And when Stumpy Courtesan heard what he had to say about it taking money to make money, that head of hers started bobbing up and down, and that was the last we heard from her on the subject. One line from Mr. Fran-something-lin made a believer out of her.

"OK, then, after all these twists and turns, our numbskull teacher finally returned to the subject at hand: 'Our third task is to do everything necessary to protect our raw material from contamination and damage—in other words, to keep it perfectly clean.' He wants us to treat our up-to-standard trainees as sanitary raw material—of course, you may be only a reserve trainee, but you're considered up-to-standard, sanitary raw material. What are you laughing at? There's never been any doubt about that.

"That numbskull teacher went on to say, 'In order to keep our raw material clean, we need to make sure that the place where it's stored is absolutely clean.' That's the fucking way he talks, blah blah blah, yada yada yada, his fucking ancestors! He said, just listen to me! He said, 'So we have to pay particular attention to the sanitary conditions of our up-to-standard trainees' quarters, that is, where our trainees live.' He wants us to think this way: The trainees' quarters are to be considered storage space for our raw material—in simple terms, a warehouse. He said that the only way we can keep our trainees, our raw material, sanitary is to keep the warehouse clean and outfitted with modern facilities. Without modern facilities there's no way to ensure sanitary conditions. What he means by modern is air conditioning. Crap like that! That way the clean raw material stored inside won't turn bad! So to keep our trainees sanitary, we have to move them into a warehouse with modern facilities. Don't get all worked up, we're not moving the girls into any warehouse. Didn't I just tell you he was upset about how unsanitary, how filthy, our place was? So—right! That's right! You said it! He wants us to move this group of trainees, this consignment of up-to-standard raw material, into modern storage facilities, put it into perfectly sanitary surroundings to maintain its quality. He absolutely refuses to let the trainees keep living in our places of business. Where are they going to live? Where would you say? Where in Hualien can you find modernized rooms, with air conditioning, toilets, and bathing facilities? You tell me where. Oh, you're getting fast on the uptake. That's right, the hotel that was just built, what's it called? Oh, right, the Prosperity Hotel, that's it, the Prosperity. Our Mr. Dong wants us to move this consignment of raw material into the hotel. A separate room for each unit of raw material. He says that only a high-class place like that is suitable for American GIs in the market for full-service treatment. After all, our national honor is at stake! He reminded us that the whole world knows how Taiwan's economy has made great strides in recent years, and foreigners are convinced that Taiwan is now an economic giant. So how would it look if the *sabisu* [service] in an ecomomic giant was dispensed in a shabby, filthy place like our Rouge Tower?

"What do you mean, great, great! Staying in a hotel is great, you say? It may be, but you'll never know. Oh, but who knows, maybe your *qiangsi* [CHANCE—blown away] to stay in a hotel with air conditioning and a spring mattress will come someday, even if you're only a reserve at the moment. No such luck? Who knows, it could happen. But do you have any idea how much a room with a toilet, a bathtub, and a spring mattress costs a night? How much? You bet! Three and a half fingers, that's three and a half! Thirty-five? Just listen to you! We're not talking thirty-five U.S. I'll tell you, one night costs three-fifty! Three hundred and fifty New Taiwan Dollars! And that doesn't include meals, you hear that? An unmarried public servant only earns a thousand a month! You hear what I'm saying? A thousand a month! And they want three-fifty for one night in a hotel. Why's it so expensive? Because it's modernized! Hell, we're even getting a discount, at that. We're only getting a three-fifty rate because of Councilman Qian's influence. Hear that? Know how much it costs to put fifty samples of raw material into fifty separate rooms in that outrageously priced hotel? Figure it out, go on, figure it out for yourself. Seventeen thousand five hundred. That's for one night! From the beginning of the training sessions until the GIs leave, we're talking about two weeks, a good thirteen or fourteen days. So how much is that? A hundred eighty thousand? Did you say a hundred eighty thousand? What are you talking about? What kind of math is that? It's more like two hundred and forty thousand! You hear me, we're not talking about ten or twenty thousand, but more than two hundred and forty thousand! You could build a palace for that! Asking us to spend that kind of money is like cutting the meat right off our bones or gouging out our hearts! And three meals a day on top of that!

"Their meals are *our* responsibility! Our not-so-refined Siwen said so! He said we have to supply the trainees with three meals every day they're in training. And that's not the half of it—the trainees are to eat only the most sanitary, most nutritious food. You should have seen Stumpy Courtesan's reaction to that. She tossed that drumstick into her bowl and started waving her hands in the air. 'Hold on, Teacher!' she said. 'Every one of your strokes of genius is a stroke of financial bad luck for us. We can't keep this up much longer! When we started this, all we wanted to do was entertain the American GIs for the sake of the country. We never thought it'd cost us so much. It's a damned bottomless pit!'

"Black-Face Li, who hadn't said anything for a while, spit out his betel nut and said: 'Teacher, oh my, you've set your ideals too high. Just too high! Please, I beg you, lower them, all right? All right?' He looked so sad there, asking 'All right? All right?' I damn near laughed out loud. When he finished he gave me the eye, and I knew he wanted me to speak up. Sister Red Hair leaned over and put her mouth right up to my ear. I don't know what kind of *kuchituni* [lipstick] she was wearing, but it had a drop-dead odor, kind of like a woman's you-know-what—OK OK OK, no more dirty talk, I'll stop it. Sister Red Hair whispered in my ear: 'Talk to the teacher, tell him this is no good. We'll go belly up at this rate!'

"Well, that teacher may look like a numbskull, but no one has faster reactions. Before I could open my mouth, he jumped in and it was class time again. He was going to teach us a lesson. The smile stayed on that porker face of his, and his butt kept shifting and sliding around. I'll tell you something funny. Stumpy Courtesan was sitting next to the teacher, and every time his butt shifted, she scrunched up her nose. I asked her later why, and she said, ha ha— Just listen! She said every time his butt moved, a terrible smell smacked her right in the face. She said, 'Our Teacher Refinement is drop-dead unrefined sometimes. He stinks!' Ha ha, that's exactly what she said. I'm not making it up! Noisy farts don't stink, stinky farts aren't noisy, ha! No wonder she didn't eat anything after he came in! She filled up on his gas. Ha ha! She had all the farts she could handle, ha ha!

"Well, we've finished one bottle. Open another. Go ahead. What can it hurt? If you want the truth, you could open up two more bottles, and your Aniki still wouldn't get drunk. Put in what? No, no, put it in yours, if you want to. Anybody who puts sour plums in wine is no drinker. None of that for me!

"What class did he put us through this time? More of that money makes money, interest generates interest, old Fran-something-fucking-lin, blah blah blah. He got on our case, but with a smile, saying the four of us had no brains. He said that all the money we spent would be transferred to the consumers, so why worry about it? And the consumers this time are American GIs from Vietnam, big-nosed foreigners with deep pockets. So why worry about spending money? Remarried, know what that means? Right, right, that's it exactly. Your capital is married off to a customer who treats it like his old lady. Hell, aren't you the pro! Well, after Teacher Refinement scolded us with a smile, he turned real serious, like a preacher. Even his butt settled down and stopped shifting and sliding—the farting stopped. And spring returned to

Stumpy Courtesan's nose—no more wrinkles.

"Our Mr. Dong started in again with his fucking blah blah blah, like a political spin doctor. There was so much American in his lecture we almost fell asleep. Sister Red Hair forgot about eating, she was so busy yawning. What was he talking about? About humanitarianism, that's what. He was talking about humanitarianism! Are you with me on this? What's humanitarianism? Go ask him. Shit! Humanitarianism, his granny's beaver! What does 'his granny's beaver' mean? Go ask that son of mine who's in college. We're no match for kids these days, they understand refinement. No more 'fuck you' and 'damn him' for them, now they say things like his granny's beaver, know what I mean? Hah, humanitarianism, his granny's beaver, his granny's beaver's humanitarianism. Shit! It has quite a ring to it, almost like poetry!

"That fat pig of a teacher wanted us to think of the training course as setting up a factory and think of the trainees as raw material, didn't he? And after the trainees became bar girls, they'd be available as merchandise for the GIs. OK so far. But now all of a sudden he turns into a saint, Amita Buddha and all that, telling us we mustn't forget that these girls who will be pulling in all those U.S. dollars are people, and that we must see them as more than just merchandise. How can we have it both ways? First he wants us to see the girls as raw material we turn into merchandise, then he tells us we can't do that. He says whatever pops into his head, even if one sentence cancels out the other, and he's a granny's beaver English teacher. Oh, he informed us that we have to treat the girls with the tenderness of a spring wind and concern as deep as the ocean! We have to value their existence and respect their personalities. He told us about a scholar way back in history, huh, what's his name? I couldn't tell you, but he had a name, that much I remember. So this scholar writes a letter to his son to tell him to be nice to the new servant, that he should always remember that 'this too is the child of man.' Oh, that's some classical stuff. This too is the child of man, hey, that sounds a little like something out of a Taiwanese opera. What it means is, even though the new kid's coming into the house as a servant, he's still the apple of his own parents' eye. So you have to cherish him like a member of the family, like your own son. Well, our numbskull teacher doesn't want us to forget that these girls who are going to make us a pile of U.S. dollars have parents of their own, and that we should treat them like our own children or grandchildren.

"Why does he want that? You can't figure out why, you really can't? Well, at least you still know how to eat. And you do *look* smart. How do you think parents feel about spending money on their kids? Think it makes them unhappy? You don't know? How can you not know? Shit! You don't know because you don't have any kids? OK, then I'll plant one for you tonight, and tomorrow you'll have one. Then you'll know what it feels like to be a parent. What's dirty about saying I'll plant one? That comes straight from my heart, don't you know that?

"You know, there's something I've been wanting to say to you for a long time. Say what? Listen and I'll tell you. We've been together for two years, two years without any news. Are you still taking birth-control pills? No? Are you telling me the truth? Then what's wrong? Maybe we should get a doctor to check you out. Check *me* out? Are you saying the problem's with me? How could *I* have a problem? I'm Big-Nose Lion. Big-Nose Lion! Haven't you heard the saying, 'Big-Nose Lion, a stud among men, generals out and ministers in?' So how could anyone as mighty as a general and as wise as a minister have a problem? That haggish old lady of mine had a miscarriage at the beginning of the year. I'll drop dead if I'm lying! She did, she had a miscarriage. It was a girl. She might have grown up to be a rich and famous singer. Maybe as popular as Bai Jiali, for all I know! What a shame, a real shame, that she didn't make it. I've wanted a daughter all my life, so now it's up to you. What did you say? Maybe you took too many birth-control pills when you were a working girl? I doubt it, I really do. Maybe all those johns took their toll on you? I doubt that too, I really do. Lots of girls who use birth-control pills and take on a lot more johns than you get married and start producing babies like hens laying eggs. OK, here's what we'll do. After the GIs leave, we'll get you checked at a hospital in Taipei. The only thing I regret in my life is not having a daughter. If you present me with one, I don't care how much it costs, even if it takes my last penny. I, Big-Nose Lion, will gladly give it all up to see that she grows up to be a TV songstress, more popular than Bai Jiali or Yang Xiaoping. And she'll be rolling in money, know what I mean?

"You have to give me a daughter, you just have to. And when you do, you'll know how it feels to be a parent, just like everybody else. There's nothing unhappy about spending money on your own kids. That's why our Mr. Dong wants us to be granny's beaver humanitarians, why he wants us to treat the girls who'll be making all that money for us like our own children, then—right, now you've got it, now you're using your head, that's exactly what he wants. By having us treat the girls like our own daughters, he can get us to invest more money in them, just like parents, without a bunch of griping or calculating. He wants us to *OK* everything without a murmur. And now you know, now you see exactly how sneaky that teacher of ours is. He's not the numbskull you think he is. Every time he opens his fucking mouth he's like a Shaolin master, with all sorts of traps that turn us into lambs being led to the slaughter. That numbskull teacher is really a granny's beaver!

"How'd we answer him this time? How were we supposed to answer him? We just stared at each other, not knowing what to say. And that numbskull teacher, now that his speech was over, just sat there smiling at us. You could have heard a pin drop in that room, except for Black-Face Li, who kept munching away at his betel nuts—munch munch munch, like somebody was doing it right there in front of us. What are you laughing at? That's what it sounded like, all right. OK OK, I'll stop, no more of that dirty talk.

"Hell, Stumpy Courtesan sat there drop-dead stiff, you know, not daring to move a muscle, like a schoolkid. Sister Red Hair and I were puffing away till the room was filled with smoke, and our teacher's fat face was a mass of wrinkles, like railroad tracks or a highway map. Why? Beats me. He doesn't smoke, and he doesn't like people smoking around him. I think he's afraid it'll make him sick. He's not the fucking numbskull or idiot you think he is. He knows exactly what it takes to keep himself hale and hearty. Pretty soon no more smile on his face, with the railroad tracks or highway map, so I put away my pipe. But Sister Red Hair was too crude or too rude to notice what was happening, and she just kept puffing away like an opium addict who'd die if she didn't have her fix.

"Well, the four of us kept looking back and forth and didn't say anything. None of us wanted to part with any more money, but we couldn't get the words out.

"So then what? Then what, you ask? This'll really piss you off. Who'd have thought anybody that cruel could live among other human beings. And a high school English teacher at that! Listen to what he said when he saw we weren't talking. He said—smiling again, I might add, a big granny's beaver grin—he said: 'Since you have nothing to say, ladies and gentlemen'—who had nothing to fucking say? We were just too embarrassed to say it!—he said: 'Since you have nothing to say, I take that as your tacit consent to proceed with my suggestion.'

"Tacit consent? We were just too fucking embarrassed to say anything, or we didn't know how to say it. Who says that keeping your mouth shut is the same as tacit consent? His fucking ancestors! There's nothing about that in the law books. Here's a fucking teacher, spouting all that nonsense, and with a smile, no less. You'd have been pissed off if you'd heard him. He said: 'Our trainees are fortunate indeed that you ladies and gentlemen are willing to treat them like your own children, that you'll cherish and look after them, that you'll concern yourselves with their physical and emotional well-being, and that you'll pay attention to their working environment,' and on and on. Then he said: 'I couldn't be happier, and on behalf of the trainees, I thank you, one and all.' And he didn't stop there, the granny's beaver. He said, 'With the counsel of such wise, knowing, and farsighted individuals, I am confident that our cooperative venture is bound to succeed beyond all expectations.' What fucking cooperative venture? Who's cooperating with him? If not for Councilman Qian, we'd have gotten someone else a long time ago!

"There's more, just listen. He grabbed a jowl with one hand and banged the other hand on the table. 'Ladies and gentlemen,' he said, 'I've had another inspiration, another great idea, a stroke of genius!' Hell, it was that 'stroke of genius' that did it. As soon as the word *stroke* hit the air, Stumpy Courtesan's face turned green, and before Teacher Refinement could finish what he was about to say, she shouted, 'Hold on, Teacher, please!' That's what she said: 'Hold on, Teacher, not another stroke of genius, please! OK? OK? Every one of your strokes costs us money. I mean it, the next one will wipe us out.' You should have seen the panic on her face. If you'd been there, you'd have seen those big tits of hers jump up and down, up and down, like she was about to die of a 'stroke'!

"And then? And then what? Just listen. Stumpy Courtesan's outburst made the teacher laugh out loud. His face turned red as a persimmon. After he'd had a good laugh he said, 'Take it easy, ladies and gentlemen, don't get all upset. I'm not going to spend your money this time, I'm going to save you money.' He paused then and gave us a big smile. And that's not all, you'll die laughing when you hear this. That numbskull teacher lifted his ass off the seat and—that's right! You said it! Bwuut, he let fly a noisy fart—no smell, just the noise. He grinned after that, hell, his eyes were a couple of slits, like a man ready for some pillow talk.

"That's what he said! 'This great idea, this stroke of genius will save money for you ladies and gentlemen. Hear me out. Take careful note of what I'm going to tell you.' Then he paused again and flashed another smile. Black-Face Li stopped munching his betel nuts and let his mouth hang open. His red tongue and red teeth made him look like a blood-sucking vampire. And Sister Red Hair stopped smoking; she flipped her cigarette to the floor and crossed her arms over her chest. Stumpy Courtesan just stared wide-eyed at the teacher, like he wasn't wearing pants or something. Hell! When she heard she was going to save some money, the color returned to her cheeks.

"The teacher said: 'In order to cut down on expenses, I don't think it's necessary for the trainees to move into the hotel for the period of training.' He barely finished before Stumpy Courtesan, Black-Face Li, and Sister Red Hair were shouting hallelujah. He followed that with 'But as soon as the training's over, the trainees absolutely have to move into a hotel with modern facilities! And, and, even though they don't have to live in the hotel while they're undergoing training, they can't stay in the shabby rooms you've got here.' 'Where, then?' Sister Red Hair asked him. 'Find a hostel somewhere that's got clean rooms. And in order to save even more money, they can double up, two to a room, which will also make it possible to encourage and keep an eye on each other.' Stumpy Courtesan reached over and patted the teacher on his meaty shoulder and got flirty-like. 'Hold on, Teacher! If they stay right here, we can save money and make it easier on everybody.' Well, he turned real stern and said, 'No good! During the training sessions, all the girls have to live in a hostel so we can supervise and train them at the same time. You tell me how many soldiers live at home when they're in basic training. How many? Tell me.' Then he giggled and said: 'Now what do you think of my idea? Not bad, hm? I'm saving you lots of money, aren't I? Is it a stroke of genius or isn't it?' He dragged out the words *stroke of genius*, one at a time. Then the corners of his mouth curled into a big smile, and we could see how pleased he was with himself.

"I damn near bellowed at him, 'On the contrary, your granny's beaver!' But I thought better of it. Good nature is a source of wealth, after all, so who the hell cares what he does as long as the U.S. dollars pour in? The head's already half shaved, so what happens if we stop listening to him? Then what?

Then the four of us got up from the table without another bite and were off again, running all over the place during the hottest part of the day, back and forth, until Sister Red Hair's face was bathed in sweat and streaked with face powder. I couldn't stand to even look at her. Running around with the teacher to find a hostel! A place with clean rooms for the girls. Hell, you'd have thought he was checking out a prospective son-in-law, not some sleazy hostel. Talk about high standards! In every single one he complained that the rooms weren't airy enough, or not soundproof enough, or too dark, or that the beds were too narrow. Balls! He went and inspected their toilets, looking them over and sniffing around. Shit! He even called us in to sniff around after him. I damn near puked, with that odor of shit and the smell of farts—his farts! Who'd you think? Balls! Those sneaky farts of his are drop-dead lethal. It wasn't until today that I realized that fat people's farts are ichiban [number one]. If you get a whiff of one someday, I guarantee you'll remember it for the rest of your life. What are you waiting for? Every word I'm saying is the truth. I'm not bullshitting you! You can go ask Stumpy Courtesan and Sister Red Hair if you don't believe me.

"We didn't settle on a hostel till four or five o'clock, you hear that? We rented every room in the Flying Fortune Hostel. Why? It was the only one that had room for our fifty gir—our fifty trainees, that's why! Was it up to his standards? One hundred percent! In fact it was about the same as all the others, no difference that I could see. Why did he choose it? Councilman Qian, that's why. He's part owner of the place. At first Mr. Dong wondered what we were talking about. Who said it first? I think it was Black-Face Li or Stumpy Courtesan, I don't remember which. But the minute Mr. Dong learned that Councilman Qian was part owner of the hostel, he said, without even thinking, he said: 'Look, we've been everywhere, and the other places are just about like this one, so I say to hell with it, this one's as good as any. What do the rest of you think?' Hell, what could we think? He gets what he wants. What else can we do? Am I right or aren't I?

"But I have to admit that the rooms were nice and clean. The windows and doors were all polished, and the sheets were spotless, a helluva lot better than anything we had. Hell, you know that pig of a teacher still made them turn to: mop the floors, wipe down the window blinds, swab the toilets—and that's only the beginning. He had them disinfect everything, until the hostel looked like a hospital. He wouldn't allow the trainees to move in until the place was clean by hospital standards. Hell, he even told the attendants to paint over all the graffiti the guests had written on the bathroom walls. He said it could pollute the trainees' pure thoughts. Hell, now we had to worry about their thoughts!

"Come on, fill me up again. All the way to the top. Don't worry about Aniki getting drunk. That's it, that's the way to show you love Big-Nose Lion.

"No more pig's feet? We ate them all—really? Is that true? *I* ate every one? *I* finished them off? See how famished I was? I finished off a whole plateful of pig's feet all by myself.

"How could I be *that* hungry? For nine solid hours, I went without even a sip of water! Nine hours, we four managers were run ragged by that numbskull teacher for nine hours nonstop, you hear that? He'll be the death of us at that rate. Hell, we'd no sooner settled on that hostel than we had to worry about what to do with guests staying in some of the rooms—Manager Liu of the Flying Fortune did everything he could, agreeing to all sorts of demands before they vacated the place. But our numbskull teacher was in too big a hurry, and he told us to move all the girls who had passed the v.d. examination into the hostel right away. Mengxie had barely gotten them back to their own quarters from Venereal Wang's by then—it was about three o'clock, yes, I'd say right about three o'clock. When did you get home—about one-thirty, maybe one-forty? You were one of the first to be examined, then you came right home by taxi. No later than a quarter to four—they were bused over, so they had to wait till the last one finished her examination, and didn't get back till after three, know what I mean? They'd already missed lunch, and now they had to throw their things together to move into the hostel. You should have heard them bitch about that! Little Yuanyuan, our champion, pouted until her lips were almost touching the tip of her nose. You should have seen how pissed off she was! Refuse to pack? Her, refuse to pack? She didn't dare. When you're on the payroll, you do as you're told.

"Him? Oh, you mean our numbskull teacher. He left when we did. He said he wanted to inspect the bar, then go back to his hotel. We hailed a pedicab for him. When we brought the girls over to the hostel he was already there waiting for us, along with his four assistants. All men. They're on loan from Councilman Qian's trucking company. Why did they come along? What's their job? Listen and I'll tell you. When they saw us pull up to the hostel, one of them came running over to tell the girls to line up at the entrance.

With their bundles and suitcases in hand, they looked like a queue at the train station. They even drew a crowd of curious bystanders. Once they were all formed up, a second assistant walked up with a list of names from the v.d. clinic and a gold pen. Hell, that pen almost blinded me. Somebody said it was American. He told us four managers to take our places at the end of the line. What for? Listen and I'll tell you. While we stood there, he read out the names of the girls, pausing after each one so we could identify whoever responded as belonging to that name. Hell, what a scene that was. One ticket-seller and four ticket-punchers. It was like a fucking voting precinct. The bystanders looked on wide-eyed and open-mouthed, like they were at some kind of *shakashi* [circus].

"Some of the girls were so hungry they dropped their belongings where they stood and ran over to a nearby noodle stand to get something to eat. This was one group of trainees that needed a lesson in following orders. Every time the assistant called out a name, one of us managers had to run off and find whoever it was, then drag her back. Some refused to put down their noodle bowls, and shouted, 'Hold on, what's your hurry? I'm almost finished, just a few more bites!' We were so flustered and so mad we screamed at them to get their asses back here. But they screamed right back at us, complaining and arguing and refusing to listen. Shit! It was like that line in the opera: 'When the general's away, he can ignore the emperor's commands.' Hell, with all that shouting back and forth, it was some kind of drop-dead farce! Real-life show business! Stumpy Courtesan and Sister Red Hair's voices were the loudest, and it wasn't long before they shouted themselves hoarse.

"And then? And then the girls who had proved they were who they said they were reported in to another assistant, who made them sign in, fingerprinted them, did just about everything but ask them for a footprint! After all that, a third assistant passed out room assignments. And that was it? Hell, no. In my college son's vocabulary, 'not by a long shot!' After they got their room assignments and keys, the fourth assistant handed them a whole bunch of stuff—pencils, ballpoint pens, clipboards, notebooks, and things like towels, soap, and toilet paper. And that took care of the registration procedures. Why notebooks? So the trainees could take notes and do their lessons. Of course they have to take notes and do lessons. This is a training course. They're expected to go to class and be trained. This isn't playtime or party time. Thank goodness you weren't chosen. Otherwise you'd have to be taking notes and doing lessons. Tests even! That's right. And you know what else they had to do? Answer a bunch of questions. Like what? I'll tell you. Hell, that pig of a teacher is one smart operator. He knows these girls are no disciples of Confucius, that to them a pen might as well be a saber, so he gave each one a sheet of paper with questions printed on it and told them to give brief answers. If they didn't know the answers they could leave them blank. That shows how smart the guy is, a real teacher.

"Lots of the girls started writing and scribbling right away, then turned their papers in to the assistant within a few minutes. The questions? 'What's your name? When and where were you born? How far did you go in school?' and 'What jobs have you had?' The last question was, 'Why did you take up residence in the red-light district?' Of course that wasn't the way he worded it, no, he made it sound far more elegant than that, like you'd expect from a college graduate. He asked them, 'For what reason did you'—no, no, that isn't how he put it—he asked them, 'What motivated you to select your present occupation?' Pretty fancy, wouldn't you say? Want to know how they answered that? Most of the Ami aboriginal girls left that question blank. But some of the other girls answered it, and most of them wrote, 'To help my family.' Some of the goofier answers were, 'Don't know,' 'Can't say,' 'I can't tell you,' and 'I'd rather not say.' Honest, that's what they wrote, I'm not making it up. A few of them actually wrote things like, 'I thought it would be fun' and 'It sounded exciting.' Honest, they really wrote that, I'm not making it up. What fucking imaginations. If you took someone's place, that's what you'd write too? You're nuts! Just leave it blank and let it go. Oh, I haven't told you what Little Yuanyuan wrote. You'll shit your pants laughing when I tell you. She said—she wrote—'Because I hated math class.' How does that grab you? She hated her math class, so she dropped out of school and came here. I wonder where she came up with a fucking answer like that.

"Oh, we weren't finished yet. All of a sudden that numbskull teacher's eyes lit up like fireflies, and that sent chills up and down my spine. I blurted out, 'Uh-oh! Uh-oh! He's got something else up his sleeve!' I was right. That smug look on his face, like heaven had smiled down on him, was all I needed to know that he had another stroke of genius and we were about to have another stroke of bad luck.

"What did he have up his sleeve this time? I'll tell you. He said that after all our hard work in choosing a group of young, attractive, hygienic, and clean trainees, it would be a shame not to do everything possible to protect them against contamination, which they might then pass on to the GIs. He called this a moral issue. We had to pay close attention to this moral issue and avoid the possibility that these GIs, coming from so far away, would take a filthy venereal disease back with them. We had to ensure their safety and their health before they returned to Vietnam to continue fighting the war. This latest stroke of genius provided that from tonight until the GIs leave Taiwan, the trainees will not be permitted to entertain any other johns, they may not make love with a single Chinese man. If you mean 'fuck,' say 'fuck'! What's this 'make love'? Refined crap, if you ask me! Why, we asked? He said: 'That's the only way we can keep the trainees' v.d. record clean.'

"Fuck his ancestors! V.d. record, hah! How much income do you think we're going to lose on that? The girls we chose as trainees are the best, the best looking, and the most desirable products we've got. If we don't let these ichiban individuals entertain johns, what else have we got to sell? All four of us registered strong objections, of course we did. Black-Face Li, for example, spit a mouthful of gummy betel nut right onto the spanking-clean floor with a loud *ptui* and argued: 'That's like stealing business from ourselves! Like stealing business from ourselves!' He kept saying the same thing, over and over, getting louder all the time. Then Stumpy Courtesan jumped in with her 'Hold on, Teacher!'s. 'What's wrong with letting them work at night? They're not a bunch of newcomers. The freshest ones have been on the job for two or three months already. They all passed Venereal Wang's exam with flying colors. Even after seeing johns for two or three months! What harm can five or six days do? You don't have to worry that they'll pick up syphilis or the clap in that short time. Please don't worry, Teacher.' And she didn't stop there. 'Teacher, we rely on the pretty girls for most of our business. We couldn't even open our doors without them. Please, Teacher! Let them work at night. How about this? They only work till eleven o'clock, or say ten. Ten o'clock, and no later! That won't get in the way of their training. Hold on, Teacher. How's that? What do you say?'

"All this time, the rest of us were cheerleading from the sidelines. We talked until our mouths were dry, but that shitty teacher refused to give in, he wouldn't be swayed. He said every john was a potential v.d. carrier, and to ensure the safety and health of the GIs, the trainees were forbidden to work while they were in training. That was one of the reasons he wanted them to move to the hostel in the first place. He'd safeguard their cleanliness by removing them from a filthy environment. Safeguard their fucking cleanliness. Shit! Then he said that in order to guarantee one hundred percent success in our training program, he's scheduled crucial classes at night for all the trainees. If they didn't attend these, there was no chance they'd ever become exceptional bar girls, and unexceptional bar girls don't stand a chance of raking in U.S. dollars. He wants us to take the long view, not just look at what's right in front of our eyes. He told us to make absolutely sure we didn't lose something big over something small. Fuck his ancestors! 'Make absolutely sure you don't lose something big over something small,' hah!

"What could we say to that? What was there to say? Because of Councilman Qian and the chance of making a pile of U.S. dollars, all the four of us could do, all we *can* do is let him order us around. Let's drink! Drink up! Just the sound of his name fills my gut with anger. Shit! That idiot teacher!

"That should have wrapped things up, you say? Hell, the best was yet to come! When the girls heard they wouldn't be working nights, they went through the ceiling, went ballistic. Their shouts sounded like war whoops, know what I mean? You'd have thought a revolution had broken out. Why? Because they didn't want to give up all that business. I'm like you, I never thought they'd raise such a stink. I figured they'd appreciate the comfort of not having to entertain johns. They're living in a hostel and eating good food, all free. They should be thrilled. Their outcry came as a surprise to me, especially as a group and with such ferocity! How come they couldn't work nights? Why was their livelihood being taken away? Not letting them work was like not letting them keep on breathing. Hell, that Little Yuanyuan, who hated math class so much, sat down and figured how much money she'd lose, and she hounded us to let her keep working, like we were all deaf. She had it figured down to the last penny. Damn, who'd have believed that someone that good at figuring didn't like math?

"We shouted and we cursed, but the girls would have none of it and refused to quiet down. They said the only reason they were in the business was to earn enough to take care of their families, and they insisted we let them go on working. Oh, we were a hundred and twenty percent behind them, but we couldn't say so while the teacher, that idiot teacher, was standing right next to us observing everything, a fucking grin on his face, like he was watching a bunch of performing monkeys. At first he didn't say a word, until the girls started getting out of hand and shouted for freedom and democracy for all, equality of the sexes, crap like that, really letting out all the stops. He could see that we had our hands full trying to calm the girls down—hell, we could have calmed them down if we'd tried, but we didn't really feel like it. Well, then that crazy teacher walked up and shouted over all the noise: 'Shut up!' Hell, it was like a teacher bringing a class to order. Those girls, hell, those girls clammed up just like that, and all of a sudden it was so quiet we even heard Teacher Refinement pass wind: bwuut, bwuut, like a tire losing air. I'm not making this up, I was standing right next to him and I heard it, drop-dead clear—I said I'm not making it up! Bwuut, bwuut, like a tire—OK OK, I'll knock it off.

"Then came the speech. He told everyone to take it easy, that he'd anticipated the problem this morning, and he'd come up with the perfect solution. As soon as he opened his fucking mouth, out came the blah blah blah, like a butcher carving up chunks of pork. He paused before going on, and every one of those girls stared wide-eyed at him, hanging on his every word. Me, Aniki, I stood listening to the bwuut, bwuut of those silent farts. Ha ha, I even heard his stomach rumble two or three times. I'm *not* making this up, I heard it clear as day. Some time passed, then some more, and still he didn't say anything, until we couldn't stand it any longer. Then he continued—just listen to me. He said, what he said was: 'Take it easy, all of you, and don't fix your eyes on pocket change. You ought to be thrilled to have such a fine opportunity to study something new, an opportunity other, less fortunate people would jump at. This is a gift straight from heaven! You should grab it while you have the chance. Instead of letting another second pass, you should work and study hard to become the best trainees possible. You have to take the long view, look to the future. One week of sacrifice is what I'm asking. Once you get through these five days of training classes, you will not only elevate your status, but you'll also increase your earning power.' Yes, that's what our Teacher Refinement said. Are you listening? He said, 'You'll greatly greatly greatly greatly increase your earning power, which will greatly greatly greatly greatly improve your standard of living, until you are among the richest people in our society. You will greatly greatly greatly greatly elevate your social standing, until you become respected members of the community.' Shit! 'Greatly greatly greatly greatly, greatly greatly greatly greatly,' it sounded like a damned machine gun! And that's not all he said. 'In pursuit of this wonderful vision, this boundless future, the tiny bit of deprivation and inconvenience you're facing means nothing.' He repeated repeated repeated repeated this great great great great pronouncement over and over, grinning like you wouldn't believe. I actually felt a relaxed air settling over us, know what I mean? By then the girls were giggling, until he stopped them with: 'You trainees won't be working while you're in training, but don't concern yourselves with that, because I'm going to ask the people who manage the top houses to make it up by handing out daily unemployment subsidies.'

"Fuck him! Unemployment subsidies! When Stumpy Courtesan heard this, she blurted out, 'Aiyo, Hold on, Teacher!' But Teacher Refinement didn't give her a chance to say her piece. Hell, he had that phony grin on his face again! He said, 'You four managers don't oppose that modest suggestion, do you? I deeply believe'—he said 'deeply believe,' not just 'believe.' He said, 'I deeply believe that you four managers are great entrepreneurs who embrace the great ideals of Datong Company.' You never heard of Datong Company? You know, the company that makes electric fans. That's right, the one with the jingle, 'Datong, Datong, our service is tops . . .' He said we truly share Datong's lofty aspirations. What aspirations are those? To generate profits and share them with all. He said we now had that opportunity, a chance for the four of us to give free play to those aspirations, and he assumed that we were willing to share our profits up to this point with the trainees, to distribute them happily. Shit! Distribute fuck-his-ancestors unemployment subsidies to the girls in training! Then with that shit-eating grin, he hit us with: 'Am I right? Am I right?' What were we expected to say to that? What *could* we say? We just smiled and kept our mouths shut. But oh no, that numbskull teacher wouldn't let us off the hook that easily. Over and over, the same question, 'Am I right? Am I right?' Nonstop, 'Am I right? Am I right?' He wore us down until we nodded our heads just to shut him up. If that numbskull teacher took a job as a fucking police interrogator, an innocent man would confess to anything just to get him to stop with the questions. Shit! He was leading us around by the nose!

"Some of the girls asked him: 'How much unemployment subsidy will we get a day?' Little Yuanyuan echoed the others in her shrill voice: 'How much a day? I take in at least this much every day.' She raised seven fingers to show us. Well, that numbskull teacher just smiled and said calmly that everyone had to look at the big picture in terms of the U.S. dollars they'd be earning instead of worrying about the amount of the subsidy. He told them the actual figure is a secret, but assured them that when they received it they would be very pleasantly surprised. Our champ, Little Yuanyuan, who puts money in the bank every single day, gazed up at the teacher with a flirty look in her eye and said: 'Make sure it's no less than this, Teacher.' She showed him the seven fingers again. What did he say? 'You could raise one more finger and still come up short.' That mouth of his sure knows how to paint a pretty picture. I could never learn how to do that. Those girls were so damned happy they almost broke into applause!

"Know how much he wants us to give them? He took us aside and told us, 'Hold off until the training's over, then give them a little something, a goodwill gesture. But you must give them something. You have to make good on your promise'—oh, that's a saying that means you have to keep your word. That's exactly what he told us to do, I'm not making it up. Hell, just giving them a little something still costs us. So the four of us decided we wouldn't give them a thing when the time came. Not a red cent. So we don't make good on our promise, so what? Him and his fucking unemployment subsidy!

"What? Are you that sleepy? You gave me a scare with that hippopotamus yawn! How could just waiting for me one night wear you out? Come on, drink up, and you won't feel so tired. Look at me. After a little wine and some pig's feet, I'm drop-dead ready to go! Remember how beat I was when I first walked in? Come on, drink up!

"That should have wrapped it up, you say? Like hell! There's plenty more. He told us to go see Dr. Yun for some kind of pills, something with a weird name—Marzitone. Yeah, right, it does sound like 'Mao Zedong,' it does. So he told us to go get Mao Zedong from Dr. Yun. They're sleeping pills, you can't buy them in drugstores—what for? He said, 'To safeguard the health of every trainee, since they need eight hours' sleep every night. During their training period, they're to be in bed at nine-thirty and up at five-thirty. We take them out for a thirty-minute jog around Huagang Mountain first thing, then it's back for breakfast, followed by English practice till seven-fifty. After that, they walk to the church for their first class.' He said to give Mao Zedong to any girl who has trouble falling asleep at nine-thirty. They're guaranteed to take you as deep as the eighteenth level of hell. A night owl like you is damned lucky you're not in the program. You'd get Mao Zedong for sure, and wouldn't that be a mess, ah-so desu!

"That should have done it? Hah, 'On the contrary.' After everyone was run ragged, that fat pig of a teacher took the four of us outside the hostel for a private chat. About what? I'll tell you, but be prepared for a shock. You won't be shocked? You sure about that? Well, our Teacher Refinement said, 'Besides having the girls entertain the American GIs, we need to enlist a few males as drinking partners too.' What for? He said that one out of every four American men is a fairy. A fairy, you know what that is? Somebody who slips in the back door. Get it now? You do? Your mouth's open, you know that? I shocked you, didn't I? How did he come up with that idea? Who knows? But he said we have to enlist some handsome boys to entertain the fairies. He said Councilman Qian has approved the plan, and is in complete agreement. And he said he already has people out looking for candidates. Shit! Another one of his fuck-his-ancestors strokes of genius! And another fuck-his-ancestors stroke of bad luck for us! What do you mean, it doesn't have to cost anything? They have to eat and have a place to stay, and they'll want an unemployment subsidy. Well, that was the last straw! The very last straw!

"I didn't know what to say in response to this latest stroke of genius, but Black-Face Li, who sat there munching on betel nuts, did. First he spit a mouthful of the gummy stuff to the floor, then he said: 'Teacher, I—' But that's as far as he got before Teacher Refinement got on his case, complaining about how unsanitary it was to spit on the floor and telling him not to do it anymore. The whole country would lose face big time if the GIs saw him do that. Black-Face Li took it in stride, though, and went on with what he wanted to say: 'Teacher, you don't have to go looking for boys. I can do it myself.' Calm down and let me finish. We were just as shocked to hear Black-Face Li say that as you are. And the smile on that pig of a teacher vanished. His mouth opened so wide it nearly touched his ears, and his eyes were as big as ripe plums. The look on his face, that look, was like a man whose balls had dropped off! But then, then he started to laugh, this drop-dead weird laugh, like he was trying to hold it back but couldn't. He said, 'Mr. Li, Mr. Li, you want to do it yourself? That that that would be too embarrassing.' Know what Black-Face Li said to that? He he he surprised us by saying, 'What's so embarrassing about that? It's not like it would be the first time.' Stop with the 'Aiyo-

aiyo's already, and let me finish. Teacher Refinement had an answer all ready. He said, 'That would be wonderful if you were just a few years younger. You see, the GIs we're expecting will be in their twenties.' When he heard the teacher turn down his offer to work the back door with the American soldier boys, Black-Face Li came right back with a counterproposal. Who knew he could be so quick-witted? Sharp as nails! No bark, but plenty of bite! He said, he said, 'Then how about this? I'll bring my three nephews over. They're all eighteen or nineteen, weight-lifters, and strong as oxen. Nothing to keep them from entertaining the American fairies, I assume.' Teacher Refinement laughed and said: 'OK OK, you've got a deal, you've got a deal! Send them over tomorrow to start learning some English.' Black-Face Li had an answer for that too. 'They don't need any training; they're high school graduates, so they can handle simple English. I'll have them come over when it's time for back-door activity.'

"Teacher Refinement blinked and wrenched his mouth to one side, saying something about Chief Qian's instructions that they keep the wraps on this. Then he said to Black-Face Li, 'They don't need any training, then, but don't forget to bring them when we need them, and don't forget to instruct them how to handle the clients.' Guess what Black-Face Li said to that. You'll laugh yourself silly when I tell you. Just listen. He said, 'Don't worry, Teacher. I'll instruct them when the time comes. But it doesn't take a genius. If it hurts, a little soap will do the trick.' Is that a riot or what? You don't think so? Don't act so virtuous. Teacher Refinement sure thought it was funny. 'Kak-kak-kak, kak-kak-kak,' he sounded like a duck in heat. But after he stopped laughing, he said three won't be enough. This time it was Sister Red Hair who chimed in. She said she has a couple of nephews she can bring. So then it was my turn, like I was competing with them. I volunteered my son, the one in college. He'll be coming home for spring break, so I'll get him into the program. And he can bring along some friends. What's with the 'aiyo-aiyo'? What's wrong with that? It's all in good fun, and it won't leave any scars, like it would with one of you girls. So what's wrong? What's the problem? Don't worry yourself. It's a terrific chance for him to practice his American and earn a few U.S. dollars while he's at it. He'll jump at the chance. And if he doesn't? I'll tie him up and drag him over. Teacher Refinement was shocked to hear me volunteer my son, just like you. 'That's not such a good idea, Aniki.' 'Why not,' I asked him, 'if there's money in it?' I said I'd do it, and I will. That's the kind of man Big-Nose Lion is! A-hen, it's no big deal! He has a good time and gets paid for it. Why shouldn't he do it?

"Hell, we thought Teacher Refinement's latest stroke of genius would be a double stroke of bad luck for us. We never figured on the quick wits of Black-Face Li, who actually saved the day, know what I mean? Nothing would have happened if he'd kept his mouth shut. But he didn't, and it was like the opera goes: A noise to wake up the dead."

Big-Nose Lion talked on and on and was still prattling away when they went to bed, telling A-hen how Siwen returned to his hotel but kept calling every few minutes to get the managers of the Big 4 to do this or that. He had them check up on the trainees to see if they were in bed or if any of them tried to sneak out to turn a trick or two, or to see if they were taking Mao Zedong down to the eighteenth layer of hell.

When Big-Nose Lion finally ran out of things to say, it was already midnight. But then he seemed about to start in again, and A-hen jumped in: "Save the rest for tomorrow, all right? I could die, I'm so sleepy." A huge yawn brought tears to her eyes.

"OK OK, I'll hold off for tonight and tell you the rest tomorrow." Big-Nose Lion rolled over and sat up. When he tried to undress her, A-hen pushed his hand away.

"Not tonight!"

"It won't take long."

"I said, not tonight. Didn't you tell me Teacher said we couldn't turn tricks, in order to keep our bodies clean?"

Big-Nose Lion reached out again, but A-hen pushed his hand away.

"You're not servicing the GIs, so what are you worried about?"

"I said no. If I contaminate my body, how will I ever face those GIs?"

"Aren't you something! Contaminate your body?"

"Didn't you say I was a reserve? What if I was called to duty with an unclean body?" A-hen shrugged her shoulders, the hint of a grin on her face.

"Fuck you! If you're unclean, you can just drop dead. I'm not one of your johns, so what's the problem?"

"I said no. How am I going to deal with the GIs if I'm unclean?"

"Well, fuck you and your ancestors! You and your body contamination!"

Chapter Thirteen

At about eleven P.M., Siwen and three of his assistants—one stayed by the phone at the hotel—went to Mercy Chapel to convert the church into a classroom. After a few hours of supervising the most important tasks, Siwen returned to the hotel to take a badly needed bath, as if to cleanse himself of the likely contamination from a day's contact with the trainees. As he stepped out of the bath, before pulling back and cleaning beneath his somewhat elongated foreskin, a major concern occurred to him. Should he adopt the school's weekly assemblies as a model for tomorrow's opening ceremony of his crash course for bar girls—start with everyone standing at attention, followed by the singing of the national anthem and three bows to a portrait of Sun Yat-sen, the Father of the Country? If we omit the national anthem and the bows, the opening ceremony will lack solemnity, won't it? While he sought respectability for his bar-girl training course, he was somewhat bothered by the thought that people might accuse him of excess. How could he think of having *prostitutes* sing the national anthem and bow before a portrait of the Father of the Country? He clutched a soapy jowl. *OK.* Let them disapprove, I'm not afraid. *See*, the Constitution doesn't say that *prostitutes* can't sing the national anthem or bow to a portrait of the Father of the Country. They're people too! Who can deny them their fundamental rights? This conclusion resulted in enormous satisfaction and, of course, a celebratory explosion of wind from his backside. This particular emission produced both sound *and* a toxic odor that made even his eyebrows arch. *But, but* having them sing the national anthem and bow three times under such circumstances did seem a bit far-fetched. On the other hand, what kind of ceremony would it be without the national anthem? It's sung at movie houses and theaters. The answer came as he pulled back his foreskin and cleaned the end of his penis. Since singing the national anthem and bowing three times might be seen as inappropriate, and not singing or bowing lacked solemnity, why not ask Songzhu's mother, the pastor, to sing a hymn and say a prayer or give a two- or three-minute sermon? That way, a solemn and respectful air could be maintained, success would be celebrated, and the gesture would serve as thanks to their host for making the church available.

Hell, there's another stroke of genius! Ecstatic, he ran out of the bathroom, covered with soapsuds, to telephone Chief Qian with the news and solicit his opinion. Chief Qian responded with a flurry of compliments—"Great idea, you numbskull! Great idea, you numbskull! That's some kind of idea, you numbskull!"—to which Siwen responded with his own flurry of farts, some completely silent, others far less so. His report finished, he hung up, then phoned his second-floor office to tell the remaining assistant to hightail it over to Mercy Chapel and pass on his latest instruction, then stick around to help out. This instruction was: Do not hang the national flag, a portrait of the Father of the Country, or maxims for youth on the pulpit . . . leave it just as it is, don't change a thing, except for the addition of the sign "Propriety, Justice, Honesty, Shame." Everything else was to proceed according to plan.

He was reminded of how on the previous Sunday night, as he joyfully cleaned his foreskin, yet another stroke of genius had provided him with a lecture topic for the Monday morning assembly at school. After agonizing over this assignment for the longest time, he had despaired of ever coming up with an idea that satisfied him. The key to learning English, the best way to choose a book, general principles of life, what it means to be young in these times, young people's ideals and aspirations, whether or not high school boys should date . . . he'd considered those before, but they were all clichés. He wanted something brand new, something fresh, something unique. From the minute the dean asked him to give the talk, he had searched for a topic, searching and seeking, seeking and searching . . . but he discarded every idea that came to him, and was on the verge of settling for the very next idea that popped into his head. Then he found it, in the midst of the satisfying task of cleaning his foreskin in the bachelor dormitory shower, he found it, and he was so happy he grabbed a handful of pubic hair and yanked it—too hard, as it turned out: Ouch! That was the only way he could prove he wasn't dreaming, that it was indeed real!

He did not reveal his topic until he strode up to the podium, and all eyes were on him—the principal, the dean, the student adviser, the faculty adviser, and the teachers, who were seated on the stage behind him, plus the students and the military instructors in the audience, everyone. They sat there like statues, dumbstruck; for a moment, the auditorium was like a photograph, still and quiet.

His topic: It's *OK* to masturbate!

Chapter Fourteen

If you've read this far, you've invested a considerable amount of time. Well, Siwen also invested a considerable amount of time, waiting for the arrival of Councilman Qian and his company's senior employees. One of these was the legal adviser, Attorney Zhang, whose appearance struck Siwen as quite uncommon. Outside of a court of law, people seldom laid their eyes on Zhang the lawyer, a gaunt, dried-out man. "Seldom" really doesn't do justice; "almost never" is more like it. Zhang the lawyer wore nothing but black and was never seen without a pair of shades, a la blind masseurs. He was like a detective on a case or a ninja in a martial-arts novel who soars onto the scene, unknown to gods or ghosts; he usually shocked the hell out of Siwen, who called him Sherlock Zhang behind his back. Today, as usual, Sherlock Zhang was all in black: black suit, black shades, black shoes. Hell, even the handkerchief in his breast pocket was nearly black. The sight of this funereal man did not please Siwen, who considered turning an ominous sight into an auspicious one via sarcasm. But Sherlock Zhang walked into the church, his black shoes click-clacking on the hardwood floor, without so much as a nod, thereby heightening Siwen's displeasure with Councilman Qian for arriving so late. He frowned importantly and was about to "Fuck!" him, when Councilman Qian turned the tables with a loud "ha ha":

"You numbskull," he said, "you're a master! You've

made history here, ha ha!" He tugged at Siwen's collar. "I see you're even wearing a suit today, quite the fashion plate!" Then he yanked Siwen's tie. "Ha ha, with you as commanding general and crafty adviser, what's to stop me from being elected provincial councilman in the next election? After that, national legislator, even the National Assembly Line!" (At the time, representatives to the central government were not democratically elected.)

Siwen knew it would be churlish to "Fuck!" the author of such effusive praise, so he merely smiled and said, with just a hint of resentment, "How come you're so late? The Big 4 and all fifty trainees are here, not to mention Pastor Yun and her acolytes! They were scheduled to go to Beipu this morning to 'Seek seek seek, seek the Holy Spirit,' but they delayed that for us until after the hymns. Then you come waltzing in this late, Chief, because you like to act like a bigshot!"

Chief Qian merely laughed—ha ha ha—and shrugged his shoulders as he ushered his coterie into Mercy Chapel. Once they were out of earshot, he said to Siwen, "I forgot to ask if Yun Songzhu agreed to hold class for the girls."

"Shit, don't mention that name to me! That son of a bitch promised he'd teach a class in personal hygiene and give the trainees an overview of Americans' sexual mores and practices—" Chief Qian nodded and said approvingly: "A worthwhile class, very meaningful!" "Yesterday he told me to my face he'd do it. So this morning he goes and breaks his word! When I called up the pastor this morning, he got on the phone and asked if any boys would be participating in the training. I said we were recruiting some, but that you wanted to keep it under wraps, so they wouldn't attend the sessions. As soon as he heard that, he said he had a golf game and I'd have to cancel the class. *Damn!* That son of a bitch!"

"What a shame, canceling a terrific class like that," Councilman Qian said, with a shake of his head.

"I begged him until he finally agreed to attend the opening ceremony and make a brief address from the pulpit on the latest developments in personal hygiene."

"He's coming?"

"He's coming, all right, but not until eleven o'clock!"

"Well then, I'll pass up the assembly meeting just so I can hear what that son of a bitch doctor has to say that's so novel." Councilman Qian lowered his voice and added, "By the way, is anyone from the county or municipal governments coming?"

"No."

"Any assemblymen?"

"Not a single one. But they sent flowers."

"That's good, that's good," Councilman Qian said with an approving laugh—ha ha ha—and a nod of his head. "A hearing is scheduled, so they must not have time for us."

"We'd better go in," Siwen said with a gesture of invitation.

As they headed inside, Siwen told Chief Qian that the Dean of Students from his school, Mao Two, had agreed to give a lesson in "global etiquette." He was perfectly suited to the important task of transforming the trainees and elevating their moral character. A short, squat man, he was unyieldingly strict with his students, always ready with a well-placed swat or a thunderous roar. Discipline was his forte.

"Where'd he get a goofy name like Mao Two?" Councilman Qian asked.

"That's not his real name, just a *nickname* the students gave him. It's short for Mao Zedong Number Two. What do you think of that? He's clearly the best choice, a cinch to make an impact. You can bet he'll teach some *good manners* to this bunch of ignorant *bar girls to be*."

Chapter Fifteen

With a young woman accompanying her on the organ, Pastor Yun led the congregation in singing "Come to Jesus, come to Jesus, come to Jesus now, now come to Jesus, come to Jesus now. . . ." The crash course for bar girls had begun. After finishing her "Come to Jesus" hymn, the white-haired Pastor Yun launched into an emotional evocation of Jesus' deeds, preaching the Gospel of the Lord, informing one and all that believers can look forward to life after death, that faith in Jesus turns extinction into eternal life, and so on, until she asked the congregation to bow their heads in prayer. She raised her white head ever so slightly, closed her bird's-nest eyes, and rested her bony hands, clasped in reverence, on the satin-covered pulpit.

"Our Father, who art in Heaven, hallowed be Thy name."

"Our Father, who art in Heaven, hallowed be Thy name," the congregation intoned, led by the booming voices of acolytes sitting in the front pew.

"Thy kingdom come."

"Thy kingdom come." . . . and so on and so forth. . . .

Councilman Qian, Sherlock Zhang, and the senior employees from Qian's company were ensconced up front in the VIP section, their heads bowed reverently, lips moving as if they were chewing gum, to all appearances reciting the prayer along with the pastor. The course leader, Dong Siwen, sat behind them on the aisle, his eyes shut in rapture, as if drawing unto himself the heavenly music. Next to him, shoulder to shoulder, sat Big-Nose Lion, Sister Red Hair, Stumpy Courtesan, and Black-Face Li. The lesser whoremasters and madams, as status dictated, were aligned behind them. Mengxie, a man named A-yong, and some other bouncers stood in the rear. To look at the faces of these whoremasters and madams, you'd think they were paragons of virtue, solemn devotees of the Word.

Sandwiched between these two extremes, in the student seats, sat fifty buxom girls—all conversant in boar pour more, unencumbered by the monthlies, free of disease. Three generations under one roof, all primed to become world-class bar girls. Most of them, nearly all of them, in fact, had their eyes shut—for they were fast asleep. It's safe to say that none had slept well the night before. Although Mengxie sent them to bed precisely at nine-thirty—lights out—they grumbled that no one went to bed *that* early! After all, they didn't have to get up to catch an early train home, so what was the purpose? Ignoring their complaints, Mengxie brandished his leather belt and bellowed, "You're wasting your breath! This is how our leader wants it, and this is how it'll be. He said if you can't sleep, take Mao Zedong down to the eighteenth level of hell. Who knows, you may never come back up!" That killed their interest in Mao Zedong! Some of the girls tossed and turned all night, not falling asleep until three or four in the morning, while others weren't even that lucky. Then, before seven o'clock, Mengxie, A-xiong, A-yong—the newly appointed monitors (more like boot-camp drill instructors)—sounded reveille with their whistles: hoot hoot hoot, hoot hoot hoot. "Rise and shine, rise and shine!" Hoot hoot hoot, hoot hoot hoot! "Up and at 'em, rise and shine!"

"Fuck off!" Little Yuanyuan screeched angrily. "What do you think you're doing?" Others echoed her complaint: "What the hell are you yelling about? You'll wake up the dead!" Mengxie and his crew pumped themselves up confidently and fired back: "What are you yelling about? Our leader wanted us to get you dumb pussies up at five-thirty, and the only reason you slept this late is that we reminded him it's the first day and you're used to sleeping in. Besides, the only thing scheduled is the opening ceremony, no classes, so you don't have to get up all that early today. We talked till we were blue in the face before he bought our arguments. Starting tomorrow, you're up at five-thirty, like good little girls. And what do we get for letting you sleep an extra hour? Bitching and more bitching. Well, you can all go to hell!"

When they arrived at Mercy Chapel, the girls gabbed and giggled, even clapped their hands and laughed out loud, not what you'd expect from girls who hadn't slept all night. But then Pastor Yun started in with her "Come to Jesus, come to Jesus," and they began nodding off as the sandman moved in; by the time Pastor Yun embarked upon her revelation of the Lord's deeds, nearly all fifty trainees had entered the foggy second stage of sleep and were well on their way to the third. Then Pastor Yun spoke eloquently about how Jesus died for our sins, abruptly clearing the cobwebs in the heads of the chosen few, who stared wide-eyed at the anguished face recounting the sorrowful tale of the man wearing a crown of thorns, of Jesus carrying the heavy wooden cross to the site of the crucifixion, of his body torn and bruised. There were yelps of "Oh, my!" from some of the girls, especially Little Yuanyuan, who had a vision of the scene. "That's so cruel. That scares the life out of me!"

As if to lend substance to this shocked reaction, Pastor Yun's acolytes, seated right up front, rocked the heavens: "Hallelujah! Hallelujah! . . ."

And then Jesus was nailed to the cross, hand and foot. Little Yuanyuan and the other girls voiced their shock and outrage; in common parlance, they were hysterical!

"Oh, my God, how could those foreigners be so cruel??"

"How *could* those foreigners be so drop-dead barbarian?"

"A bunch of butchers!"

The outbursts nearly drowned out the "Hallelujah" chorus, with a long, drawn-out "ahhh" swirling above the heads of the congregation and refusing to go away, so embarrassing Big-Nose Lion and the others that they turned to glare at the trainees.

But then, as Pastor Yun informed one and all that God is the light, that God is love, that everlasting life is promised to the believer, resurrection awaits, . . . most of the girls, Little Yuanyuan among them, reentered the second stage of sleep.

By the time Pastor Yun fervently intoned the words "For Thine is the kingdom, and the power, and the glory," the girls were well into the third stage, right on the verge of being "out like a light."

What about everyone else? you ask. With the exception of Pastor Yun's acolytes, most of the congregation meekly, and weakly, repeated, "For Thine is the kingdom, and the power, and the glory. . . ."

One of the lesser madams, who was sitting directly behind Big-Nose Lion, muttered softly to the person next to her, "What's this all about? Is this a church service or an opening ceremony?"

"Forever, Amen!" Here Pastor Yun raised her voice, apparently to underscore her devotion.

"Forever, Amen!" The sonority of Dong Siwen's voice matched that of Pastor Yun's. But he used the foreign word, *Amen*, not the Mandarin imposter, as if only thus could his fervent prayer reach the ears of the alien God.

Chapter Sixteen

Councilman Qian's ascent to the pulpit breathed life into the proceedings at Mercy Chapel. The girls appeared rested and wide awake, a la the resurrection of Christ. As he laughingly gripped the edges of the pulpit, one of the girls greeted him with a giggle and a shout of: "Aiya, Pantless Qian is going to do a striptease!"

Like a current running through the congregation, the shout created waves of noise that came crashing down on Councilman Qian.

"Oh boy, a striptease!"

"Take it off, my dear councilman!"

"Strip! Don't be shy!"

"We'll pay to see it!"

"Hurry, hurry! Strip! Not only will we pay, we'll give you our sacred votes in the future!"

Just then the stern voice of an aboriginal girl rose above the uproar. "Councilman Qian, in your campaign you said you'd have highway buses pass through our town of Fengbin, and I thought you meant it. Well, we haven't seen hide nor hair of one yet!"

"What did you expect?" another girl chimed in. "That would be a lot harder than taking off his fucking pants!"

She barely got the words out before the place was rocked with laughter so loud it would hardly be an exaggeration to say it raised the roof. Big-Nose Lion, decked out in a bright red sport coat and shocking green bell-bottoms, jumped to his feet, then quickly sat back down. Trying hard not to laugh, he turned to Sister Red Hair, gave her a sign with his eyes, and jerked his thumb to the rear. She stood up, filling the air with her bulk, and turned partway around. The rose in her hair fluttered as she scowled and said menacingly, "I want you girls to shut up!" She paused for effect, then hissed, "Do you hear me?" The laughter stopped as abruptly as a movie when the film snaps in the projector.

Still staring daggers at the girls, Sister Red Hair turned back around and sat down. Dong Siwen leaned over and said "Thank you," then sat back in the pew and looked up at Councilman Qian, his only thought, Do we need a class in global etiquette, or what! He was hopeful that Mao Two was up to the important task of teaching the trainees some manners.

Councilman Qian Mingxiong stood at the pulpit laughing. "Ha ha ha, ha ha ha." He laughed right along with the girls who were having so much fun at his expense, a reprise of his election campaign the year before, ha ha ha, ha ha ha. Once the girls had quieted down in the wake of Sister Red Hair's menacing hisses, he ha ha ha'ed a time or two more as his eyes swept the congregation, a trick he had learned from Dong Siwen—the *po-si* [*PAUSE*—deathly rude]—then began to speak.

"Ladies and gentlemen, first I want to thank Teacher Dong—" He nodded twice in the direction of Dong Siwen, a show of respect to which Siwen quickly responded by clasping his hands in front of him and demurring: "You flatter me. It was nothing, really." "—if not for Teacher Dong's dedication and hard work, we would not be witnessing this historic event in Hualien today. And you trainees sitting out there would not have this wonderful opportunity to practice your American, learn how to entertain foreigners, earn some extra cash, and raise your social status! So you should give Teacher Dong the respect he deserves." Siwen lowered his head modestly. "You must work hard, study diligently, become useful and accomplished students in order to be worthy of his high expectations. I am reminded of Lin Yutang. Lin Yutang, you know who he is, don't you? You don't? One of the world's great jokesters, and you don't know who he is? Then you must study even harder and apply yourselves even more diligently. I can't believe you've never heard of one of the world's most famous jokesters! I'm shocked (he ha ha ha'ed as he shook his head). One of his most famous lines was: 'A speech is like a woman's skirt, the shorter the better!' "

"What's so great about that?" one of the girls shouted with a laugh. "I say go all the way!"

"Ha ha ha, that's the ticket. Strip to the buff, like Councilman Qian there, if you want to do it right!"

Once again the trainees rocked the room with laughter until the roof tiles rattled. Instead of deferring to Sister Red Hair, Big-Nose Lion stood up, and this time stayed up, turning to the rear and hissing, "Quiet down, OK? Where are your manners?"

At that moment, Dong Siwen heard a muttered comment—in Mandarin with a strong Hakka accent—from A-cai, one of the lesser whoremasters sitting behind him: "So *this* is how high-class girls act, eh?"

"I thought at least they had some upbringing!" one of the lesser madams echoed authoritatively.

Once things quieted down again, Councilman Qian, still laughing, swept the congregation with his eyes, making sure he didn't miss anyone, then continued, "Speeches are like women's skirts, the shorter the better, so I'll *su-ta-pu* [*STOP*] here. I wish you all success in your studies and a great future! Thank you!"

Siwen rose from his seat and looked first at Councilman Qian, then at the congregation before saying excitedly, "My thanks to Councilman Qian for taking time from his busy schedule to honor us with his presence at this opening ceremony. Thanks too for his passionate and encouraging remarks, and for his earnest good wishes. What could be better than encouragement and good wishes? We are grateful to Councilman Qian for supplying them just when we need them most. Thank you from the bottoms of our hearts!" He raised his hands and began to applaud. "Come on, everybody, a warm round of applause for Councilman Qian. Come on, everybody, join me! No need for modesty, not when you show gratitude. Come on, everybody, join me!"

The congregation began to applaud, including the aboriginal girl in red who had complained a few minutes earlier about how Councilman Qian had broken his word regarding highway buses in Fengbin, although she clapped unenthusiastically, barely bringing her hands together and making about as much noise as a soft breeze against her face. At the opposite end of the spectrum were Big-Nose Lion, Black-Face Li, Stumpy Courtesan, and Sister Red Hair, managers of the Big 4, whose resounding claps sounded a bit like the smacks they frequently applied to the faces of their girls.

Councilman Qian stepped out from behind the pulpit, bowing and scraping, acknowledging the ovation with clipped laughter and sweeping waves of his hand before taking his seat up front.

Filled with the excitement of the moment, Dong Siwen faced the congregation and announced, "Now I hope Attorney Zhang will honor us with a few choice remarks." Dong Siwen raised his hand toward Attorney Zhang, who was sitting next to Councilman Qian, like a dancer offering the stage to another; the smile creasing his chubby face made his head seem even puffier than usual, like a man with water on the brain.

The black-clad Sherlock Zhang demurred with a shake of his head. Dong Siwen bent down and said with a smile, "No need to be modest, Attorney Zhang. A few words of encouragement is all we ask." Then he faced the congregation again and said, "Attorney Zhang is only thirty-two years old, yet he's already been a prosecutor and a judge, and is now one of Hualien's most renowned lawyers. As legal consultant to Councilman Qian's company, he has accepted an invitation to offer a two-hour class, Friday at two o'clock, for you trainees on elements of the law. Let's give our youthful and talented attorney a warm welcome, and I'm sure he'll honor us with a few remarks." Pa-pa pa-pa, he clapped loudly, but drew only a smattering of halfhearted applause from the girls, as if they had just watched a disappointing concert.

The gaunt, puny, and probably impotent Attorney Zhang—who had once hinted to the drivers of Councilman Qian's trucks: "If you ever run anyone over and the person doesn't die right away, back up and do it again to make sure you leave no witness to the incident. You'll buy a lifetime of grief otherwise"; who once gave judgment in a case that could only have taken place in a martial-arts novel (an old man in his seventies leaped off the roof of a two-story building and crushed a fortyish woman with whom he was engaged in a land dispute); and who would later travel north to Taipei, where he would make a killing in illegal emigration—actually blushed from embarrassment as he waved off the invitation. Back and forth it went, until Sherlock Zhang rose reluctantly and walked to the first pew, where he bashfully turned to the congregation and timidly adjusted his shades.

"I, I—" It was a struggle to even open his mouth. "I'll just speak from here—" Siwen tried to coax him up onto the stage, but he repeated, "I'll speak from here! I'll just speak from here!" until Siwen had to defer to his wishes. "A moment ago, Mr. Councilman Qian quoted the world-famous joke Lin Yutang, oops, sorry, that's not right (no one but Siwen and Councilman Qian caught the slip, which they greeted with a meek ha ha), what I meant to say was the world-famous jokester Lin Yutang, who said a speech is like a woman's skirt, the shorter the better. So I, I—" He swallowed hard, as if he could scarcely get the words out. "I only have one thing to say, only one thing" (in fact, he had already said more than one thing, a lot more). He swallowed again, then continued somberly, "I ask you all to keep in mind that it is against the law in our country to go out on strike. What that means, in simple terms, is if you're dissatisfied in any way with your boss—maybe he gives you wages you feel are too low because it would be a hardship for him to give higher wages—you then join together in a work stoppage, which results in financial losses that force him to give in to your demands. That is a simple explanation of a strike. I ask you all to keep in mind that strikes are not permitted in our country. They are illegal, punishable by death (several of the girls oohed and ahhed at that). Please keep that in mind, don't ever forget it. Thank you." Having said his piece, the gaunt, puny, unmanly Attorney Zhang, who would one day make a killing in illegal emigration to America, quickly sat back down.

You could hear the sounds of breathing.

On the following Friday afternoon, Sherlock Zhang would remind the girls during his "elements of the law" class, "You mustn't go out on strike, strikes are illegal." He would also talk about how U.S. dollars are foreign currency, which they were not permitted to keep for themselves nor use in cash transactions; they must turn them all over to their bosses, who would take them to the bank. Keeping or trading in foreign currency was a punishable offense. And he would tell them they must ask a fair price from the Americans for their services, or they would be breaking . . . in dealing with the Americans they must give full value for the amount paid, or they were liable to be sued. . . . The girls would sit through both classes with wide-eyed, slack-jawed attention, some even paling at what they heard. But Little Yuanyuan would remain unruffled throughout, even turning to the student next to her to whisper, "Don't worry, he's making it sound more serious than it is. We live in a democracy, where the kinds of things he's talking about—where everything you do violates section such and such of the criminal code, and where they can put you in jail or shoot you—are unheard of. He's a stinking windbag!"

Once Attorney Zhang had said his piece and was back in his seat, Siwen found himself in a dilemma. He had not anticipated the prospect that not a single member of the county government or the various invited councilmen would show up. *Damn!* Even worse, Chief Qian and Attorney Zhang turned out to be devotees of Lin Yutang. *Damn!* The shorter the skirt the better, the shorter the better. That left him with more time than he'd planned on. Yun Songzhu wouldn't arrive for another hour, for crying out loud! How was he going to fill a whole hour? His nerves must have gotten the better of him, as he turned seriously flatulent. Happily, it was muted; that and the fact that his expression didn't change combined to make it all but impossible to guess who might have been the messenger of gas. "Drop dead," one of the girls muttered, "who cut the cheese?" Siwen pinned the gabby girl with a look of righteous indignation, so embarrassing her that she lowered her head as if *she* had been the cheese cutter.

His gaze shifted to Black-Face Li, just as the latter reached into his black martial-arts outfit for a handful of Shuangdong betel nuts and was about to pop them into his mouth. He quickly jammed his hand back into his pocket. "Aha!" Siwen exclaimed, in the grip of another stroke of genius. Another stroke of genius! Without wasting a minute, a single moment, he bent over and invited Big-Nose Lion up to the pulpit to address the congregation. Big-Nose Lion shook his head spiritedly. "I've got nothing to say." But Siwen was too quick: "Just tell the trainees where the GI bar is located, how close to completion we are, and when they can go inside to familiarize themselves with their new surroundings." Shying away from something he hadn't expected, Big-Nose Lion continued begging off, refusing to mount the platform. So Siwen turned to Sister Red Hair with the same offer, and she responded with the same spirited head-shaking, which turned her red hair into a burning bush. Stumpy Courtesan's response was a rapid-fire series of "Oh, Teacher, I couldn't! I couldn't!" In his turn, Black-Face Li turned mute: Oh oh oh! Not another word emerged above the frantic waving of his hands.

Siwen could hardly call a break and send everyone outside to mill around until Songzhu arrived, then summon them back inside to recommence the interrupted opening ceremony. How would that look? *That's ridiculous!* Siwen felt another build-up down low. But now, awash in propriety, justice, honesty, and shame, he squeezed his sphincter tight, took a deep breath, and succeeded in sealing the offending gas inside. With the matter of breaking wind resolved, at least for the moment, Siwen's mind suddenly Ah ah-ed! Another "Ah ah" stroke of genius!

"Honored guests, esteemed students, ladies and gentlemen, welcome!" He placed himself behind the pulpit, gripping its edges with both hands. "Our benefactors, the tireless managers of the Big 4, have shown how modest they are. I guess I'll have to speak for them. These Big 4 managers have been the midwives for this training program. Without their generous contributions, the program would never have been born, and you students would not have an opportunity to earn some cash from the Americans. No opportunity to enhance your income, to improve your lives, to raise your social standing, or to become respected members of society. It is only fitting and proper that we offer our heartfelt tribute to these four individuals."

"Hold on, Teacher!" Stumpy Courtesan protested. "Please don't say that!"

Sister Red Hair was so embarrassed that her forehead was touching her ample bosom. Big-Nose Lion and Black-Face Li shook their heads and laughed. "You flatter us," they said, "you really do."

A girl in a white dress shrugged her shoulders and whispered to her neighbor, "We're the ones who filled the Big 4 managers' pockets with all that money. Heartfelt tribute? Bullshit!" Even in a whisper, her comment was audible to the girls around her, and drew a round of sniggers.

Like a man speaking Chinese to foreigners, Siwen continued in measured tones. "These four managers have willingly spent their hard-earned money—" The girl in white sneered and whispered: "Bullshit!" "—to invite the best teachers they could find to instruct all of you. We are privileged to have, for instance, bartenders all the way from Kaohsiung who will teach you how to mix drinks and then how to drink them, and Hualien's most renowned dance instructor, who will teach you the latest ballroom steps. We have arranged for Hualien's finest lawyer to instruct you in aspects of the law . . . not only have our four managers invited the cream of the crop to offer classes, but they have also spared no expense by renting Hualien's most up-to-date hotel for you to entertain the visiting GIs. I doubt that Hualien's wealthiest families can boast such modernized facilities, which is to say that you students are the city's most fortunate citizens!"

Several of the girls exchanged whispered questions like, "What the hell does modernized facilities mean?" Little Yuanyuan had the perfect answer: "It's bullshit!" All within earshot laughed in spite of themselves.

"I have even more good news for you." A pregnant pause had the girls holding their breath. Big-Nose Lion, Sister Red Hair, and the other Big 4 managers either cast their eyes downward, feigning embarrassment, or kept them fixed on Siwen in sweeping gratitude. "What is that good news? Just listen. Our Big 4 managers are going to host a banquet at the Noblemen Lounge to celebrate the success of our endeavor, and you are all invited to enjoy a meal of the finest and cleanest Japanese food."

"I'll be damned, they're treating us to a meal!" said one of the girls, whose bangs came down to her eyebrows, a la Chinese actresses from the '30s and '40s. "I thought—"

"What did you think?" her neighbor leaned over to ask, the mole beneath her left eye looking like a lonely teardrop.

"I thought they were going to give us some extra money to make up for our losses during these training sessions, that's what!"

The girl with the teardrop mole grunted. "Fat chance!

All the girls who heard this exchange laughed spiritedly—tee hee hee, tee hee hee—keeping their voices so low that some of the laughter sounded like coughs from next door. Girls out of earshot cursed good-naturedly, especially Sister Red Hair's shrill-voiced adopted daughter, who had taken A-hen's place. "You drop-dead windbags, what are you gabbing about? We can't hear what Teacher Shi Song's saying, thanks to you!"

Just what was Dong Siwen saying? With mounting excitement (it would not be inappropriate to use the descriptive term "the spittle was flying," though it might be a slight exaggeration), he was describing his feelings the night before, after paying a visit to the provisional bar erected by the four managers across the street from the Heaven's Omens Theater on Nanking Road, downtown Hualien's hotspot. A first-class establishment, he was saying. Everything—stools tables easy chairs bar artsy lamps even planters and glasses—was top-quality, items brought down from Taipei.

(What he failed to mention was that this provisional bar lacked even a provisional toilet. Anyone needing to go number one or number two had to use the all-purpose toilet in the frozen-dessert shop next door. Whether squatting or standing in that old-style crapper, you couldn't avoid the disgusting sight of flies and maggots crawling all around the pit. After the American soldier boys came, when they were inside pissing or shitting, they would hold their noses and mutter over and over, *Oh, my God*! An officer with the same name as Agent 007, James Bond, no sooner stepped inside the crapper than he retched loudly and emptied his stomach of all the *cognac* [gan-yi-niang, fuck your old lady] he had consumed.)

Easing into his Ah ah speaking style, Siwen detailed how the bar was built entirely of bamboo, "ah ah, using blood-and-tear speckled bamboo ah! Ah ah! Know what I mean? This beautiful bar, incorporating the best of Chinese traditions and culture, is, without fear of contradiction, a cultural milestone in Chinese history, a pioneering masterpiece!" And in conclusion: "Permit me to wrap this up with a biblical quotation. Ah ah! You students are truly blessed to be able to serve the American GIs and enrich our nation with foreign currency in a place of unprecedented perfection!"

The young girl in bangs reminiscent of a 1940s Chinese actress asked earnestly: "What's foreign currency?"

Siwen giggled. "It's those precious U.S. dollars!"

The lesser whoremaster named Ah-cai piped up: "U.S. dollars are great! Each one's worth forty NT!"

"Are you kidding me?" Sister Red Hair's foster daughter, A-hen's nemesis, shouted incredulously, gleefully.

"Of course I'm not!"

Siwen nodded to the madam to show his approval, then glanced at his wristwatch. *My!* After all that, I've only been talking eleven or twelve minutes! *My!* Songzhu won't be here till eleven-twenty, another thirty or forty minutes. How do I kill *that* much time? At school, whenever he finished his lecture before the end of class, his favorite means of killing time was to have the class stand up to recite the lesson, one section per student. Usually after six or seven students had finished, the class bell rang. Sometimes he added comments of his own, refuting this and criticizing that. (Don't be fooled by his resemblance to the lovable Shi Song, because when he starts in on his comments, he's anything *but* lovable. He once got right in a student's face and said, "When a teacher offers private lessons on the side, it is a scholar's shame. Ah ah! It's a national disgrace!" He also had unkind words about school policy; when probing public servants—it sounded like "toxic serpents" the way he said it—visited, the administrators ordered students who wore glasses to remove them, so as to bring glory to the school as an institution where no one is short-sighted. "Ah ah! Hypocrisy! A scam!" He discreetly admonished the students that they mustn't take as their models those who should die a thousand deaths. The school's administrators were not pleased, but what could they do? No one told them to break their own rules. He was equally critical of education in general. "Ah ah!" he said. "Nearly a century of education, and look where it's gotten us: it's the ruination of our students, the ruination of the future masters of our country. There can be only one explanation: traitors lurk in our educational system, ah!" Later, after going to work at the TV station, he often made comments that displeased his bosses there, criticizing them for giving amateurs authority over the professionals and for bestowing upon clerical personnel, who had the cultural qualities of a bedpan, leadership roles over programmers. No wonder the TV programming is like an old lady's breasts, sagging more and more every year!)

Siwen had nothing else to say, and by now his forehead was a river of sweat. How to *kill* another half hour? What do I do? Turning suddenly tongue-tied, he cast a beseeching look in the direction of Councilman Qian, but it was completely lost on the Chief, who just smiled back as if to say, "Good speech, and I can hardly wait to hear what else is new." Attorney Zhang was also smiling at him. Big-Nose Lion, Sister Red Hair, Stumpy Courtesan, and Black-Face Li, managers of the Big 4, along with the minor whoremasters and madams, were smiling too, seemingly on pins and needles as they waited to hear if he had any other surprises in store for them. They looked like they'd be awfully disappointed if he stopped now. He couldn't stop, he knew that, but what was he going to say? He'd already exhausted his repertoire. Our talented and fearless Siwen had a sudden case of nerves, and was in danger of springing a leak. Self-restraint was called for here, so he took a deep breath and forced back what threatened to be a very loud emission. As he straightened up to take a deep breath, a slogan tacked to the wall caught his eye, a line of rich black characters on a sheet of pink paper! At that moment, that very moment when he spotted the glorious pink, a barely audible "Ah" escaped, and the brilliant glow of excitement lit up his fat face.

In line with his award-winning style, he ought to have said: "Ah ah! Pink, beautiful pink! Pink, lovely pink! Once again you have bestowed your favors on me. Once again you have presented me with a stroke of genius that shows the path I must take, ah!"

But instead, he turned and, in the "Bright lanterns and colored banners bring me great joy" musical manner of celebrating Retrocession Day, announced to the congregation: "I deeply believe that there are many people who doubt my ability to take a bunch of girls who don't even know their A-B-Cs and, in four or five short days, teach them enough simple English to communicate with foreigners—"

Before he had a chance to finish, Councilman Qian grinned impertinently. "I never doubted you for a minute! I have complete confidence in you! Anything you put your hand to is a cinch to succeed!" (While this was going on, Mao Zedong was still alive and overseeing his Great Proletarian Revolution; if he had not been, at this moment Councilman Qian would have quoted Mao's deathbed comment to Hua Guofeng: "With you in charge, I am at ease!").

Then it was Stumpy Courtesan's turn, as she held on to the red flower in her hair to keep it from falling off. "Hold on, Teacher! We all have complete confidence in you! We're completely confident that you're the best English teacher anywhere! With you in charge of the training, everything will turn out perfectly!"

Big-Nose Lion, Sister Red Hair, and Black-Face Li nodded enthusiastically in support of Stumpy Courtesan. Siwen's face creased in a smile and he nodded, his way of saying thanks; he wiped his sweaty face with the back of his hand, wishing with all his heart that his assistants were there with him. Back when he and those four know-it-alls were planning the course schedule, they never stopped asking if he thought it was doable. "Can you really teach these girls English in four or five days? That probably won't even be enough time to teach them the twenty-six letters of the alphabet." When he not only said it was doable, but even told them how he was going to do it, they fell back on the same old refrain. "Is it doable? Is it really doable? Can you possibly do it?"

To see is to believe. He shouldn't have let them stay home to catch up on their rest today, even if they had spent the entire night getting the church ready. He should have made them attend the ceremony, so they could witness old Dong Siwen's abilities with their own eyes. *Damn!* I never considered the possibility that I'd have time left over.

"I am touched by your confidence and praise. But I still believe that at least a minority among you have your doubts about me. I tell you in all seriousness, there's nothing wrong with doubt. If someone doubts you in a particular endeavor, that only proves that you are trying something new, something unique, something others have never experienced before, and so they doubt you'll be able to carry it through. Can it really be done? For every new discovery in the history of man, the discoverer carries a heavy cross on his back, filled with countless nails of doubt, of sarcasm, and of derision. . . ." An aboriginal girl sitting in the back stifled a yawn and asked the girl in front of her, "What's a cross?" But before the girl could answer, Mengxie hissed from the back, "Stop that, shut the fuck up!"

"I repeat, there's nothing wrong with having people doubt you, since what you are doing goes beyond the imagination and intelligence of ordinary people." Once again Siwen wiped his sweaty face with the back of his hand and gazed expectantly at the congregation, waiting for them to erupt in applause. Unhappily, it never came. Realizing that no one was applauding or shouting, Siwen managed to hold on to his smile, although his face seemed a few shades paler. "Now, and now, please allow me, at this point permit me to demonstrate the newest and most effective method of teaching English."

Without waiting for the sought-after permission, nor for an invitation to go ahead, he launched into his performance (here the term "put on a show" would be perfect, if not for the fact that it hadn't been invented yet). He asked one of the girls to come up as he moved to the blackboard; removed his suit coat, which he draped over the crucifix; then turned to the girl, who looked very nervous, and said soothingly: "Don't be scared, I just want you to assist me in demonstrating this new method of teaching English, so everyone will know exactly what it's about, and will then have complete confidence in our training course, not to mention the highest expectations." The sweaty, chubby face turned back to the congregation, who sat in rapt anticipation. "I am now ready to begin, so please pay close attention."

Everyone held their breath.

Siwen rolled his cuffs up to the elbows and stepped toward the girl, who tensed noticeably. She was only seventeen or eighteen, fair-skinned and pretty, except she didn't have the rosy cheeks or youthful luster you might expect in a girl her age. And she was skinny enough to remind Siwen and just about any of her educated johns of Lin Daiyu, the female protagonist of *Dream of the Red Chamber*. So when this modern-day Lin Daiyu saw Siwen approach her, she was so rattled she looked down at the floor, sending a shock of sallow hair tumbling down over her forehead; from the shimmying of her green dress with its red floral pattern, she appeared to be trembling. Leave it to a teacher to notice that this modern-day Lin Daiyu was petrified, trainee or no.

He wasted little time in giving her a sweet smile and a consoling word. "Don't be scared, I'm just going to teach you a little English, so you can do business with the Americans." Siwen's smile spread outward from the nose that anchored it. "I'm not going to yell at you or hit you, so why are you so tense? Come on, look up. Higher, raise your head higher. Atta girl. Now you look like a real student. Now then, listen carefully to what I say. Pay close attention! *OK*?"

Off came the smile, replaced by a grim, funereal look as his eyes swept the congregation before engulfing them in an outburst of English, one sentence, which he repeated over and over for their benefit (Little Yuanyuan mumbled, "What the hell is he saying?"). Then he turned to the modern-day Lin Daiyu.

"What did I just say?" he asked her. "Did you understand me?"

She shook her head spiritedly. She was obviously still frightened.

"Have you ever studied English?"

She shook her head no again, panic showing on her face.

"I was using English just now. I asked you your name."

"I'm Li Shunü." She lowered her eyes again and stared at the baskets of flowers arrayed at the base of the speaker's platform.

"Li Shunü, fair-maiden Li, what a nice name." By now the girl's face was tucked into her bosom. "But for the moment, it isn't your name I'm interested in. I want you to listen to the sentence in English. Now listen. *What is your name?* That's how you ask someone's name in English. *What is your name?* Now memorize it. Don't forget it. I'll help you, listen carefully."

And off he went, saying the same sentence over and over and over, at least ten or twenty times: *What is your name?* He'd had a dog at home when he was in high school, and every day he'd say to the dog: "Sit! Sit! Sit!" shoving the dog's rump to the floor with each command. And that's how it went—"Sit! Sit! Sit!"—for four or five days, and of course it produced results. Every time the dog heard him say "Sit! Sit! Sit!" it did exactly that.

Li Shunü was just like that little dog, and after hearing *What is your name?* she ought to be able to grasp its meaning and memorize the sound. So after repeating it several times, quickly, he asked her what it meant. Without so much as a second thought, she answered, "What is your name."

"Wonderful, that's exactly right!" A look of smug satisfaction leaped onto Siwen's face. "The first principle of language acquisition, and the most important one, is that training in speaking and listening should precede training in reading and writing. Most English teachers these days have it the wrong way, as we Taiwanese say, 'bass-ackwards,' so our college graduates can't even carry on a simple conversation with an American. It's sort of like that popular song goes: 'My mouth cannot speak the love in my heart' [I love you more than I can say]. This drew laughter, mainly from Sister Red Hair and Stumpy Courtesan, as if they were the only ones who detected the humor). Many years (two or three years is closer to the truth) of teaching experience have shown me that this method of teaching simply doesn't work, it doesn't produce results, and ought to be scrapped. But no matter how many times I say it or how loud I shout it, nobody listens to me." Heh heh heh, he laughed. "But who can blame them? My discovery is so new that no one's ever heard of it. Remember Edison, who discovered electricity? Well, no one dared use it at first, either. My method is so new it must be considered revolutionary. And now I plan to go public with this teaching method, holding back nothing, and using it on this group of trainees. I beg all you students to cooperate with me fully to make this unprecedented experiment a rousing success."

The first sounds of clapping came from Councilman Qian and Sherlock Zhang, but they were soon joined by Big-Nose Lion and the other Big 4 managers, plus several of Councilman Qian's senior employees and the lesser whoremaster who spoke Mandarin with a heavy Hakka accent.

"As long as you students are willing to work hard, to give it all you've got and cooperate fully, I, Dong Siwen, guarantee that within the space of four and a half days (classes were scheduled to begin on Tuesday afternoon and continue through Saturday morning. Tuesday morning was reserved for the opening ceremony, and on Saturday afternoon the trainees were to go to the pier en masse to greet the American GIs), you will be able to understand spoken English and speak enough to get by. Oh, and there's one more thing. My assistants and I will not, under any circumstances, apply the obsolete teaching method that relies upon scolding and beating. We believe in the positive approach to learning, and want you trainees to be relaxed, to feel free, and to accomplish your learning in an atmosphere of fun and games. So there's no need for any of you to be nervous. Just treat this training period as fun and games, and embrace the biblical adage of 'Be happy as you learn.' That way, the fruits of our training will be as splendid and brilliant as gold in the sunlight, of that you can rest assured.

"The last thing I want to say to you is this: I plan to teach you only thirty English sentences, that's all, a mere thirty sentences of *bar-girl English*—" Once again it was Sister Red Hair and Stumpy Courtesan's voices that were heard above all the others: "Only thirty? Is that going to be enough?" "Hold on, Teacher! Thirty won't be nearly enough!" "—I plan to teach you only thirty sentences of simple bar-girl English. As long as you understand and can utter these thirty sentences, which even an idiot could learn, you'll have no trouble doing business with the Americans, and you'll be rolling in U.S. dollars!"

"Honest?" several of the girls shouted out in amazement. "Thirty sentences is all we need?" Little Yuanyuan, the math hater, did a quick calculation. "Thirty sentences in four and a half days means seven sentences a day. What could be easier than that? You could teach us that many at lunch, between clients. So why waste time hauling us all over here to the church, when we could be working and making a living?"

Stumpy Courtesan, apparently quite worried, repeated her earlier concern: "Teacher! How can thirty sentences be enough?" But when she saw Siwen nod and smile reassuringly, she fell silent again. Yet after the ceremony, she would grumble to Big-Nose Lion: "Thirty measly English sentences, that should take no more than two days. But he says four or five days, and if that's supposed to be a joke, I'm not laughing! Do you know how much we'd save by cutting two or three days off this training period? Not only that, we'd have the girls turning tricks all that time."

As silence settled over the congregation once more, Siwen smiled and went on with the "show."

"That's right, only thirty sentences. I guarantee you that these thirty sentences of bar-girl English will be enough to handle any situation. A cure-all, a panacea, just like those American steroids." (Some years later, the government would outlaw the use of these wonder drugs.)

He had racked his brains to come up with these thirty simple yet useful samples of bar-girl English in the final moments of making arrangements for the training sessions; then he had gotten too busy to add to their number. It wouldn't be until that afternoon, barely ten minutes before classes started, that he would think up another half dozen or so important additions, such as: *"Hello," "Welcome," "Come in," "What's your name?" "Will you buy me a drink, John (Peter . . .)?" "Another drink?"* and the like. Lastly he would teach them to say: "*What's it like in Vietnam?*" That question was sure to get the men talking a blue streak, and all the girls would have to do was sit there drinking and saying *ya ya* once in a while, or maybe just nod and keep their mouths shut. Sometimes, when the speaker got particularly animated and looked them straight in the eye, as if to ask if they'd ever seen or heard one thing or another, all they'd have to do was look surprised and say *Really?* and that would do it. After he finished talking about the war in Vietnam, they should say, "Tell me about your family! You must be homesick." This was sure to reenergize him.

The next day Siwen would teach his students how to say to the American soldier boys, "Jimmy (or John . . .), after you pay the check, how about coming to my place?" Then at the hotel, to say, "Don't be shy, just make yourself at your home." Finally, to ask, "Would you like a drink? I've got *cognac* [gan-yi-niang—screw your old lady] and *Johnny Walker* [qiang-ni-wan-gao—I'll swipe your rice-cake]. What would you like?" Then when he starts getting a little frisky, they should say, "Let's go to bed!" Teacher Dong then instructed them on what they should say before they climbed into bed, drawing upon something he had read in *Catcher in the Rye*: "a quickie is so-many dollars, an all-nighter so-many dollars. What level of service are you looking for, sir?" "Settle on the price up front," he said, "that's a cardinal rule of business. When that's taken care of, you get undressed and move around to show you're part of the action. No need to worry about A-B-C, Dog bite pig-gy! then." When they sensed the orgasm was near, he told them to say, "*Are you coming?*" Then, when it was over, they were to say "*You are wonderful! You are marvelous!*" Either that, or simply shout, "*Oh, my God!*" over and over. "Your GIs will be on cloud nine." By the end of the training session, he would have taught them a couple dozen of these useful bar-girl English phrases; the remaining half dozen simply wouldn't come to him no matter what he tried, though he might have been holding back a bit, just in case. But it was still a far cry from "*Hello,*" "*How are you?*" and "*Want to do it?*" wouldn't you say? A glance at these sample sentences makes it abundantly clear that Siwen, a man who was deathly afraid of contracting a venereal disease (this did not include herpes, since no one back then had heard of this frightening strain of v.d.) and had never tiptoed through those particular tulips, knew a great deal about the fine art of clouds and rain, like an authority on the erotic novels *The Carnal Prayer Mat* and *Golden Lotus*, or a specialist in the *Classic of*

Women. I'll bet that got a rise out of you!

"Students, ladies and gentlemen, your attention please. I am now going to perform an educational experiment. Please give me your undivided attention. No talking, please, as that will break my concentration." Siwen took a handkerchief from his back pocket and wiped his sweaty face, then turned to Li Shunü, who had been standing there all this time with her head bowed, and said, with a clap of his hands: "Student Li, come a little closer." Miss Li, the modern-day Lin Daiyu, shuffled about half a pace toward Siwen without looking up. "A little closer." Miss Li raised her head timidly, then lowered it again and edged a bit closer. Her eyes were still fixed on the baskets of red and purple flowers on the floor. "That's fine. That way the pulpit won't block everybody's view of you." He took a step forward and faced the congregation, the tips of his leather shoes nearly touching the flower baskets. "Ladies and gentlemen, students, I now start the experiment! I ask you to remain quiet and give me your undivided attention. If you see something that could stand improvement, please bring it to my attention later. Don't hold back on my account."

His rotund body swiveled to face Miss Li, and he said forcefully, *What is your name?*"

Miss Li didn't miss a beat. "What is your name?" she replied in Chinese.

"*Very good*. Now I will teach you how to answer this question in English. You are Li Shunü, so you say: 'My name is Li Shunü.' Now how is that said in English? Listen carefully and watch my lips. If you want to speak English well—and not just English, but any language—the most important consideration is how you shape the letters with your mouth. If it's not right, your pronunciation will never be accurate, no matter how long you practice.

"Student Li, listen carefully, and watch my mouth. It's not what you'd call a pretty mouth, but there are worse looking ones. You needn't be scared, Miss Li, just watch carefully."

Some of the congregation laughed. Councilman Qian turned to Sherlock Zhang, author of "Death Penalty for Strikers," and said, "That numbskull knows a thing or two about humor."

Some of the girls giggled and said, in a mixture of Mandarin and Taiwanese, "It's a cute mouth, like Shi Song's. Not bad at all!"

"A kissable mouth like that, how could it not be pretty?"

"*Kawain e* [cute]!" one of the aboriginal girls said in Japanese.

The tee-hee-ha-ha outburst from the congregation pretty much stripped Miss Li of her fear, and her natural beauty quickly replaced the pallid look of a moment before; there was even the hint of a smile. She riveted her clear eyes on Siwen's cute mouth, as she was told.

"This is how you give your name in English." Siwen paused and took a deep breath, as if about to submerge himself in water, before pronouncing the fateful sentence: "*My name is Shu-ni Lee.*" His lips formed a circle, like the letter O, then formed a horizontal slit across his face; then it looked like someone was stretching his mouth this way and that until all his front teeth were exposed. "Foreigners put their family names last. Like President John Kennedy. John is his given name, Kennedy is his family name. So, Li Shunü, in English your name becomes *Shu-ni Lee*—" His mouth was twisting all over the place, and in order to make it sound even more foreign, he pronounced the *Shu-ni* in a monotone, dropping the original tones, and *Lee* in a drawn-out, falling tone.

"*Now follow me*, say what I say. *My name is Shu-ni Lee, My name is Shu-ni Lee*—" He stopped in mid-recitation, rolled his eyes, and smacked himself on the forehead with his meaty hand. "Aha! Students, I've just had a wonderful idea—" Big-Nose Lion turned and smiled weakly at Sister Red Hair. "Fuck him!" he said. "Another stroke of genius. Please, please don't send us back to our wallets!" "—I think it's too much to ask the Americans to pronounce the names in Chinese. How can we expect them to distinguish among all those *zhi chi shi, zi ci si, yi* and *yü* sounds? So I've come to a decision, one perfectly suited to the situation: I'm going to give every one of you a name in English that is elegant, sounds pretty, and is easy to say." He made this pronouncement in the manner of an imperial edict. "Names like *Kathy, Mary, Jenny, Stella, Helen,* and *Vera* are elegant, pretty-sounding foreign names. Then there's *Elizabeth*, one of the prettiest of all—we pronounce it Yee-lee-sha-bai. The world's most beautiful movie star is Yee-lee-sha-bai Tai-le, and the Queen of England is also Yee-lee-sha-bai. They share the same name."

Little Yuanyuan moved like lightning. "I want that name! My family name is Wang, so I'll be Yee-lee-sha-bai Wang [queen]." She even remembered to draw out her last name—Waaang!

Siwen bestowed upon her a tender parental smile. "All right, the name is yours. *Elizabeth*, what a lovely name. There are other lovely names too, like *Victoria, Margaret, Judy, Julie, Shirley,* and *Teresa*, plus the even lovelier *Penelope*—"

The girl with the tear mole beneath her eye gasped in amazement. "Aiyo! Whoever heard of an ugly name like *Pian-ni-lao-mu* [trick your old ma]?"

The aboriginal girl who had attacked Councilman Qian for going back on his word on bus routes shrugged her shoulders and sneered. "Who wants an ugly-sounding American name that means 'trick your old ma'?"

Cloaked in the mantle of authority, Siwen glared at the offending girl. "It's not pronounced Pian-ni-lao-mu, it's pronounced *Pe-ne-lo-pe*, hear that, *Pe-ne-lo-pe*. Isn't that lovely? The sound alone gives expression to a girl's faithfulness and moral courage, leaving nothing to the imagination." He turned to Li Shunü. "Student Li, I'm going to give you a name that's even prettier than *Penelope* and easier to remember. *Patricia*." He turned back to the congregation, opening and closing his mouth in exaggerated fashion. "*Patricia, Pa-tri-cia Pa-tri-cia*. I ask you, everyone, is that lovely or isn't it? And easy to say, isn't it? I love that name. I'll level with you. I had a girlfriend once, and *Patricia* was her name. The name was what really attracted me to her."

One of the lesser madams said in Cantonese: "Good, real nice! I like the sound of that!"

But that was not a unanimous opinion. "It doesn't sound so good to me, and I sure can't pronounce it without twisting my tongue all around itself!" one of the girls complained.

"Student Li," Siwen said, his fat face oozing the excitement of a man climbing into a woman's bed, "your name will be *Patricia*. Whether you add your family name or not is up to you. A pretty, good-sounding foreign name is really all you need. *Now*, repeat after me: *My name is Patricia*."

Nothing.

"*Speak*."

"Ma—" As her face crimsoned, student Li seemed to be calling for her mother before her voice gave out.

"Say it, *My name is Patricia*."

"Ma—"

"Raise your head."

Miss Li looked up, her eyes filled with embarrassment, and stammered: "Ma, ma, ma-nee—"

"Mai, mai, it's pronounced mai, not your mama. Try it this way: mai, mai, *My name is Patricia*. Go ahead, say it."

Sweat began to drip from her scalp into the corners of her eyes, then continued down her cheeks and onto her neck; the crystalline marks looked like tear streaks. "Ma—Ma—"

"It's mai, mai. Say, *My name is Patricia*.'

"Shay—"

"Not all of it, just *My name is Patricia*. Hurry up!" Siwen was starting to squirm.

Miss Li's face turned ghostly white, and she clenched her tiny fists as if that were the only way she could keep from shaking like a leaf. "Ma—nee—ma—nee—"

"What's this, *ma nee* [give you hell], *ma nee*?" Siwen tore off the Christian Dior tie Councilman Qian had given him and swirled it over his head like a whip. "Ma nee, ma nee, that's exactly what I ought to do, give you hell! How are you going to entertain the American GIs and extract all those U.S. dollars from their pockets if you can't even master a simple sentence like this?"

With an angry, hateful grunt, he turned his bulbous head so he wouldn't have to look at the object of his contempt; the anger then moved to his foot, which stomped down on one of the colorful flower baskets.

There wasn't a sound from the congregation; it was a morgue. A palpable sense of trepidation settled over everyone. The 1940s girl turned to her neighbor and whispered: "This teacher isn't anything at all like Shi Song. He's mean."

The modern-day Lin Daiyu's frail body (she was, however, young, and had nice full breasts, which is probably why she was picked in the first place) began to quake. She kept her eyes on the floor, not daring to look at Dong Siwen, or at the congregation, for that matter.

Siwen snapped his head back around, swung the tie over his head, and said, nearly yelled, at Li Shunü: "Hold your head up!"

It took everything she had, but she managed to raise her head enough so that everyone could see the terror in her eyes, as if a string of firecrackers had gone off in front of her. Ah Ah! (a la Siwen), she looked like she was about to jump out of her skin, ah!

"I put this teaching method to the test in my class, with a hundred-percent success rate. So why do I get a hundred-percent failure rate when I use it here? *Damn!* Student Li, I'm going to keep at it until you get it right, until victory is in my grasp. Student Li, you must put your mind to it, you must work with me, allow this experimental teaching method to bear fruit!" His mouth was dry, so he licked his lips. "Now listen to me carefully, and watch my mouth. *My name is Patricia*. Say it."

Siwen tried goading her into saying it, over and over and over again, until she was quaking from head to toe; and still the same problem: "Ma nee, ma nee. . . ." Siwen was ma-ed into a real tizzy; his sweaty face was the color of a fire engine, and all he could do was say "*Idiot! Blockhead!*" to replace a drumroll behind him: bwuut, bwuut.

Siwen's roars turned Li Shunü's eyes redder and redder.

"*My name is Patricia*."

"Ma nee, ma nee—ma nee yee si—" Finally, Li Shunü managed to get as far as the word *is* [yee-si], and she was nearly in tears.

"You and your ma nee, ma nee! *Idiot*, retard! OK!" Siwen nodded in resignation. "Ma nee ma nee! Well, ma nee it is. *Go on go on*."

"*Gou-wang* [husband]?" Shunü's teeth were chattering.

"It means go on from there! You and your gou-wang gou-wang!"

"Ma nee yee si ma nee yee si—"

"*Go on*, don't stop there!"

"Ma ne yee si yee si—" That's as much as she could manage.

"*Patricia*."

"Ma nee nee yee si ba—*ba* [beat]—" Li Shunü burst into tears. "I can't say it! I can't! I can't, honest!" Two clear streams of snot snaked out of her nostrils.

As if he couldn't even see student Li's tears and snivel, as if he couldn't hear her plaintive voice—"I can't! I really can't!"—Siwen snapped his tie over his head like a horse whip and set his face hard.

"*My name is Patricia*. Say it, hurry up and say it!"

Li Shunü's chin fell back onto her chest as she clamped her hands over her mouth.

"*My name is Patricia*, say it!"

"Ma—"

"Say it! Say it!"

Nothing.

Big-Nose Lion roared angrily, "The teacher told you to say it, so say it! Do you hear me? Say it!" He sat up in his seat, looking for all the world as if he were getting ready to run up there and smack her.

Li Shunü, the modern-day Lin Daiyu, forced herself to raise her tear-streaked face; her lips quivered, until she finally managed to do as she was told. "Ma nee yee si ba—"

"*Patricia.*"

She chewed on her lip and whimpered for a moment, then pressed on to the finish and got the whole alien name out. It sounded to everyone as if she had said *ba dee kee she ya* [I'll beat you to death]!

Siwen frowned and was about to say "Wrong," but changed his mind at the last minute. "Say it again."

Teary-eyed Li Shunü looked down at the flower basket Siwen had knocked over. "*Ma nee yee si si ba dee kee she ya* [I'll give you hell and beat you to death]!"

She'd done it, she'd said the whole thing! Siwen was beside himself with joy. Who cared if her pronunciation was a little off? "Again!" He said excitedly.

"Ma nee yee si si ba dee kee she ya!"

"Right, that's right! She got it right!" A look of sheer joy suffused Siwen's face, his rotund body was energized; he could have flown to heaven. "*My God!* My experimental teaching method is miraculously effective! Miraculously effective!"

Councilman Qian, Attorney Zhang, and the senior employees of Councilman Qian's company all clapped excitedly; not to be left behind, Big-Nose Lion, Sister Red Hair, and the other Big 4 managers clapped just as fervently. If Pastor Yun and her accolytes had still been in the congregation, it's quite likely the strains of "Hallelujah" would have swirled in the air. As applause rained down on him, Siwen, contented as never before, released a magnificently sonorous fart. Apparently, it went unnoticed.

Chapter Seventeen

It wasn't until seven or eight minutes later that the congregation had another chance to hear Siwen's celebratory wind-breaking. No one was disappointed, for it was even more sonorous than its predecessor; an apt comparison would be to the first explosions of New Year's firecrackers. Just imagine: even Yun Songzhu stopped in midsentence and couldn't continue his sex-education lecture for several seconds; even then the tremor in his voice made it was clear that he was badly shaken.

It was a repeat performance: the same excitement and joy combined to drive the wind loudly out of Siwen's backside. An indication of mood, perhaps? The purgative excitement and joy on the first occasion resulted from seeing the fruits of the English-language teaching method he had created; this time, however, he had found something that had remained elusive for so long, and it nearly did again, a great and timely discovery whose loss would have haunted him to his dying day. An inspiration, a revelation, presented to him—surprise of surprises—by none other than Dr. Yun!

When introducting Dr. Yun as the next speaker, he wrote the surname on the blackboard, saying that contrary to what anyone might think, it was not pronounced *hui*, as in a dirty face, or *hun*, as in the word for low-down bastard, but *yun*, as in pregnant, with child. The congregation laughed at this little joke. He then went on to say that Dr.

Yun was Hualien's richest physician, a man whose wealth was astronomical. More laughter from the congregation. But Dr. Yun was not in a jovial mood. When he walked in the door and saw a room filled with gabby women, much of his enthusiasm melted away on the spot, and he passed on the greeting rite of pinching Siwen's nipples. Then as he listened to Siwen's so-called humorous introduction, one look at his pallid face showed how displeased he was.

No wonder he stepped up to the pulpit and opened his lecture with: "Ladies and gentlemen, your attention, please, no talking." That and the dark expression on his face seemed to turn the ceremony into a judicial proceeding. Every eye in the room was glued to his face, all ears were ready to receive his message; even teary Li Shunü, her hands covering her mouth, still shattered from her "Ma nee yee si si ba dee kee she ya!" experience, raised her head to see just what hormonal crap Songzhu was going to pass on to them.

Not long into the presentation, Siwen rose from his seat and rushed out of the church as if he had urgent business to attend to. How could someone like him, a virgin, sit there and listen, actually sit there and listen, to Songzhu's feverish disquisition on the shape and characteristics of the male organ, its components and their functions, the stimulants that cause it to swell and grow rigid? You may not be prepared to believe this, but it's absolutely true. And when Songzhu got caught up in the subject of his own lecture, he was transformed; his look of displeasure was replaced by one of utter bliss. He embellished his lecture with illustrations at the blackboard, larger than life and accurate to the smallest detail. Councilman Qian chuckled to himself the whole time as he watched and listened—ha ha ha; Sherlock Zhang was mesmerized, adjusting his shades from time to time so as not to miss a thing. Big-Nose Lion and Black-Face Li sat in stunned disbelief—or maybe they were in awe of Songzhu's talents as an illustrator. Sister Red Hair and Stumpy Courtesan kept their heads down, but sneaked a peek from time to time. Some of the girls did the same, covering their faces but looking out through the spaces between their fingers; but a significant number took one look and turned away, muttering to themselves and to their neighbors, "Haven't I seen enough men's nasty equipment in my life? Why bring me to church to take *this* tour? Bullshit!"

Songzhu, in high spirits, moved on to words and pictures of men's erogenous zones: the groin area here, and here, below the armpits, the lower belly, the anus . . . and a few hints on how to use those areas to best advantage. As he was explaining how to stimulate the armpit, he raised his right arm to expose, beneath a thin shirt, his own hairy armpit; then with the fingers of his left hand he toyed with the hair through the thin layer of cloth, and by then poor Siwen had begun shifting his backside, not to break wind, but because he couldn't sit still. Councilman Qian, on the other hand, was listening with rapt attention—no more ha ha has from him. There can be little doubt that he was trying to commit to memory every trick and technique of foreplay, in order to pass them on to his wife or. . . . Little Yuanyuan, winner of the most-johns competition, turned to the girl beside her and said, under her breath, of course, "Caressing and getting into the right mood, all bullshit! Do you know how many tricks we could have turned during all this? Making money is like they say in that laundry soap commercial: Two shakes and you're ready for the next load. Isn't that right?"

"How should I know?"

"You don't know? You're a bitch, that's what you are!"

They both giggled at that, and the girl behind them, the one with the lonely tear mole beneath her eye, leaned forward and patted the shoulder of the girl who said she didn't know. Pointing to Songzhu up on the stage, she commented, "Like the way he sees patients. One every couple of minutes. Now do you get it, bitch?"

"I don't know."

Little Yuanyuan gave her an elbow and cursed her softly. "You can drop dead if you don't know, bitch!"

Big-Nose Lion turned to see who was bitch this and bitch that-ing, then spun back around to reimmerse himself in the sex talk by Songzhu, who by then had worked his way up to a smiling and detailed account of male orgasm and what the man's partner did to welcome it. Not surprisingly, the happiest people in the congregation at that moment were Councilman Qian and Big-Nose Lion. Most of the girls sat with their heads down, not daring or not caring to listen. Siwen's ample backside was really in motion by then, and the tortured expression on his face showed his discomfort. By the time Songzhu had turned to introducing—with considerable excitement, by the way—all sorts of techniques to get the most out of the male organ—such as the woman straddling the man as he lies on his back, or crouching on all fours and presenting herself to him—most of the girls had heard all they could bear to hear; since they could hardly cover their ears with their hands, they looked away, focusing attentively on the arched roof or the congratulatory flower baskets or the slogans—"As ye sow, so shall ye reap," "Dignity is all that matters"—or at the crucifix behind the pulpit, with its "Propriety, Justice, Honesty, Shame" banner.

Siwen the virgin could not, simply could not listen another minute, so, as we have seen, with his coat in one hand and necktie in the other, he made a beeline for the lawn outside the church, startling four or five sparrows into the leafy protection of a breadfruit tree. He took several deep breaths before sitting down on a rock under the tree. It took a few moments for the effects of his embarrassment to wear off; when they did, he laid his coat down beside him, calmly retied his necktie, then paced back and forth beneath the breadfruit tree, beginning to regret having slipped out before the speech was over. So he put on his coat, thought it over one last time, and convinced himself that he had no choice but to go back inside and hear the rest of the talk.

Instead of returning to his original seat, he stood by the bookcase at the rear. That way, when he heard things that someone who hadn't yet dipped his wick ought not to hear, he didn't have to worry about looking embarrassed. He no sooner took his place by the bookcase than he heard Songzhu announce authoritatively:

"You must be careful, all of you! Before you get down to business, make sure the American GI is wearing a condom. This bears repeating. Before you get down to business, make sure your American soldier boy puts on a little raincoat. If he won't, you have every right to refuse him. Don't give in under any circumstances, because if you do, you're at risk of contracting that super strain of gonorrhea. It is one nasty dose of v.d. No cure has yet been found. Once the virus works its way into your brain, you turn into an idiot. This super strain of gonorrhea is rampant in Vietnam, and as scary as the Viet Cong. It's everywhere. But what's interesting about this horrible venereal strain is that it carries a beautiful nickname." Yun Songzhu paused for effect; his eyes opened wide under his long lashes. "Saigon Rose, Saigon Rose, the perfect name. Everyone knows that a rose is a beautiful flower, but be careful of the thorns. Ladies, please, please be careful of Saigon Rose, of this prickliest rose of all. Never never try to pick one." At this moment, at the very moment when Dr. Yun was rose this and rose that-ing, Siwen's backside betrayed him. It was New Year's eve, firecrackers popping, and for a moment confusion reigned in the church. Dr. Yun could not go on with his lesson, for there was an explosion of laughter from the girls, whose heads swiveled as they sought out the culprit. Siwen's head turned and craned with the best of them as he joined the search, laughing along with everyone else.

He was ecstatic, really and truly ecstatic, his dimples resplendent beyond belief; his Yaminagaya hair tonic exuded a powerful fragrance. The solution to a problem that had haunted him for days came at that very moment, and what a solution it was! In Siwen-ese it would be "Ah! Ah! A stroke of genius, ah!"

It was all that and more. The bar girls he had taken such pains to train must sing, they must sing, they must sing "*Mei-gui, mei-gui, wo ai ni*" to greet the GIs arriving for R & R. "Mei-gui, mei-gui, wo ai ni," "Mei-gui, mei-gui, wo ai ni," and in English: *Rose, Rose, I Love Rose; Rose, Rose, I Love You*." That's it! That's the answer! In his heart, a single phrase repeated itself over and over: Thank God, thank you God for reminding me of the old song, "Rose, Rose, I Love You," the moving "Rose, Rose, I Love You," to welcome the American GIs. The perfect song for the occasion. He began singing it to himself:

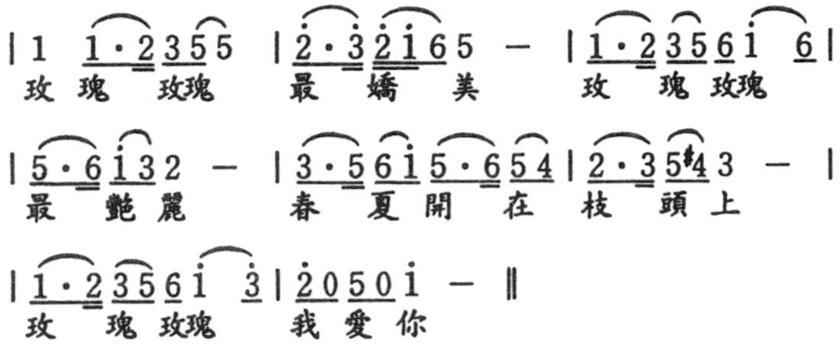

| 1 1·2 3 5 5 | 2·3 2 1 6 5 – | 1·2 3 5 6 1 6 |
玫 瑰 玫瑰 最 嬌 美 玫 瑰 玫瑰

| 5·6 1 3 2 – | 3·5 6 1 5·6 5 4 | 2·3 5♯4 3 – |
最 艷 麗 春 夏 開 在 枝 頭 上

| 1·2 3 5 6 1 3 | 2 0 5 0 1 – ‖
玫 瑰 玫瑰 我 愛 你

Rose, rose, so sweet and charming,
Rose, rose, so lovely to view,
Flowering on the bush each spring and summer,
Rose, rose, I love you.

He was already making plans to invite the school's music teacher to teach the girls to sing "Rose, Rose, I Love You"; he was already making plans to use ten minutes at the beginning and end of each day to teach the trainees "Rose, Rose, I Love You"; he was already making plans to hire a band to accompany the girls; he was already making plans to have each girl pin a fresh rose on her breast as she sang "Rose, Rose, I Love You"; and he was already making plans to teach the girls the English lyrics to "Rose, Rose, I Love You"; he had decided that they would sing the song in Chinese first, then in English. By now, the fertile furrows of his heart were so inundated with "Rose, Rose, I

Love You" that he missed the tail end of Dr. Yun's lecture—warnings that the Americans' organs were much larger than those of Chinese men, and that the girls needed to be psychologically prepared for the couplings so as to avoid ruining those happy moments with shouts of "Ouch!," and similar gems of wisdom. By the time the last strains of the song—"Rose, rose, such deep affection/Rose, rose, the tenderness of love . . . the heart's vow, the heart's affection, a sacred and pure light shines down on earth"—faded away in Siwen's mind, the melody gone, Dr. Yun had reached this point in his lecture: "And now, from the depths of my Christian heart, I wish each and every one of you constant renewal and unending progress. At the same time, let me solemnly remind you: for your own health and, even more important, for the health of all your countrymen, be very very careful not to be infected by Saigon Rose! Thank you, ladies and gentlemen, thank you very much!"

There was fervent applause, but only from the hands of Siwen, Councilman Qian, Attorney Zhang, Big-Nose Lion, and the senior male employees Councilman Qian had brought along with him. All the rest, including the lesser whoremasters and madams, sat there dumbfounded.

As Dr. Yun turned to leave the stage, Siwen called out from the back of the church, "My deepest thanks to Dr. Yun for treating us to such a fine and moving lecture on personal hygiene. Thank you so much. Since you are a devout Christian, Dr. Yun, would you honor us by leading us in a prayer to close our opening ceremony?"

"I'd be delighted!" With a dignified air, Yun Songzhu buttoned up one side of his shirt—he had intentionally left the top buttons undone—then stood up straight behind the pulpit with his hands folded, as if he were about to sing a glorious aria. There was no pocket on the left side of his gauzy, powder-blue shirt, so his dark nipple was exposed to the gaze of people in the front row—that and the little tuft of hair around it. "How's this, we'll close the ceremony with the Lord's Prayer, with the congregation repeating the lines after me."

"Did you say the Lord's Prayer?" Siwen called out.

"That's right."

"The pastor already recited that one, she opened the proceedings with it."

"Oh! That wasn't right. The Lord's Prayer should come at the end, it should be the very last thing." Without waiting for Siwen's reaction, Songzhu said to the congregation, "Bow your heads, please, and close your eyes (the pastor, his mother, had forgotten this part). I'll recite a line, then you repeat it after me. OK, bow your heads and close your eyes, like you would if you were observing three minutes of silence. Be of pure and solemn heart and clear your minds of all thoughts except for those of the the Lord Almighty. All right, now listen carefully." He shut his eyes and gazed heavenward.

"Our Father, who art in Heaven."

"Our Father, who art in Heaven," intoned the congregation. Except for those in the first pew and Siwen and Mengxie at the rear, the girls lowered their voices out of shyness; some barely made a sound.

"Hallowed be Thy name."

"Hallowed be—Thy—name."

Siwen edged up to the last pew as he intoned the words.

"Thy Kingdom come."

"Thy—Kingdom—come."

"Thy will be done."

"Thy—will—be—done."

"On Earth as it is in Heaven."

"On Earth as it is in Heaven."

There in front of Siwen—soon to become bar girls—social status about to be raised—riches about to roll in—two young trainees sat with their heads bowed, but their eyes open. After Dr. Yun intoned each line, they engaged in a hurried conversation, with an occasional stifled giggle, shamelessly tossing praises to the Lord to one side.

"I'm scared."

"Scared of what?"

"Saigon Rose."

"Just do like the doctor says. Make sure the GIs wear their armor, and there's nothing to be scared of."

"But what if—"

"No crazy thoughts."

"And then they shoot you if you go on strike, and they put you in jail for holding on to foreign money."

"That was just that crazy lawyer bullshitting us."

"The doctor says the Americans are really big. That's what scares me!"

"What's to be scared of? If we can squeeze out a baby, we ought to be able to handle anything those big-nose guys are equipped with, don't you think? They sure can't be any bigger than a baby's head, so what's to be scared of?"

"Yeah, but what about trying to speak American to them? I don't know how I'm supposed to twist my tongue around all those wild sounds. What if

I can't learn it at all?"

"Simple, don't say anything."

"Then how do I do business with those big-nose guys?"

"Simple, do what Councilman Qian did, take off your pants."

"Aiyo, you crack me up!"

"I'm not joking. Take off your pants, and you're in business! You have to be nuts to waste time with that ridiculous Ma nee yee si si ba dee kee she ya!"

"But we have to treat them nice, since they're coming all the way from Vietnam."

"Treat them nice? Whip your pants off as fast as you can, that'll do it."

"My, aren't you the naughty one?"

This private question-and-answer session was carried out in such muted tones, while everyone else was following Dr. Yun in reciting the Lord's Prayer, that the training director, Dong Siwen, missed out on it. But even if he had heard every word, he wouldn't have paid any attention; all the while he intoned the prayerful words uttered by Songzhu—"Give us this day our daily bread/And forgive us our debts, as we forgive our debtors/Lead us not into temptation, but deliver us from evil"—a completely different image, a bright, glorious picture, had formed in his mind's eye: fifty bar girls, painstakingly trained by him personally, as perfectly packaged as Japanese export goods, decked out in gorgeous, shimmering cheongsams or eye-catching aboriginal dress, a single fresh rose adorning the head of each and every *darling bar girl*, and another garden beauty pinned to her breast, are arrayed on the pier in three neat rows; the band director—suit, leather shoes, white gloves—stands before them, a fresh aromatic rose also pinned to his lapel; as he leads them with grand waves of his arms, the hundred-member band behind them fills the air with

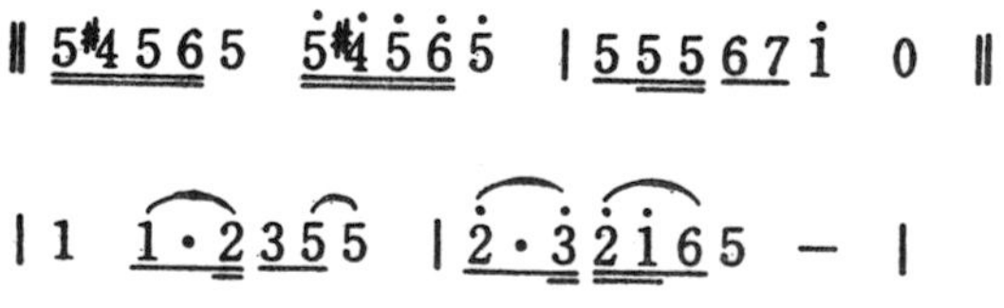

‖ 5#4 5 6 5 5#4 5 6 5 | 5 5 5 6 7 1 0 ‖

| 1 1·2 3 5 5 | 2·3 2 1 6 5 – |

Siwen's fifty bar girls, roses in their hair and pinned to their breasts, sing their song of welcome to American soldier boys who have traveled all the way from

Vietnam, from the city of Saigon, just to be with them:

Mei-gui mei-gui, zui jiao-mei,
Mei-gui mei-gui, zui yan-li,
Chun xia kai zai zhi-tou-shang,
Mei-gui mei-gui, wo ai ni.
Xin-de shi-yue, xin-de qing-yuan, sheng-jie de guang-yao
zhao da-di
Xin-de shi-yue, xin-de qing-yuan, sheng-jie de guang-yao
zhao da-di
Mei-gui mei-gui, wo ai ni.

Then, as if by magic, the three rows of lovely bar girls form into a single line, a long dragon, and every Dong Siwen bar girl is holding a lei made of charming, beautiful roses. Each one of Siwen's bar girls shouts *Welcome! Welcome!* in perfect English as she lovingly drapes her floral lei around the neck of an American soldier boy, then joyously looks up into his beaming face and accepts his kiss of gratitude.

Then, again as if by magic, Siwen's *darling bar girls* re-form into three rows and, with the resounding accompaniment of the band, continue their song:

Mei-gui mei-gui, qing-yi zhong,
Mei-gui mei-gui, qing-yi nong,
Chun xia kai zai jing-ji-shang,
Mei-gui mei-gui, wo ai ni.
Xin-de shi-yue, xin-de qing-yuan, sheng-jie de guang-yao
zhao da-di
Xin-de shi-yue, xin-de qing-yuan, sheng-jie de guang-yao
zhao da-di
Mei-gui mei-gui, wo ai ni.

Teacher Dong Siwen's world-class bar girls form another single line in front of the American soldier boys who have come all the way from Vietnam, from the city of Saigon. Flowers in their hair and on their breasts, the bar girls jubilantly wrap their arms around the American GIs, they fervently kiss their hair, their cheeks, their lips. . . . After the hugs, after all the kisses, they raise their voices, filled with strong affection and deep love, to sing in English:

Rose, Rose, with your slender stem,
Rose, Rose, your prickly thorns,
Wound the tender stem and precious bud,
Rose, Rose, I love you.
The heart's vow, the heart's affection, a sacred and pure
light shines from above
The heart's vow, the heart's affection, a sacred and pure
light shines from above
Rose, Rose, I love you.

Yun Songzhu, solemn and respectful, had now reached the closing line of the Lord's Prayer: "For Thine is the kingdom, and the power, and the glory, forever, Amen."

The congregation, gathered together for this solemn ceremony, echoed him halfheartedly: "For Thine is the kingdom, and the power, and the glory, forever, Amen."

Afterword

The Mandarin song "Rose, Rose, I Love You" has had a long and florid history, spanning half a century and two continents. Written by Chen Gexin, with lyrics by Wu Cun, it emerged from 1930s Shanghai during the Chinese craze for Hollywood films and popular music. Following World War II, it was the first popular Chinese song to return to America; recorded in English, it became a minor hit in the U.S. and among British troops stationed in Hong Kong.

According to one authority on Chinese music, "Rose, Rose, I Love You" was first recorded in Chinese in 1937. Then in 1940 it was one of ten songs performed by "Golden Voice" Zhou Xuan, the most popular chanteuse in twentieth-century China, for the movie *Tianya genü* (Wandering Songstress), with recordings by Pathé. Its snappy rhythm and sappy lyrics must have held Shanghai in thrall, for twelve years later (1952) the song resurfaced in the Shaw Brothers Hong Kong movie *Hong meigui* (Red Rose), featuring the leading lady Li Lihua; as the movie's lead song, it was performed by Zhou Xuan's protégée, Yao Li (sister of composer Yao Min), who would be known as the "Silver Voice" and would later be influenced by Patti Page. *Red Rose* was shown throughout Taiwan in 1953.

In 1954, a film entitled *Meigui meigui wo ai ni* (yes: Rose, Rose, I Love You) was released in Hong Kong; the title song, however, was written by Bai Lang, with lyrics by the renowned composer Li Junqing, so it was most likely a different song with the same title. This, of course, attests to the popularity of Chen Gexin's song.

"Rose, Rose, I Love You" reached its apex of popularity in 1959, with the release in Hong Kong of the Cathay color blockbuster *Longxiang fengwu* (Calendar Girls),[1] an MGM-inspired musical that featured four Zhou Xuan songs, including "Rose, Rose, I Love You," for the first time lavishly choreographed. Easily the most popular Mandarin movie of its time in Hong Kong, Taiwan, and Southeast Asia, this film is likely the source of Wang Chen-ho's inspiration, for the title song was enormously popular in Taiwan and became a favorite tune in dance halls.

A final note on the most popular of flowers. As we learn in the novel, a particularly virulent form of gonorrhea was nicknamed Saigon Rose. The Chinese rendering of the South Vietnamese capital's name is *Xigong*, a literal translation of which is "Western tribute." Thorny indeed!

1. In *Calendar Girls* the song is credited to Lin Mei, a name otherwise unknown in Chinese pop music. Given the strident anticommunist climate in Taiwan at the time, we must assume that this is a made-up substitute for Chen Gexin; interestingly, the attribution carries over onto a compact disk of film theme songs from Guangzhou, China. There are inconsistencies among published versions of the song, and I have followed Wang Chen-ho's version in my translation.

For help in untangling the history of "Rose, Rose, I Love You" I am indebted to the work of Jeffrey C. Kinkley, Huang I-min, Shui Ching, Wu Hao, Andrew Jones, and especially William S. Tay.

Rose, Rose, I Love You[2]

Music by Chen Gexin
Lyrics by Wu Cun

Rose, rose, the loveliest
Rose, rose, most gorgeous of all
Blooming on spring and summer stems
Rose, rose, I love you.
The heart's vow, the heart's affection, a sacred and pure light shines down on earth
The heart's vow, the heart's affection, a sacred and pure light shines down on earth
Rose, rose, I love you.

Rose, rose, heavy with love
Rose, rose, fragrant with love
Blooming amid spring and summer thorns
Rose, rose, I love you.
The heart's vow, the heart's affection, a sacred and pure light shines down on earth
The heart's vow, the heart's affection, a sacred and pure light shines down on earth
Rose, rose, I love you.

Rose, rose, a delicate stem
Rose, rose, your prickly thorns
Wound your tender stem and dainty buds
Rose, rose, I love you.
The heart's vow, the heart's affection, a sacred and pure light shines down on earth
The heart's vow, the heart's affection, a sacred and pure light shines down on earth
Rose, rose, I love you.

2. This is how Wang Chen-ho remembers the song. At least two other, somewhat different, versions have appeared, one on a compact disk from Guangzhou, China.